THE MAN WHO WALKS

Alan Warner was born in Oban, Argyll, and now lives in
Ireland. His first novel, *Morvern Callar*, won a Somerset
Maugham Award and was filmed by Lynne Ramsay. He
is also the author of *These Demented Lands*, which won
the 1998 Encore Award, and *The Sopranos*, which
received the Saltire Scottish Book of the Year Award. In
2003 he was chosen as one of *Granta*'s twenty Best of
Young British Novelists.

ALSO BY ALAN WARNER

Morvern Callar
These Demented Lands
The Sopranos

Alan Warner

THE MAN
WHO WALKS

V

VINTAGE

Published by Vintage 2003

2 4 6 8 10 9 7 5 3 1

First published in Great Britain in 2002 by
Jonathan Cape

Vintage
Random House, 20 Vauxhall Bridge Road,
London SW1V 2SA

Random House Australia (Pty) Limited
20 Alfred Street, Milsons Point, Sydney
New South Wales 2061, Australia

Random House New Zealand Limited
18 Poland Road, Glenfield, Auckland 10, New Zealand

Random House South Africa (Pty) Limited
Endulini, 5A Jubilee Road, Parktown 2193, South Africa

Random House UK Limited Reg. No. 954009

A CIP catalogue record for this book
is available from the British Library

ISBN   0 099 28546 0

Papers used by Random House UK Ltd are natural, recyclable products made from wood grown in sustainable forests. The manufacturing processes conform to the environmental regulations of the country of origin

Printed and bound in Great Britain by
Bookmarque Ltd, Croydon, Surrey

Michael Karoli (1948–2001)
All gates are open now, friend.

Valerie Weber, Kate Gambrill
and Leonard Bliszko who wrote
asking for more of The Man!

How the First Helandman of God was Maid

God and Sanct Petir was gangand be the way
Heiche up in Ardgyle, quhair thair gate lay,
Sanct Peter said to God, in a sport word,
'Can ye nocht make a Helandman of this horss turd?'
God turned ower the horss turd with his pykit staff,
And up start a Helandman blak as ony draff.
Quod God to the Helandman 'Quhair wilt thow now?'
'I will down in the Lawland, Lord, and thair steill a kow.'

possibly Alexander Montgomerie (1545?–1610?)

There is no document of civilisation that is not at the same
time a document of barbarism.

Walter Benjamin

You should never put the new antlers of a deer to your nose
and smell them. They have little insects that crawl into the
nose and devour the brain.

Kenko (1283?–1350?)

The Man Who Walks

It wasn't just during winters the ghost bags came in, rolling over across the dawn-hard fields from distant miles, tumbling for so long on themselves, inside out or inflated, bloated, as when Murdo in The Albannach *found the ballooned-up dog, buried just beneath the sand, or in* Gillespie: *a living eel emerged from the drowned fisherman's mouth, from its coiled home in his swollen stomach.*

Maybe the ghost bags have rolled and bounced all the acres from mini-markets in the next villages, maybe further, from roadside skip bins; perhaps one hundred miles or more from distant cities or freed by some reversing bulldozer on the council landfill?

Rarely seen in the distances, though your eye is alert to all those types of strange horizon movements – some ancient instinct for far and dangerous fringe movement. So you generally never see the ghost bag arrivals. They stir and move on through these territories under cover of night or only when mankind is absent – unless: find the ghost bags at first light where they ended their nocturnal wanders!: snared on the top barbed-wire of the roadside fences – vibrating, thrumming wild in prevailing westerlies, non-degradable ends ragged, the wind alone and the continual resnaggings of the wayward, tattered ends have masticated the plastic rags down to a texture of sickly grey, dead flesh. Supermarket bags with weathered and fading blue logos from the multinationals, torn-off slicings of scratched polythene from hayricks and black domestic bin-

liners, hopelessly multi-wrapped on the barbed-wire, lodged forever: flapping, twittering deep in the night.

Sometimes he takes his hunting knife and cuts the tethered ghost bags free, watches them chatter off across the fields and suddenly swerve, he is furious at their unpredictability.

At dusk, the fresh ploughed fields on either side of the roads make sky darker. Tractors are still working, turning back at cliff edges, letting the full beams of headlights cane out and drum across the surface of the black seas or lochs until they swing, deeply downgear, and shake back unto you. In fair weathers they'll work all night, and seem quite beautiful in the darkness, halted mysteriously behind a copse, hotly illuminating fore and aft and with lights out on specialised, shaking booms as if some kind of mobile location unit creating a strange new cinema.

When he walks the backroads in daylight, the ahead crows wait till a last taunting moment to lift slow from the macadam before him where they pick at the flattened, sun-dried ruins of their own kind. The crows avoid the ghost bags, spooked by their withering vibrations. The hungrier the crows get the more they come to feed off one another's corpses and all the more of them burst under the wheels of vans, cars and trucks until a steady theme of increasing slaughter and cannibalism leads him north.

Highland Clearance

The Nephew was lain silent up atop the paper sacks of pony nuts near the roof of the agric supply warehouse, dreaming about ghost bags, when his mobile diddled 'Rule Britannia, Britannia rules the waves'.

The rat he'd been waiting on scattered along the main rafter, as the Nephew'd seen rats running the tops of fish-trap walls across loch shallows at low tide, craftily avoiding a two-mile detour. This lengthy rat came against the Nephew's shaving mirror and free-falled, plopped into the aluminium drum of water placed twenty foot under, on the hay-flecked, ochre-washed concrete. The rat's snout and paws barely scratched, circling in the watery-bin.

The Nephew nubbed off the anthem.

'Check your sheds and outhouses,' the Foreman's voice whispered, 'that's your Uncle cracked up again. Your mother just tinkled, tells me he's lighted out for Ballachulish, cross-country as per usual and at a fair old rate of knots; but no before he's murdered your four bloody budgerigars. Again!'

'Never!' the Nephew breathed. 'Not Ian, John, Reni and Mani?'

'Aye, all four birds slaughtered, just like the last four: Mr Green, Mr Yellow, Mr Blue and Mr Blue, least it was quick this time; just scalded each to death with a cigarette lighter, then took both your mother's sets of false teeth for his own mouth, marched down the Mantrap and stole their World Cup kitty. For a man with a glass eye, your Uncle's pretty long-sighted when it comes to pub kitties. Last count there was near seventeen grand in it. They've agreed not to call in the Feds. Keep it a family thing and see if you can find him first. *I'll* give you the days off. You'll no get many lifts if this petrol blockade steps up. Get going and find Old Two Bags. Don't dare lose my mobile there.'

'Right you are,' the Nephew says.

Ears still droning from the baseball batting he gave the sides of that water bin, till guts hung out the rat's mouth, the Nephew came down the caravan park. Inside their caravan, burned bird feathers smelled like singed human hair. The Old Dear had ventured out just far enough to float his wee dead birdies into the bulrushes and down the Black Lynn, which flows beneath our town, to where it emerges at the tunnel mouth by the sea, no doubt with a haughty stare from the swans clustered there. The Nephew thought, If I horsed it to the Farmer's Den, descend the cellar's steps, could probably just catch their cheery-coloured, scalded feathers drift past smuggler's slipway in the green tunnel, away downstream and salute them bye, bye forever. A tear came to his eye and he shivered with violence.

His Uncle, The Man Who Walks, had never took too kindly to birds since he found her lemon canary still happily singing over the corpse of his dead Mum on the lino, her skin scorched by three days of concentric urine circles round her. His Uncle shut that canary up in the attic, close to the lightning during a thunderstorm, and it never sang again.

The Nephew sighed, 'Well, least I'm *doing* something in response to this latest little family crisis, Mum!'

'Hey, you hold your horses, I'm only just got out of my bed!' Old Dear coughed curdles of smoke, mascara all run. Without false teeth, the Old Dear looked old right enough, in her easy chair, goggle-stared at a sheep-herding champion omnibus on telly.

The satellite dish on the floor was aligned to western hemispheres. Fixed on the caravan carpet were outlines in different coloured parcel tape, figured to the dimensions of the dish's base plate. Written on the different coloured strips of parcel tape were words: Lies (24 hrs), Irish Network 2, TV3, Porno, Illegal (Amsterdam), Weird and, written in the Nephew's higher-case hand, Discovery. By directing the satellite dish base to each position on the floor they got a semblance of reception. At least it beat the days his Old Dear and latest boyfriend'd make the Nephew stand outside the caravan in the driving rain, holding up an antenna to the skies, whenever Scotland played a soccer match.

Yon programme the Old Dear watched was called *One Man and His Dog*. The presenter was interviewing a shepherd wearing a dark green overcoat. To each carefully teasing question the shepherd was replying: 'Aye.'

'Aye.'

'Aye.'

'Aye.'

'Aye.'

Wasn't making for many pure television moments, but when it worked, telly was always stuck on that station, ever since his Uncle, denied his ration of pony nuts, chewed up the remote control.

5

'Shift yourself, you always did interfere with the reception,' the Old Dear snapped. 'And get my teeth back.'

Behind the basking sharks and grey seals of his Sea Life Centre shower curtain, the Nephew fished into one of the bin-liners of manky washing, selected the lesser of many, many, evil boxer shorts and, scant word of farewell, thumbed it west towards a new darkness.

First to stop was a cattle wagon droving from Lowlands to ferries and marts of this territory. Could hear weighty shifts and stumbles of heifers in through the back of the cab, beyond the pinned-up Confederate flag. The driver was just a wee man whose arms seemed hardly able to reach the extremities of that big, horizontal steering wheel before him.

The driver back-palmed the gear stick into second and jammed on music: old eight-track. Kris Kristofferson doing 'Border Lord'.

> Take it all
> Till it's over, understandin'
> When you're heading for the border,
> Lord, you're bound to cross the line

'Old Kris, eh?' the Nephew shouted, trying to get a bit of blether initiated. 'When Kris was in the US Air Force, trying to send his songs to Johnny Cash, Johnny wouldn't answer any letters so Kris just flew in, landed his helicopter right on Johnny's front lawn!' The Nephew smiled.

'I'm cab crazy, son.'

'Aye?'

'Cab crazy, cannie get enough of it. Cannie get enough of

this long and winding road. There may be nae petrol but there's derv, son! Tell ya, I've got white line fever, white line fever, laddie!'

'Aye?'

'Used to do the juggernauts; driving into Rome, boy, big motorway circles Rome, all the way along it, mile after mile, *whoors*! Whoors stood there mile after mile, sonny, each one illuminated by a bonfire of cardboard boxes. Look all sorta hellish, with their faces lit from below, kitted out in red plastic skirts. No just big lassies either, transvestites! You ever tried it with a man, sonny?'

'Eh?'

'With a man, have you ever tried it with a man? Don't believe what they say, it can be as good with a man as with any woman. Look, son, I'll be straight with you. I'm no poofter but I'll give you a fiver if ya gobble me as I drive?'

'Can you stop here, please,' the Nephew says.

Fixed to the back of the cattle wagon was a triangular yellow sign: silhouette of a kangaroo. 'I Swerve for Kangaroos', declared the legend as the lorry vanished into darkness.

The Nephew had travelled about nine hundred yards from the Port and found himself stood at sole roundabout in that territory. Cause it was sole roundabout, the only cars which circled, several times as they kept missing the townward exit, were L cars from the Driving School: Ramraider's glum, Raybanned sons sat beside each learner inside each identical car: staring at the Nephew, who had his thumb still out as the vehicles circled and circled, whining in high first gear till they finally got the exit.

A young couple arrived on the back of a big Kawasaki motorbike; brand-new plates. Lassie with no helmet, in leather jacket and breeks, got off and walked, centre of that grassy roundabout, took a digi camcorder from her pocket and began filming the guy on the motorbike as he circled the roundabout again and again, upgearing ever more excitedly past the Nephew's thumb in silver-blue rolls of exhaust fume he'd redisturb on each circuit. The girl steadily followed the bike's circuits with the camera, till he side-skidded in and she remounted, faced wrong way round, laughing, painted finger-nails split open the zip on her jacket front, two curving no-bra breasts, glint of a piercing, spilled out with blonde hair in that slipstream, hiding her face as the bike wildly accelerated back into town, beyond the '30' sign; speed cameras blushed out a silver flash: photographing her stuck-out tongue, her astonishing tits swung free and her cowboy boots neatly crossed over and obscuring the number plate as she filmed back.

Inland, the Nephew had his back to eased-off sea blusters as he walked through foothills, thumb canted to the clouded-out pole star, not giving eye contact to invisible drivers, admitting they would pass before they did. Suddenly the ground before his boots got illuminated by double-upped redness of brake lights as a passed saloon car smeared to haltingness along there. The Nephew stooped into a wee trot toward twin exhausts. Driver, an old fellie, spoke before his electric window had reached all the ways down, says a surname that the Nephew instantly forgot, and the Old Fellie thrust out a arm to shake hands. The Nephew shook.

'And this is the lovely wife,' the Old Fellie added.

The Nephew kneeled and nodded. Wife, ancient purple rinse, face like a busted couch, was in the back, though there seemed no reason.

'I'm headed Ballachulish way.'

'Oh, we were just going that way; *over* the bridge. Weren't we, lover?'

'Yes, dear, how lucky for the young man.'

'Yes, come on, clamber aboard, son.'

When the Nephew'd clicked seatbelt, the Old Fellie had goes, 'Just got to pull over to our house, pop in for some bits and bobs, then we'll be happy to drive you up Ballachulish.' He put the car into gear and they grundled forward. 'Not in a desperate hurry, are we?'

'No desperate, no, I'm actually looked for my Uncle who's sorta done a runner. He's no full shilling, the Unc, no right in the head, in *so* many ways. Used to be in Out Patients, Lochgilphead loony bin; Lochgilpheadcase, as we call it; he sometimes does a wee runner.'

'Oh, how *exciting*!' Purple Rinse goes, just behind his earlobe.

The Nephew says, 'Uncle burned out on yon hippie trail during the sixties, flipped ever since I was a laddie; never uses transport, just walks all places. They call him The Man Who Walks cause you'll see him, out in most farthest of far places, stomped along vergesides in all weathers and woe betide if you offer *him* a lift; curse you till he's blue in his face.'

'Mmm,' the Old Fellie nodded.

'I remember when I was little, I had this cuddly wee elephant called Markus. Markus the bellyphant with saddest face,' the Nephew sort of mumbled, thoughtful.

'Ooooo, cute!' Purple Rinse's voice goes, right up close to the Nephew's lug, way she was leaned all forwards, tits squeezed up between the two front seats.

'Aye, Markus was my favourite toy cause he was stuffed full of lentils and beans so he had this heaviness when you dropped him, made this kinda crunch noise when he flopped on the floor what with the dry lentils inside of him. Then I remember yon

9

time, Uncle, The Man Who Walks, had turned up at Granny's house, down off hillsides, sleet and snow in his hair, carrier bags of froze water by his side. Gran was out on an early and there wasn't any nosh in the house, so Man Who Walks slips free his Swiss Army knife, slices open Markus and empties all the lentils into a pot to make a soup, used Markus' skin to wipe his beard clean. Aye, that's my fond earliest memory of my Uncle, The Man Who Walks! If he stayed with the Princess and her Pea he'd soon enough have her dried pea in the soup!'

'Oh, ho, ho, ho, ho,' went Purple Rinse.

It was really pouring down now; Old Fellie had wipers on, rain like white ash, shifting west in the headlight scallops of the bouncing wash ahead. There was such a half inch of water on the tarmac it looked like that rain was landing on the sea itself.

Purple Rinse had been nod-nodding, really absorbing that story, she says, 'Look, isn't that just atrocious, just as well you got a lift off us!' and they were hanging a right into that estate of snooty, new, bought houses just outside Tulloch Ferry. Some were still getting built and you could see pale pine wood of roof beams in the rainy dark up there.

'Come on in, it's right cosy in our house.'

'Nah, you're grand, I'll just sit it out here. Got radio? Aluminumville FM is a scream.'

'No, won't hear tell of it, we'll be a good fifteen minutes, you get in our front room with a cuppa.'

'Och, that's awful kind and all, but look at the state of my boots, can't be trailing muck all over your carpets.'

'They can come *straight* off at the door, son.'

'Oh, you can be no worse than him, in from the garden Sundays!'

Boots left under the coats in their hallway, the Nephew was

plonked on part of a garish three-piece suite. They had a yappy Jack Russell, called Trafalgar, sniffing round all ankles. 'He's had six homes and he's only five,' cooed the Rinse. Trafalgar. Very grand name for a bloody wee rat-catcher, the Nephew thought.

The house was the usual dismal décor of boring folk with o'ermuch cash-money to hand: flowery wallpaper, yon sickly stripe round entire rooms halfway up, big red curtains that Purple Rinse had soon tugged closed, and dreary wee ornaments: porcelain Jack Russells on shelves in an alcove above telly. Now *that* was a real beezer, digital wide-screen affair. The Nephew coulda fair kitted this den out proper compared to the Settled Community: an always-dreamed-of house, his beloved books, squeezed up thegether on a pine shelf in *strict* alphabetical order: Aeschylus, Apuleius, Barker, Beckett's *First Love* bound in cloth and autographed, Cicero's *Murder Trials*, Crowley, Flavius Josephus, Herbert (Frank), King (Stephen), M.L.R. James, Kenko, James Kennaway, Lao Tzu, Longus, Lovecraft, Lucretius, Machen, Andy McNab, Masterton, Ovid, Pausanias's two volumes, Sir Walter Scott, Seneca, Smith (Delia, then Wilbur).

'I guessed you were a *lots*-of-sugar sweet-toothed boy!' she screeched. Purple Rinse had materialised, big hot Jack Russell-emblazoned mug of tea and what if she hadn't a platter of pieces (chicken spread and spam)! She remoted telly on and left him there, fairly tucking in.

There was a weird film on, that he half looked at: some ride of a campus lassie, boarded in a spooky old Girls' Private School, was being pursued by this guy vampire, then a scene came along where some photographer lassie invites the ride campus lassie to her rooms to get photos took and, was his luck no in, if they were quick, before the wrinklies' return! What with hot sweet tea and spam sandwiches the Nephew was chomping on fit to bust, what if the screw lassie didn't start stripping off and you can see both her and girl photographer are into it! The Nephew's wondering about this stuff broadcast so early in evenings when he noticed that wee red light twink: it's a video tape! The door busts in: the Old Fellie and Purple Rinse dive across the floor stark bollock nude! Wee Trafalgar yapping up at them. The mug tea goes flying one way, still–full platter spam sandwiches the other, all across the carpet and that dog's tucking in straight away.

'Fancy some party games, son?'

'Last of the original swingers!' Purple Rinse yells, opens her arms and, to the Nephew's horror, it's not just on her head the hair is purple, she's gone for it all over, and the Old Fellie with a boner, the Nephew thinks, Jesus, we all get old, but talk about Willie Whitelaw doing salsa in the shower! Yacuntya.

Just a jiffy: the Nephew is strode across all those still–unfenced lawns, ducking washing-line whirlies, holding a boot in each hand. All these battalions of movement-sensitive security lamps are sparking off, like speed cameras, from the eaves of every house as if these bampots each have Rubenses hung off their walls.

Clear of glare, he paused, cursing by that cattle grid, to slap clicky plastic ends of laces on his boots over sodden socks and yank them tight; then he shrugged under buckets of thunder-plumpings just gushing torrential down out of the heavens and he hucked in his trot towards Ferry Hotel.

Sir Walter Scott has written, 'It's one of the privileges of a story teller to begin his tale at an inn.' Some privilege, look at the place, yacuntya! Nae need to describe this Highland hotel: just another name for a pub with a few beds above it, we've all come to know them so well, these pubs – *unremarkable* in every way and more to come, sure as fate.

The Nephew stepped in the Ferry Bar as a girl walked out the toilet and called to the barmaid, 'Hoi, nae toilet seat in the Ladies!' Barmaid, yon Hole of Morar aka the Gap of the North, nodded as she drew off lager for a fellow bar-sat. The Nephew struggled to shut the door behind him; the bitching wind was so blowy out there, when the Nephew got the door shut, he felt his ears pop with the pressure change. Everyone cast the glance at the Nephew, that mute hostility of small communities, then everyone nabbed up their pint or scuttled off behind the pool table. The Hole spied the Nephew and that lassie from the toilet too, who quickly settled with some excuse for a boyfriend. The Nephew wiped hair off his forehead and plonked a wet arse on a stool. He whispered, 'Pint lager, bag of prawn cocktail crisps.'

The Hole did a nod, began tugging out lager.

'Man Who Walks in the day?' he says quiet.

She looked at him queer, says, 'Aye, think he was this afternoon,' pretend-concentrating on that pint, working up any level of intrigue from any non-happening she could. She put down a pint lager and he lifted it almost before she'd took her fingers from its sides.

He could see disruptions to condensation her pudgy mitt had made on the glass and they annoyed him. She placed crisps on the bar and he says, 'Lea & Perrins.' The crisp packet got tore open, Worcestershire sauce busily unscrewed and fairly scuttled down within, so's pools would be gathering in both corners of that packet's disintegrating, lowest crisp layers. Oh, how he loves his seafood. All along the Nephew was looking Hole in her face. 'How much did he have?'

'Eh?'

'And what is it that he was drinking?'

She shrugged. 'A fair scoot of drams. As per usual.'

He glanced along all whisky bottles to pricey malt for daft tourists. 'It'd be Talisker?'

'Nut, he was on that Irish stuff.'

'More treachery! So what's a fair scoot in your bed? Three, seven, eleven?'

'He'd sixteen, didn't even try for a tab, paid up in used twenties. He was well behaved; stood in that corner there with a wee radio pressed to his lug hole tuned to Aluminumville FM.' She looked down at the bar and, pretending it was needing a wipe, slithered a stinky cloth with a thready white tail along. Clarty slut; it'd been the first time that day.

'Sixteen doubles?' he raged, 'Yous've all jaloused fine it's no good for him! Out he goes on his raiding and foraging missions and the whole family's made it apparent over the years to purveyors of liqueurs and beeveridges in these vicinities that he should *not* be catered for, yet our family's requests go *grossly* unheeded!' The bar went silent but then:

'Excuse me, but I'm really *needin* to pee!' that wheedly, moan-moan voice went ahind him.

He chewed, then yelled, 'Hover, like most women, or you'll catch something more!'

'Will yous mind the bar?' the Hole called quick, looking over the Nephew's head. 'I'm away up the stair.' The cowardly bint vamoosed off.

Soon the Hole was back, crossing the floor with a toilet seat tucked under her arm. The girl ran right into the Ladies after her. Fat behind that she couldn't wait to lay on the pan, the Hole'd be lucky if she didn't get her fingers peed on, the Nephew thought, and shifted on the stool glancing over at the boyfriend. It looked at him, then It looked away. He crossed over to It. 'Blag a fag offof you, pal?'

'Aye, sure,' It says quick and slid the pack across.

John Player. You'd think It'd a Formula One parked outside or something, farmed salmon slithering between the steer wheel in this fucking weather, the Nephew thought. A Spar lighter snugged inside the pack, up against the remaining cigarettes. He lit up and goes, 'Ta,' to It.

The Nephew recrossed back to the bar and sat on the stool. It was good for the Nephew to suck smoke down, let it merge into lungs, let it become part of him, then blow out, downwards, and bite a white creamy, pigtail curl of smoke back into his mouth, taste it way inward again, then lean back, a long, relaxing release, smoke reduced, thinned almost away, absorbed down, into his own self, like a Eliphas Levi book says, Catholics believe smoke manifests spirits! He sucked so hard on that ciggy, it burned and fizzered quicker along edges, leaving that rod of less-burned tobacco up its middle. The Hole emerged out the bog and made a show of under-ducking the bar as if *her* arse was anything special. She didn't wash her hands.

'Where'd you get the lavvy seat?' the Nephew goes.

'Number 14, they're away out for dinner. Get the night porter to screw it back on before they get back.'

He took multiple gulps of lager and says, '*Bet* you will. Plenty queens'll sat on yon throne. So did he go right or did he go left?' The Nephew wiped his mush with the back of his hand.

'I'm no sure.'

'Och, come along! You count how many flies are trapped against the windows in this place. You noticed okay.'

'Can't swear on Bibles but I'm sure he went thataway.'

He nodded, thinking, That would make sense. In that state his Uncle wouldn't be able to swagger up a road embankment to the old cantilever and away north. Christ, this might be as fundamental as picking him up down by the loch, 'easy peasy'.

It was flatshore all to Hacker's boathouse. Man Who Walks was getting old now, might of let himself tumble down onto kelp, wrack and laver; snore it off, planning to cross the cantilever and away north, following the old railway beds at dawn, away up through the closed stations. It would be good enough here as anywhere.

Otherwise it was uncomfortable to think of yon long walking miles north across Boomtown, far as Appin lands. Cindery crush of old railway base from lifted track under your boots. Mile after grudging mile of it and rickety, unhinged gates to clamber that farmers have blockaded the lifted line with and spaghetti'd those spars round with oranged barbed-wire to stop their cattle or sheep grazing down the track bed to an unfenced portion and away. Yellow jackets fizzing, bumble bees dangling in dead-man's bell clusters, clegs smittering about eyelids trying to bite, dusk midges requiring at least a pack of twenty fags to keep them at bay from devouring your face, then trying to get in a few hours of kippage in thirty-minute chunks, lay free of earwigs and ants on the softer areas under a decent sycamore, wrapped in a bin-liner, dreamed of hotel rooms, stiff towels and the Olympic Breakfast in Little Chefs.

Any sane mind had to consider above us to the north, a land, greened up with age, curves of saw-tooth lochs cutting east. Clawing black salt sea, lips lined with shining straps of sea kelp: disturbingly far inland. Tides rushing madly to and fro all the livelong day between rock shores beneath the mountains, their flanks still brown despite summer, as if built out of rusted steel plates from dead ships. Enough to make you dizzy, those lochs under knobs of pointless land, layered with humus and smeared bluntly westward; sick sweet knottles of whin bush and daisies, daisies so close meshed they look like a sleet fall in the grass. And that's just when it's raining, woe betide the circumstances a few hours of shuttled sunshine produce as crawling things spill forth: wasps, slugs, bluebottles, moving as if magnetised, clegs, eerie-wigs, slow worms, shell-less snails. Man has never been able to sufficiently impress himself on this land, men can only turn on one another under these heartless mountains, useless as beauty.

Tried to calm hisself by draining the lager pint, noticing fungusy, smegma specks moving in the shaking dreks.

'Phone working?'

'Nut.'

'As per usual, eh. Just popping out to the callbox.'

He grabbed his backpack from under where he'd hid it, in the damp-smelling porch, under a pile of softened, ink-run tourist brochures scattered on the table; none for the Sea Life Centre. The top one, hydro-electric, read: Discover the Heart of the Hollow Mountain.

Out, it was still raining. He tutted hisself for no ripping them off two pints. He walked down past the bus stop, spat out in dark, beeped up the mobile phone and dialled.

'Aye?'

'I'm in Tulloch Ferry. He was on the sesh. Ferry Bar,' the Nephew says quiet, stood in dark, hearing that sound of his own voice, breeziness and rain blips on shoulders. The Foreman didn't say a thing so the Nephew went on, 'He'd been too plastered to get uphill to the old cantilever and aways north, so I'm gone sweep the shore.' Quieter, with a tone of triumph, the Nephew goes, 'He could still be *right* here.'

'What about his house?' the Foreman's voice goes, then you heard that downturn of the last word, silenced by a cigarette going into his mush. There was a sort of second, silent presence there. The Nephew knew fine the Foreman was shagging his mother, though both them refused to acknowledge this. Christ, a few hours out of town and the Foreman was moved in with her!

'The Old Dear,' he paused for effect, 'says The Man Who Walks got estate agents to board it all up.'

'I *know*. He's used the old railway path last two flights, but he might be after a bolt-hole in this weather.'

'Tell me about it,' the Nephew muttered.

'Hoi, son!' the Foreman raised his voice. 'Twenty-seven grand. A bit of clean rain'll no do you any harm. Any local resistance?'

'A few freaks. Nothing I can't handle.'

'Good laddie.'

'Thought it was seventeen grand.'

'I'm getting new intelligence.'

'Jeez-o,' the Nephew whistled through his teeth. 'Less he went to his house before the pub there's no ways he could reach it: slopes all the ways and once the booze saturates his inner ear his balance is shot; he can't go up nor down the slightest gradient or he falls flat on his arse . . .'

'Well, maybes he did go before; even after, if he went round the way, up, 'long, unner and past. Pretty gentle risings?'

The Nephew shook his head though none to see. 'Nah, no that way, the gradient round the main road by the Loch and under the old cantilever is too much for him, and besides, who would want to pass in front of the police house? He had sixteen double nips. The deluxe shite too.'

You heard quick adding up and the Foreman going, 'Forty-six quid already. Check the house. Phone *minute* you get the money.'

He'd hung up.

The Nephew slipped the phone in his jacket. He didn't fancy an excursion into The Man Who Walks' house. Who would willingly enter that lair? It'd more environmental health writs than the Chinky restaurant in the Port, but other, worser concepts plagued him. Man Who Walks might no be able to rise or move down through Ordnance Survey map's gracious contour lines that curl up on these lands and bundle in corners like oil in a puddle, but there was no physiological reason why his Uncle couldn't cross water. Course, the stories that have become legend, and sometimes been recorded and written down, or even entered into print, are all, unfortunately, true. It is a fact Man Who Walks once walked across silty beds of New Loch, 'neath the surface, a huge boulder under one arm holding him down, breathing through a giant hogweed stalk; suffering no such side effects as the bends or, unfortunately, drowning.

There was no way Man Who Walks could swim Loch Etive here though: deadly black deep, salt and fast moving with rapids under the old cantilever. But what if, twenty-seven grand snug on The Man Who Walks, he found a vessel, even some debris or driftwood to cling to and swing out there in the currents and the eddies, away north during darkness to make safe landfall, the way those lizards in the Caribbean, during hurricanes, were spotted, floating away between the atolls on tree trunks?

The Nephew quick-crossed the crash barrier, clambered down onto shore and began, flummoxed, stumbling the tide lines in the direction of Hacker's railway-sleepered boathouse and its leaking roof of de-plugged bolt-holes, in each hole a single star always multiplied and held in the circle of jewel-clear raindrops. Hacker was no called Hacker in them, before computer and computer-fraud days.

The Nephew smiled, thought of Hacker's nightboat, so welded and so riveted by the both of them out aluminium, all that metal made the compass go fucking haywire! That craft could only be navigated by Hacker at night in good weather, using settlements and lighthouses to guide him and cross between islands or over horizons on the water. No ways was the Nephew going out on any boat. Once Hacker'd tried to use the craft as far as outer islands: night passage: urgent hush-hush business for Junkie Seamus. They never saw lights of any islands, dawn started and they was circled lost and helpless, compass spinning, Junkie Seamus spewing over the side on a featureless sea.

The Nephew scanned limits of tide line, kicked out for a few dark things – usual fish boxes, a fence post enwrapped with wire and seaweed, a jerry can and something smelled godawful, like a carcass of one those angler fish freaks with dangly forehead rod that illuminates way below in the thousand-foot depths, drawing in victims with a hapless weakness for the limelight.

He could see tide limits, heavily tumbled by dead tree roots, lawn trimmings, other garden garbage from big Bed & Breakfast guest houses up on the main road. That kind of trash brings in hoards of water rats who nest in there.

He remembered that contract job, helping one of Old Dear's boyfriends, further up-village, the Nephew still in primary school, before he was took out, again! They'd to clear a top paddock of rhododendrons. Getting roots of those bitches dug out aye was a heart breaker. Tougher than loading artics with scallop shells, he grinned, I must've flung a million ashtrays in my time! he thought.

Couple weeks after rhoddy job, old owner of the house phones up. They'd dumped all rhoddy roots down yon shoreline and they was just infested with water rats and the owner had wee grandkids dotting about.

Poured jerry cans of two-star petrol down them nestings,

tossed in the burning rags. Nothing for minutes, then those crazy fat rats came flying out, just jumping through the air on fire, swarms of them tipping over, burning down to their tails on the shore or, best of all, spiralling out in flame as roots exploded, leaving tracer trails and as those bastards hit water they just exploded. Must of been temperature change against their boiled-up guts hitting a freezing loch, pop! Then the men dove in with shovels for as to beheading of them but they was all dead. The Nephew'd took a shovel to one and halved it. Shows how young and daft he was, cause he remembered saying, 'There, it's double dead now,' but the old owner goes, 'Nope, laddie, when something's dead it's dead. Always remember that. There's no double dead on this earth.' And old owner through wars and everything must of thought the Nephew was a right wee nonce. The Nephew remembered, A rat'll take a whole aviary of budgies in one night; his scorched dead wee birdies, and he cursed his Uncle through grit teeth.

The Nephew came off shore into dripping trees, leaves rain-heavy, near those low cliffs where he and Hacker used to summer-play, heaving off biggest boulders they could lift; that tight suck, kaplump and hish. Where they found that chain, fixed into rock, like as to Prometheus, leading down those tide stains, into water, enswirled with sea kelp, the links vanished into invisible deepness! Hacker wanted him to strip off, follow the chain on down, borrowing his leaky diving mask. The Nephew had to chicken out of that one. He swore to himself again at his cowardice of water. And old Prometheus got his liver ate out by a hoody crow too.

Mockit the Psychotic, a trawlerman acquaintance, knows the Nephew is afraid of sea alone: keeps him up to date on

TOPEX/POSEIDON satellite Surface Height data. You imagine oceans flat but no, oceans slope and currents race, strongest where the slopes are greatest! The Nephew balks at the horror of oceans; at the findings of WOCE (the World Ocean Circulation Experiment) which determine when water mass was last exposed to atmosphere; disgustingly, most water has never been near surfaces! Years, the Nephew had the terrifying ocean-floor contours, the jagged, submerged mountains, the inhuman depths, as a coloured poster above his bunk, depicting 'Salinity in Relation to Depth', from Antarctica to Alaska across the Pacific, oh boy! descending to the ocean floor in his dreams and through the ocean interior, his non-buoyant balls sinking down snug atween his legs pointed deep into 3,000 feet of the Clipperton Fraction Zone, yacuntya! But worst of all are the floating ghosts he can't get out his mind; drifting with the currents, CTD sensors ballasted at neutral buoyancy, thoughtlessly constant in their predetermined depth, floating, as they drift like drowned corpses round and round this world in its deep, deep oceans, constantly monitored by earth-observing satellites!

The Nephew shook his head to rid his demons when he reached the railway-sleepered boathouse, then he tried to peep in holes, feeling his way round the sides gingerly, ca'-cannying about water lap at door and slip. Heard the metal clunk of a boat insides, so that was secure.

He stepped in that self-same cold briny right then, well in over his sock! He'd been edging round to the boathouse front door and a foot just shot down into water. It would be that sluicy bit between these concrete slips and he'd be passing up starfish getting blowjobbed by a cross-eyed mermaid; before you could say 'Davy Jones' he was back up at the shed corner where the grass was aslime. Man Who Walks would be drowned before he'd gained entrance to any vessels in there, the Nephew thought.

The Nephew circled the shed, around oil drums, floats and all sorts of chandler's crap, but found he could get to the doors on that other side and figure out how they were held by loose chains so as, with a tug, you could swing the doors a bitty and gleer in beyond ill-fitted door planks.

No boat: a green and white Castrol oil drum floated in black water, and bumped emptily against the concrete. It could clear under the door now so he sunk the drum a fraction with his squelchy boot, then toed it out and it sailed over, towards rocks where the current started and it was took away out, till invisibled by the darkness.

Oh, he'd be gone okay, Man Who Walks loved to row, maybe attraction of no seeing where yous were goed? His Uncle'd been down on shores so he'd be leaned back pulling on the oars, with a writhing orgy of baby crabs trapped tight under that Pittsburgh Steelers' baseball cap. The Man Who Walks'd gone to Hairodynamics before, with alive crabs and winkles buried right down in his hair till a screaming lassie's varnished fingernails found them.

The Nephew sighed; so long in the dark, the hands of his watch weren't aglow, he looked round; instinct . . . training, not wanting to make a night target of himself. He got the mobile in one hand, pulled out his jacket, to shield, then engaged the phone, using its light to illuminate the watch face. He moaned at the hour and still so much further to go. Yon crisps had made him hungry and the taste of thwarted spam pieces too!

He took slash against the Hacker's boathouse, aimed down of course, so spattlings and spinterings didn't come flecking back too much, thinking of Gulliver first making water before the

Lilliputians who 'immediately opened to the right and left on that side, to avoid the torrent which fell with such noise and violence from me'.

Then the Nephew set off, trying to memory-trace paths of twenty year ago through these brambles. He couldn't find the path and in two steps, bramble jags tugged his breeks like puppy teeth and kittens' claws, so he stopped, stock still, and daintily as you like, reached down, letting fingertips pitter-patter to find them and sure enough, even in the dark, as he ever so carefully touched the jaggy thorns into neutralness, he came upon the little soft bramble berries, pulled at them trying not to tear, each colder than the air, like living flesh, and the Nephew sniffed at its smell of Gran's sour jam, then, smiling at memories, put them, one after the other, into his mouth. Mumbled, almost silent as breath.

> I am a warrior
> I serve the death machine

Fingers came to little frocken berries; they would be as transparent as cod-liver oil capsules.

> Losers or conquerors
> All flash past on my silver screen

Tore on, lifting his calves high, cursing racket and tugging at thorns, spitting out chewy wee berry bits, then skirting tangled privet hedge of Hacker's folks and up there onto the wee loop road.

> So fate will have to wait
> Till time can heal the scar

My heart is ruled by Venus
And my head by Mars.

Phil Lynott, God rest his soul, only black man in Ireland. They says when the Nephew was a kid, his filthy Uncle, Man Who Walks, was there when he was hid out o'er on the green garden in the sea, gazed back to the Greater Island.

Varieties of routes presented themselves to the Nephew for reaching his Uncle's place over other side of the railway as varieties will insist on doing. All avoiding the police house, though Fed wouldn't be in. The Fed'd likely most be pulled up in a leather swivel chair at station back in the Port, tin of beer lifted from knacker drinkers in his fist, confiscated blue movie on the Evidence Video. Those praying Feds, yacuntya, man! He remembered the time the Feds lifted his gang after they done that offy. Kids' stuff. In through the corrugated roof and all they tanned was two crates of beer. Feds kept all beer-can ring-pulls from his pockets that you could send off for a car competition: 'This is evidence that would stand up in court,' yon Sergeant McPherson goes, holding up a solitary can ring-pull, and the Nephew'd just laughed in that Fed's face. Two month later the Nephew read in the paper the police pool had won an Opel Manta.

The Nephew knew all this land too well from childhood days, their old caravan pitch: parked by the electric substation on the backroad from his Gran's: what's now Man Who Walks' legal property. The mysterious clicks, the quick bangs of electrics all night long, contacts opening and closing as the electric juice poured down from the hydro's hollow mountain and morning kettles went on in the Settled Community between real walls of bricks and mortar; while his brothers and sisters were using candles and storm lamps in the caravan. But happy summer evenings! Commandos up the bushes with the gang; kiss, cuddle or torture with the McCallum sisters from up the councils. 'Lift our skirts and what do you find?'

He walked ahead: to get himself on hands and knees and in the mood for Man Who Walks' house, he considered getting in back of the guest houses and up there onto the hill where the beehives used be. You drop into the dip, ascend the bracken-rich fairy brae, where you find a drainage tunnel in the railway embankment. When kids, they could get into it and walk, back bent towards sunlight glitter of other end.

He crossed the main road, looked all ways, made it through back garden of the unlit holiday home with a tin roof, so he launched over the back fence and moved past the water supply tank towards the dark outcrop, dodging thistles that came at him, from out in the darkness, thistle heads coated in mouse fur of seed, almost tall as his waist.

McCallum sisters, he thought. Right enough it was up by the beehives the Nephew got showed his first scud mag that Hacker'd found.

The Nephew minded the gutty sink in his tum as him and Hacker peeled open those pages, shiny, preciously fragile from rain, some inks of the fleshes of one girl poured into another's. Both him and Hacker on knees there, silent, peel-curling each page gingerly so the revealings wouldn't tear, breathtaken at what things they saw. Hacker had looked at him, cautious-like. 'That's what babies come from, man puts hard-on in, spunk makes a baby grow, like Christine McKneel Along's, from the council houses, tummy.'

'What!' the Nephew had goes.

'That's what shagging is.'

'Are you bonkers?' the Nephew'd says.

'Naw, dead gen, Old Man done that to the Old Dear.'

The Nephew turned to goggle him, then he looked back at her on the page, and that leather cap she was wearing, tilted at that angle, and he just saw fury.

That effing Hacker licked his lip.

The Nephew had stood, started kicking out like billy-o at poor Hacker who'd knew he couldn't fight back, so's Hacker curled up in that cowardly ball he always would do. The Nephew didn't try to open him up, using boots to the kidneys to get at his face; after all, he was his best friend; so just booted at random as to be covering any possible slights on his Old Dear, like as if she was one to talk in those words! cause the words in the magazine weren't their words, they were the other words of other languages away in countries where whoors like that would talk, all slutty. Then there was a translation into words you could read, right at page bottom, below other, at least, European language, showing what she was said to two guys doing those things to her on that carpet, between those grit little teeth, before you came to the centre-page spread!

The Nephew'd kicked on out, more the harder, all good and proper, cause he knew what he was getting, so's Hacker grat all the more; but that hard-on just got bigger up against the Nephew, partly at the coloured, wet pages lying in the grass, but somehow at Hacker too, all curled up there, his bare back too. Then the Nephew took the nudie mag and walked away with himself for a while and then hid it in one of the rotted old beehives only he'd know.

He'd cooled down when he came back. Hacker was sat looking over at a tilting glider from the club above the abandoned seaplane base on the other side of the cantilever and the Nephew knew he'd to make up, cause he was sorry for kicking him in, so he'd says, 'C'mon, let's go find McCallum sisters.'

A few days later in primary playground the Nephew was having a confab with some of the gang down the boys' toilets. They were whispering about the McCallum sisters. Smiler comes right out, says it as Hacker came running over.

'He says you says shagging makes babies happen.'

'That's what big boys told me,' Hacker says.

'That's pure pish,' says Pure Pish Pete.

Someone kicked the football and they all followed it on out across the misty playground, except Hacker.

'That's not all, boys,' Hacker shouted after them. 'Santa Claus doesn't exist!'

They all bust out laughing, shaking heads. They were almost out of earshot, kicking the football around.

'Nobody could live in Greenland up there, it's too cold,' Hacker yelled.

Fucking Hacker, he should call that cunt up. When he gets out. Took years for them to get him in his hastily abandoned rooms, cigarette still burning. His fingertips so worn away they couldn't get no fingerprints offof the keyboards. Hackers' Manicure, they call it. Fairly smiling to hisself, the Nephew was moving on up through bracken spread, feeling first bobbles of ballast under his heels and the huge embankment of railway blocking his way. The Nephew fell forward, fingers in the grush and moss of embankment, putting his squelchy-boot first, in sideways, to get a grip and shoving on up, breathing heavier straight away. Using bendy baby birches, to heave on, and pull himself up the slope with his arms, into the complete black, an eidetic country, made out of memory alone, lay before him as the Nephew came over the top, saw the dark rails in front him.

This was still a working Mickey Mouse railway, shitely policed. Get on and off at any stations down the line: Tulloch Ferry, Back Settlement, Falls Platform, and guards wouldn't charge you a ticket. If there was an inspector from the city on board they'd put you off at the next station if you couldn't pay. But the twelve engine drivers were great. All owned bread vans and lobster boats and would get their sons to drive for them on certain days. They'd stop for you way out on the moors if you waved and take you up in the engine with them. Not for The Man Who Walks though. They wouldn't stop for him. Nosiree. Learned their lesson there! Those engine drivers'd throttle up if they spied his gangly silhouette on a horizon!

Talk about public transport! all sorts were using this railway's liberties: on a mart day in the port, Bobby Dougald, shepherd, had took fourteen Suffolk Ewes onto the train at Back Settlement; just herded them sheep in, all shiteing purlies right up and down the coach among Jap and Yankee tourists, Bobby arguing with the guard, if dogs were allowed on why werenie his prize Suffolk ewes? Yacuntya, what a place, the Nephew thought, if only I could get out. To where? I'll tell you where: to some place proper, if only! he thought. That money. Twenty-seven grand, an astronomical sum altogether, right there in a split second in one hand. That would get you somewhere *proper*. (Or a pair of hands? How many wads is twenty-seven grand of twenties?)

He heard a sound. A rapid, mad scuffling further uptrack, so he wheeled on himself and crouched, squinting into dark. No, surely Man Who Walks couldn't'd made it up here? Jesus, unless he'd tried to walk it out of the Port using the railway track! Smart old lizard. The gentler gradients, of course, one in five hundreds and all that carry-on. You never thought of the Uncle having gumption enough to use the working line, you just thought of him walking the old dead lines, the gone ones, 'axed' yet partially put under trees! Like the gone airfields from the wars, and rail lines gone since Beeching Acts. All mixed up in the Uncle's mad mind, where each new whisky dram was like drops of water in a frying pan of scalded oil, fizzing crazy, believing himself still at one of his ancient real jobs before he went down south, got all caught up in the 60s and had his mind burnt out by hard drugs. Aye, the gone ones; those were the railway lines Man Who Walks based his travelogues upon, sleeping in one of those gravel skips or platers' bothies aside the track that'd been his bolt-holes for yonks, while he was on the railway and then, again, after he was shot from it.

Still-crouched, the Nephew began to move up the railway stealthy, stepping from one wood sleeper to another, that beautiful smell: burnt diesel and axle grease up there. He could jump his Uncle right here.

Skufflerings again, strange, frantic, just at the start of the cutting. Like as maybe he was defecating – taking a jobby, and maybe that was Man Who Walks scraping over his businesses, just like a animal does; pilchardy skitters, bitumite sandwiches and whatever other horrors he'd been surviving offof. Caking loads on his boots, the mink. I'll need to watch out for a kick when I grab him, thought the Nephew.

This time the noise was right queer, a massive busy digging then falling sound. The Nephew sniffed. Blood. Smell its honk a mile off. And this time: movement, then he saw it. *There* was a load of idle speculation for you. It was a deer, flat out on its side on the railway track, most likely hit by the late train there.

He took a few steps back of disappointedness and also cause they bastards can be nasty when hurt. His heart was thumpering, though he felt completely on top of it; couldn't help it though he wasn't feart. It's the nearness of death. He came in closer and let his eyes into those obscurities.

They must have hard times getting insurance, these stags and deer, cause they're always buying it in some nasty manner, offof cars and lorries, getting stuck in ice or shot down by the well-to-do's rifles. Female, could see its back leg had been took right off by the train wheels, and just then it smelled him fine through its own blood stench and was up.

The Nephew leapt back as she managed to lift on the two front legs, a throw of ballast and grit came shooting backwards from where her took-off hind leg was trying to work, but he saw what was down there: first the mad, trembling look of its eye on the back-turned head, seeing its own awful damage; then the round, shiny ball joint of the half leg she was trying to rise up on and the other leg – gone, with a rope of lumpy intestines dragging too; must have yanked out from the abdomen when the leg got tore away.

The Nephew turned his back and walked away. Thought of the deer there all night suffering but he'd need a hefty boulder to put *its* skull in and there wasn't time to be jaffing about on mercy killings when there was enough of that to be done to The Man Who Walks; besides, the midnight freight would polish the deer off for good and drag it north to heaven.

The Man Who Walks' Nephew came down quick, slope skirting the old electricity substation. Could hear its frizzy hum before he saw it, feel his hair get more static until finally it would go on end. Like old Mr Vassel the engineering teacher, would make the Nephew and other class troublemakers stand in line holding hands, rev up the Van der Graff generator and electric-shock them!

His boots crunched on broke glass at the passing place on the single-track back road where their caravan used to be pitched, then he turned west, towards the old pool on the burn, filled in with silt these days, and his frizzled hair fell low.

Aye, that pool brought back fond recall and its ever-attendant shame: young lassies from the two villages in their swimming cozzies slapped to their wet wee tits, skinny laddies shivering, all in pumps and plimsolls against the dreaded glass of drunks' broke bottles supposedly all on the river-bed; the Nephew don't know why they didn't wear gloves too, since the laddies were as much doing handstands, bicycling around their wet black plimsolls in the air, showing off to the lassies.

When little, at start of summers, the Nephew'd came down to watch bigger laddies in swimming trunks, stood in yon dam pool with shovels from their daddies' gardens, scooping out winter's silt accumulates from below the diving board, sending an all-afternoon gush of brownness downstream and through the village, past the parish hall.

Day after, lassies arrived in giggling gangs, trannies yawling, holding them away from themselves and fizzing the tops off cherryade bottles; screaming and undressing inside big coloured towels that others held, strictly, in place for them; all lassies pale as the driven snow, no healthy an swarthy like his skin.

The Nephew'd just watched that first day from a distance, then the next it was even more heatwaver. He plucked up the mettle to go down to water's edge. What jollifications they was all having! He laughed too, looking for acceptance: a big inner tube floating, boys boinging off the board slickin in, lassies' heads bobbing in the amber water, their long hair going all different when wet. He minded a lad took a big fist of mucky sand and tried to ram it down one lassie's cozzie bottoms; when he succeeded, the lass cooried down by the outlet, and you'd see minutes of brownness crawl away over the boulders from in there! So that day, sudden-like, the Nephew pulled off his snake-belted trousers and T-shirt, then just jamp right in over his head. By time he'd come up the pool was empty.

'Yugs, he just swims in his Ys,' one of the towel-wrapped lassies goes.

'Get out there, Tinky,' one of the bigger boys says. 'We're no swimming in same water as you.'

Sure enough, even after he'd climbed out in his soaken underwear and dragged his trousers over the heather, he saw they left it a good half hour for the water to clear of him away downstream before they jamp back in.

Up at the caravan Old Dear was sat smoking in a deckchair held together with barbed wire. 'Mummy, can I have a pair swimming trunks?' he'd goes.

'What do you think this is, Butlin's holiday camp?' all she says.

Playing alone in the leech ditches, the Nephew found a dead adder that afternoon; the snake was mostly dried out, jewelled with bluebottles, so's he picked out about fifteen leeches and put them in a old hubcap. Come nightfall, he flung that leech-filled hubcap and the dead snake into their swimming pool, booted and heaved at the diving board till it was all in collapsications, then rolled those boulders into that pool and floated that diving board away downstream in the moonlight.

Couple days later, the big boys were back with one of their dads. Had a cement mixer and built up that diving board so's you'd needed a pneumatic drill to destroy it. You can't beat the Settled Community, you know. Yacuntya.

Spat out at the rain in memory, looked uphill at The Man Who Walks' house, above him on the crest, its pointy-up, evil-looking windows on second floor. The Amityville Horror. Grandma's before his mad Uncle's; all Gran's carefully hoarded money went to Old Dear that she squandered away with various men and the house was bequeathed to the queer ticket himself; the odd fellow, known in this territory as The Man Who Walks or in other counties as Prowler or The Dead Christmas Tree Man.

When Man Who Walks first took over the house on Gran's death, the lot of them spent an Easter here. The tea always tasted eggy cause Uncle boiled all his eggs in the kettle. You could find every one of the hidden Easter eggs just by following Old Dear's footprints away from them in the snow. Had to stay on for days, cause when boyfriend of the time got a punch off of the Old Dear, lens of his spectacles flew into the snow. Couldn't drive his Ford Cortina one-eyed like Uncle could, or old Angie who once drove the train blind, he knew the line so well; so after calling off the search parties at dusk with their fingers perishing cold, they had to wait for the snow to thaw so's they could get the lens of his glasses back off the green grass and then drive away.

At night, Man Who Walks would come tuck the Nephew in, Twister mat under the sheet, case of his bed-wetting due to nerves; The Man Who Walks'd read to him the ghost story 'Whistle and I'll Come to You', leave him terrified with a smoke detector clutched under his arm, its battery light blinking. 'In case it's tonight Uncle burns the place down,' Man Who Walks'd whisper, lighting up his strange-smelling pipe, closing the door.

Years went by and after social services got Man Who Walks out of there, they'd some boffin couldnie-catch-a-bus type, up from a university to take a gander at the state of the place. The *Daily Star* came to take photos but never did an article. Always seemed to the Nephew there was but one simple answer: The Man Who Walks had sad memories. But the house deeds are still in his Uncle's name with nothing they can do about it, no matter how crazy he gets. Till he dies, then the house would go to next-of-kin. Him.

The garden was not kept with accuracy. There was no differences between the scrub around the house and the actual garden when it began, so long since the fence had rotted away. The Nephew stepped quiet cause through weeds you could still feel the gravel path round the house. At the back, he checked coal cellar flaps but they was shakily padlocked. He walked forward and tripped straight over something; as he went down, he held back a curse as hardness banged into his shin. He was up like a shot and tested it with his boot. A sink, one of The Man Who Walks' vast collection, summer-high grass all grown up through plughole and overflow.

Front door was locked too, but nice old glass at the side with yon colours in it had been cunted out by kids. He listened in, but not a cheep. He moved round and lifted the sink, walked Frankenstein-like to the back of the house, raised it above his head and horsed the sink through the back window. Two black crows lifted from a tree close by. He used his backpack as a lever so he wouldn't cut his hand. Hoiked himself up and in there.

Crouched beside the throwed sink, it smelled in there still: that in-Man-Who-Walks'-house smell. Canned pilchards, sweat and something else, worser, but at least it was out of the rain. His boot crunched flat one of the tunnel sections. As eyes adjusted he could see how most tunnel sections had been tore open by social services or whoever, trying to catch his Uncle on his hands and knees as he scuttled around through the tunnels, scattering empty pilchard cans and scallop shells.

In the nook: the old Coke machine, carried on Man Who Walks' back from outside the Spar, that actually used to function when fed a same 20p, painted yellow for some reason, but stocked alone with Special Brews. Before the electricity was cut off and you had to just reach in. Before the water was cut off.

It's the Nephew's experience that houses are not normally furnished with cisterns, drinking troughs and mangers, but Man Who Walks' is. Something to do with his water obsession that saw him, in all weathers, crossing bens and from away up the glens, ever so far, forever bringing in the water with two thorn-holed carrier bags at his sides and later a barrel on his back. There was also scavanged old baths, plugholes blocked up with a slap of concrete – previously drinking troughs in fields of beasts. According to legend, Man Who Walks once stole a plastic bathtub from Gibbon's Acres and used it as a canoe down the Esragan Burn to bring himself halfway home. Also, within The Man Who Walks' residence, stylistically speaking, bar stools featured heavily; for years Man Who Walks'd been notorious for bursting into pubs, always in most isolated and obscure corners of that territory, spying a red-cushioned bar stool, snatching it, often from under someone's arse, then horsing out the pub, up a snowy hillside or into the mist, over hills and far away.

After he'd barricaded himself in, Man Who Walks' sole sign of sanity seemed to be his passion for current affairs in magazines and Scotia's swankiest newspapers, such as the nationalist broadsheet: *Rise and Be an Erection Again*, the *Scudsman*, the *Glasgow Hard-On*, the *Piss and Journal*, the *Daily Retard*, *Scotland on Binday* and other great organs of truth. For years The Man Who Walks collected newspapers from litter bins and roadside picnic areas and from Moleigh county-council rubbish tip, waltzing between the bulldozer spreaders. When *in* money (dole, invalidity benefit, recycled Christmas trees, etc), broadsheets as well as bevvy was Man Who Walks' vice, often, oddly, several copies of the same day's newspaper. No one connected the apparent obsession about the contents of the *Financial Times* with his wallpaper-paste bulk buys from Bobby's ironmongers in the Port. Trying to shut out the past memories of his mother's death, the layers of beige wallpapers and cloudy sepia photographs tacked to every wall, showing generations of only the respectable line: the sawdoctors and lawnmower mechanics, orra men, ditchers and drainers, crofters and contractors; even photos of The Man Who Walks himself, as a young plateman and track walker in the railway uniform or in new, weekend suits.

Boneheads from social and community services and loony-snatchers from mental hospital come and finally burst in yonder spring day. They found that, over the years, Man Who Walks had constructed and lived, crawling around, within a complex network of papier-mâché tunnels and igloos throughout the rooms and corridors of his house, like a badger's sett. At first just a main cupola raised up in the centre of the living room, then a more ambitious dome in the blue room – a real Pantheon (with tobacco-stained oculus) – all connected by corridors. There followed a structurally ambitious tunnel network with staging posts of ascent up the stairs to various chamber igloos in the bedrooms, comprising the Uncle's accommodation. Each igloo featured its own unique furnishings along with the baths, sinks, mangers and drinking troughs (topped up by yards of connecting tubing to a lilo footpump and 45-gallon drum in the garden). Beds with straw mattresses were made from plastic beer crates, sealed together with a blowtorch flame. From within his cells, Man Who Walks invited the crazies and freethinkers from miles around, even some international ones, to join him in the guest crawl through his tunnels.

As you did, the Nephew moved cautiously, further into the scullery, testing lino before with the tip of his boot; gingerly nudging for that old coal cellar hatch. The Nephew remembered the time, just before his Uncle's confinement, that they lifted this lino, suspicious why Man Who Walks had laid it and the stench rising from beneath. It soon became apparent The Man Who Walks had been sharing the kitchen with living chickens, keeping them there inside his own house for eggs till he'd slaughter them too and, rather than muck out, just chucked down some scavenged, ill-fitting lino!

Sure enough, cellar hatch was left open, flagrant as you like so's you could break your neck. The Nephew stepped down those stairs, specially widened for his Gran. Down into the glory hole there; he could hear the rain patting on those coal-hatch doors, he could feel wet shiny slick of ancient coal dust underfoot. There was a bar stool down there, up on it the Nephew could touch the hatches, so he protected his fist with his backpack, then hit out with all strength. There was a loud bang but he could feel the old doors were still clamped flush by the outside padlock. He paused, took a breath and hit out again: with a loud snap you heard the padlock plate break free of the woodwormed dooring and the left flap jamp up so's a glimpse of light-polluted night sky blinked and he got a downpuff of fresh air and the flap fell shut.

Always give yourself choice of two exits or walk away, any half-decent cat burglar or pioneer is going to tell you. The Nephew had the back window to the west and the coal flap to the north. His foot came against a bin-liner, it was pushed full of something soft and rustly, newspaper no doubt, so he decided to just use this new bin-liner and dig well in for the night. Not as exposed to windows as up the ground floor – no danger of getting trapped upstairs and the cellar was long enough that even if the devil himself lifted the coal flaps he would need to hang right in, like a vampire, to see the Nephew, slept on that soft, rustly bin-liner.

Using his own bin-liner on the concrete floor and the crinkly stuff under him, he tried to get comfy, but the springy insides wasn't making for good mattressing. The Nephew took the rustling bin-liner. You could compress it right down, cram it into the backpack, make a good pillow. Laid out like that was best kippage he was going to get, probably for this whole odyssey, so he lay there hearing rain, comforting himself he wasn't outside like his adversary. Already the Nephew was beating his Uncle, The Man Who Walks, using the old brainbox better.

Later, midnight freight went through up the embanking, big diesel drumming and rasping. The deer. Double dead.

The Nephew strode back into the Port like Dick Whittington, kit-bag shucked on his shoulder, and he was settled in his first pub, the pint being poured, willing acknowledgement in a few held stares but heads turned away. There should be some law against it. Banishment from town boundaries or whatever.

Some say he stayed above the Politician pub that still kept a few rooms in them days, on a bed that reached the window, sleeping solid for two nights, shouting away the bitch who changed the sheets and settling in English notes; others say that he stayed up the tower in the best guest house in town, his resources falling short of a hotel. Some might say that he moved direct to the tinkers' campsite, drank a few whiskies in the Farmer's Den, then went banging on the caravan sides till he found his mother's. Ten days anyway and he was chucking sacks in the agric supplies barn below the hanging rows of peat cutters and rubber waders. Clearing rats with expertise.

Nights and afternoons off he kept to himself, avoided the pubs where anything happened, sat away from the men who most certainly don't have wives in the Upper Bar in top town or in Outertown Lounge. He would make each pint last exactly forty minutes and read paperbacks, canny enough to make sure they were nothing too lofty.

Morbidly curious, the Nephew's only society was splitting a can Special Brew with the disgraced train driver, him never the same after *his runaway foster-daughter drowned crossing the Sound on the little illegal ferry – no more than a sloop with nary enough life-jackets; and her a smart piece and a right little ride that wrote some novel book no less, that you saw, thumbed and passed among the young ones in the pubs. It was always said she was the best bit of real writer that ever rose above these bogs and a hot-buttered looker of a girl too that ended up and got her tender bits shared out and devoured down among the crabs and fishes which cautions her kind right for letting few enough of us get a taste of them; aye, her book didn't help her float no better, the Nephew was heard to remark after her foster-dad had stumbled out.*

Donald, where's yur troosers?

The Nephew came into woke-ness of vibrated daylight knowing there was Fed sniffed round outside Man Who Walks' house. Do they Feds never learn, man? They always have their walkie-talkies turned up to squawk assistance, yet they're never done yap-yapping between themselves; specially these backland Feds: *cannot* shut their cake holes for a moment: never so much as thirty seconds' radio silence; you can hear that distinctive static voice buzzle furlongs away.

Once on his feet in the cellar, stood in cool shadow, the Nephew only had to wait and Fed might climb in that busted scullery window. When he heard glass tinkle into the sink, the whisper, 'Up, Stalker; hup, boy,' it was enough. Enter your own property and that's them sent the dogs in on you! he thought. He shouldered his backpack, plonked bar stool under, opened the coal hatch to a collapse downwards of painfully bright light, and hunckled himself up. Outside he scoped both ways, let coal cellar door close quiet, then he hit out in a disembarkation hunch for a first line of tree cover, as if off a barely touched-down chopper.

Even when well and truly along the slope lines shielding him, there was no sign of mutt nor master. The Fed would be *inside* the rooms, yielding to the novelty of his r/t, reporting a clean sweep. The Nephew hoped the Fed went straight down the cellar hatch and broke his neck, and the Nephew threw himself to his stomach, crawled last fifteen feet over stony ridges of moorland. Sure as fate: a sleek, souped-up Fed Mondeo was parked on their old caravan pitch at the passing place they were always lecturing his Old Dear it was illegal to park in; a gash sunlight off its windscreen; the Nephew turned his head both ways to take in the cathedrals of blue above; it was going into being a real scorcher of a day. Sure enough, the Nephew had seen the signs: cuckoos singing at dawn, swans flying north and in the rivers the eels turning up their silver or golden undersides or the minnows and perch leaping and the frog's skin, normally blacker among the rotted grass, had been blushing up into mustard and green.

There was no soul around but he waited a jiff, just in case a second Fed was away in trees for a slash or pulling off the gander's head, fantasising about Juliet Bravo handcuffed to a bed, but that car was unoccupied. Even spotted now, the Nephew knew he could outrun any dog upslope, towards rail embankment, and scramble the drainage tunnel. Do the dog there, in the . . . confines. Do it clean with the hunting knife. Drag its gutted sack for trains to sweep away.

The Nephew glanced back towards Man Who Walks' house; sashayed to that police car, reached out and opened driver's door as his hair went static. He looked: ersatz leather, if no the real thing, and all state-the-art electronics, radar guns, no-expense-spared-tax-payers equipment. Not that the Nephew paid tax; no need to let your imagination completely run riot! But just then he saw a most amazing outrage: top the dashboard a sort of miniaturised video monitor was relaying the moving picture sequence right there an then – inside-swerving infrared down through Man Who Walks' papier-mâché tunnels, right there on that wee screen, view scoping left, then right, the Nephew saw massive mitt of a human hand flutter near and he realised: it was a camera strapped to a collar atop that stupid dog's head, like as used in bomb or terrorist situations! Made him seethe, such equipment in this territory, like the time, just when the pub's come out, the hydro went down with a power cut, no juice was going to them new CCTV cameras in main street: those Dose brothers put in every shop window and looted just for sheer spite, brassières clipped round their oilskins!

There was a dirty sheet of hardboard where the tarmacadam turns to moss and ancient moor begins, so he scoped round. Over by thistle clusters was an example. Using the hardboard he cooried in and slid it on: semi-fresh cow shite, usual glittering array of summer flies and vermilion-tinted bluebottles tense with activity on its crusted top, holed by beetles. Insects scattered with the under-easing of the board. As judged, like a slobbery French omelette, lower portions were green runnings. Looking over his shoulder the Nephew returned to that open police car door, checked the giveaway monitor, then let cow shite smear from the board and plomp heavy onto the driver's leather seat. Smeared it round a bit, allowing some cakelets to fall onto a fitted-carpet floor in by brakes and accelerators.

The Nephew tossed that board, wound down yon window to get some flies in and, knowing sound will carry a mile here in the morning foothills, softly clicked closed police car's door. Reglancing at that monitor (the Fed dog was climbing stairs) off the Nephew swerved, uphill following moor grass doups and swells, case he'd to hit deck, but the Nephew was way in those birch leaves before there was sight of any soul.

Whole scents of this earth was rised up out of it into the Nephew's face, the sun blanching these grasslands. Splashed round his eyes; on the springy moss by a wee stream, rinsed his mouth, lips close to the rock, and spat out, but there was no time for dilly-dally. He'd put down far too many roots already this side of a loch that it was time to get over . . . across. Course he daren't use the old cantilever and away north, not now. Be a sitting duck on its five-hundred-yard dash with no escape but bailing out over that side: hundred-foot drop to rapids below. He shivered.

He crossed the embankment without a glance up the deer cutting and tumbled down through beehives where he'd beaten upon Hacker those years ago, then fell into thistle ranks behind guest houses, rehopped back of the tin-roofed holiday home and hesitated by a rowan in the garden to get a clear crossing over the road and hither anon he was back down on the bright shoreline, squinted against silvers, greys and blacks and the top slicks of current on the moving loch mass, coiling and turning like severed worms; he was headed for Hacker's boathouse through plague-clouds of gnats until he was cooried among fecund verdure, pale undersides of bramble leaves swaying close to his cheek, so he turned aside, trying to jalouse how to cross a loch, when he spotted that outline he'd missed in the night's darknesses when it had been black as the earl of hell's waistcoat. There was a bulk in among wild thorn bush just off the pale shore stones.

The Nephew didn't want to come out onto open shore yet, so he just tossed a pebble at yonder bulk: looked like something long, plastic-seeming, wrapped in hessian. Stone missed, so he under-lobbed another, like a grenade, and it hit that wrapped thing which made a fibre-glassy echo dunk. He crawled forward and tugged at that wrapping. Right enough, it was a long, faded-orange canoe, wrapped in rotted sack and blue, sun-bleached fertiliser bags that'd been violently slashed open to increase size. The canoe'd been pulled in under thorn bush, right-way-up, but fertiliser bags had stopped it filling with rain. Though a dip where the opening was had a layer of rotted autumn leaves so's it'd lay there since winter past – at least. A paddle was slid inside. The Nephew stood, stooped and dragged that canoe backward, into deeper overgrowths, like a just-shot corpse, he thought, and this movement stripped it of its coverings. The canoe was aswirl in graffiti, couple big quotes in spray paint, smaller quotations most wrote in those silver magic markers:

And I turned myself to behold wisdom, and madness, and folly: for what can the man do that cometh after the king? Even that which hath been already done.

He was no dafty nincompoop or dopey-docus. Ecclesiastes, only gumption in Bibles, he thought, and he could mind whole sections himself because he still had that little pocket Bible that had once belonged to a very, very naughty young woman and it excited him to read it, especially the lines she had underlined in her untutored hand, knowing all the most lustful things that woman had done! There was Romans 8:22, Isaiah 54:3 and much of Ecclesiastes. I sought in my heart to give myself unto wine, yet acquainting my heart to lay hold on folly. I got me servants and maidens, and had servants born in my house and whatsoever mine eyes desired I kept not from them. As it happeneth to the fool so it happeneth even to me: and why was I then more wise? And how dieth the wise man? as the fool. Questions, questions, but the Nephew licked his lips at this, for he had most niggling wee suspicion, was not this the entire story of Man Who Walks and his pursuits of him? Were he and the Foreman any better than The Man Who Walks, the fool? You can do the midnight rosary with as many servant girls as

47

you want, but you will never know all the excessive pleasures of past kings and concubines, this is the lament of the sybarites, chasing dreams – seeking ones as yet undreamt and, in the end, fool, imitator of the king, king himself: we all will perish unremembered. Nothing new under the sun on account of all that has gone before, is one conclusion of these musings or, as Sam Beckett, Nobel Prize for Literature 1969, put it, 'And for other reasons better not wasted on cunts like you'.

Whole bloody canoe was scrawled with these creepy Bible quotations, but the Nephew tried to put mere thoughts and fears of dark waters out there to one side. Such bright morning took dominion and he made himself ready for crossing.

He sat to tug off his combat trousers over boots in case they got all mankyised in that canoe bottom, stood, slipped the mobile in his lumberjack shirt pocket and dropped down his jacket. He opened his backpack to check his hunting knife and that's when he saw yon bin-liner he'd crammed in as a pillow the night before, still there and all forgot about. He yanked it out. Opened the bin-liner and he thought it was reams and reams of cine-film, a 16mm ribbon of dreams that was coming out. Whole thing stuffed with it, but then he saw it was actual typewriter ribbon, miles and miles of the stuff; maybe a report one those boffins was writing up on The Man Who Walks, so he crammed it all back in, but he couldn't fit combats and jacket too, so he spraffed them up back of that pointy-ended canoe.

He took the paddle square in two hands and practised a wee bit, stood there in his shirt and bockers and, guessing there was nothing for it, shouldered on the backpack and pulled the canoe down to water's edge.

He'd never been long enough at the high school to've done this carry-on, the old canoe rolls with helmet banging off bottom of a pee-filled shallow end, but he'd watched the mugs do it one winter's day through the steamed-up outside window of the new swimming pool in his truancy phase. Phases.

There was a lot of creepy popper seaweed close inshore, so it was going to be awkward to gain deep water. None for it but to push the canoe ahead, splash out, bow pointed to opposite shores. Not far at all, he kept thinking; then, using the paddle on rocks under water, he managed to lift sodden boots an snug hisself in, arse soaked right away on the canoe bottom that he thought he'd need to be laving out so much muckwater. He leaned over to one side, took up his paddle and, lo and behold, he was sat steady in a canoe on fearful loch water, squinting at the fast-moving currents ahead, seeing it was rushed west, at a fair old rate of knots, but preferable to being taken upstream to rapids under that old cantilever! If he did coup, he'd be carried outward, but the long, slung sandbar by the old seaplane base would be something he could kick in for. There was nae choice; he set forth.

The Nephew began to paddle and his canoe moved over the loch surface surprisingly quick, out past seaweed slops in the shallows and in and among those currents. He'd imagined force of the black water frothing against sides of the biblical canoe but, by angling the paddle blades down, he could easy counter its sweep and he turned his head round, seeing how far he'd already come in the orange canoe. In a crazy flush of confidence he even considered rounding the sand bar and paddling up to the beach over the clear water and across the wreck of the *Breda* herself, for landfall, walking down to the old station and cutting off Man Who Walks there and then, maybe carry this bloody canoe, balanced on his head! Steady now, old mate, the Nephew thought.

He was well out on that firth, seeing the village off to his right from a new angle over the straits. He couldn't have been far off halfways across – sun all way above. Ahead, the peninsula mountains with the superquarry buried deep in them like a skelf; behind, Ben More, clear as a huge, mad projection on the wall of horizon. So eerily quiet out there, deep under him silence, then a peeping bird hugging the glassy surface made past, saw it dip a wing to miss, pass behind . . . the stern. Far across the perfect polished floor of water, against his squint he could see the wee ferry *Flora MacDonald*, a thirty-footer with a putt-putting Evinrude: full-house, it was towing an unpowered rowing boat heavy with anorak-clad touristos rocking in its lively wake.

The Nephew sang:

> Michael, row the boat ashore
> Hallelujah,
> The river's deep and wide
> Hallelujah
> There's milk and honey on the other side
> Halle-oo-oo-jah.

What he thought was a lobster creel buoy was a sky-pointed seal's nose, its fibre-optic whiskers showing water drops he was so close. Maybe he could come to love the sea, one those late conversions in life he'd often read about!

The seal sunk for cover as the mobile phone shrilly rang 'Rule Britannia' in his breast pocket. Damn and blast! He parried the paddle across, hanging on with the right hand, and picked out that phone with the left; the canoe began to drift to bad places as he thumbed up the button.

'Caught me at a poor time here. Delicate ops.'

'Are ya with a whoor, boy?'

'A grey seal, phone you back.'

'AH YAH!' The Nephew yanked the phone away from his ear.

There was the most intense, jabbing pain on his left leg, then another, so he fiercely jerked, kicked up splashes at the canoe side, thought himself having a heart attack.

'Oh fiddlesticks,' he grimaced. 'Ouch, oh, OUCH!'

A little voice in his hand trembled, calling, 'Whaass matter, laddie . . . ?'

He tried drop-pocketing yon mobile in his shirt but another sting on his bare leg! Phone missed, bounced once on fibreglass and slithered down the canoe flank with a neat plop into that sea, extinguishing all the Foreman's protests, for the moment at least.

He had to try to stand and get away from those pains and, as he lifted his torso clear of the canoe, he saw his bare thighs and lower legs were crawling with clung masses of yellow-jacketed wasps! The canoe wobbled down to the left, in a sinking sway as if the top could be breached by the suddenly clear loch water. The Nephew yelled aloud and tried to balance other way as more wasps came fury-buzzing upward from the opened hole in the canoe body. He swiped out at his thigh, got stung on the hand and dropped the paddle. Down in the canoe bottom with a little muddy water he could see a bust-open half of a whole wasp's nest shoogling from one side to another as he balanced; nest must have been built in there all summer, yacuntya, he thought, looked round, wide-eyed, middle of fucking black lochs under faultless skies. Choice was clear: drown or stung to death – got a last piercing just below his balls and chose: the Nephew leaned, went over with his feet still in that biblical canoe.

Underwater the Nephew kept eyes tight shut, not wanting to

see savage serrations and wicked arêtes of a sunken mountain range below, the Foreman's phone bubbling his voice, sinking past scallop meadows and cliff-edge lobster villages, the headless seal's body at surface above. What he felt then, his eyes shut against the salt, believing this was his end, was not fear to be in his worst of feasible scenarios; not fear but huge sense of solidarity with the historical drowned, like that foster-daughter, and a deep spurt of detestation and violence for that animal fool Man Who Walks, his blood Uncle who he clearly hadn't tortured nearly enough.

His face slid out on an oily surface among patches of floated drowned wasps on their backs, wasps' little legs like girl eyelashes held to yonder sky. He spat and spun cause already that capsized canoe had drifted over him and away. What was keeping him floated was his backpack, strapped to his shoulders, so he spun it off cause the buoyancy was forcing his face forwards. He could see it was air trapped inside the bin-liner of typewriter ribbon was all that was keeping him up, so, holding it out in front of him with both arms, he began to kick and mush furiously towards that sand bar.

In moments he realised he was actually going to make it to the shore, the current not nearly carrying him as violently as he feared, but his feet were deep cold within his boots and he was fearful of any rock crops with their kelpy sheetings, but, unspectacularly, he came to first levels of seaweed float; found he was already in his own depth.

Drooked, the Nephew had to declare he stuttered through the waves and limped out the loch that morning, onto stone and shattered construction debris of the northern shores, only in boots, clinging shirt and underwear, he shivered and emptied water out his backpack looking for a quiet spot to sneak up onto the trusty old A828 and north.

Numbing cold and salt must act antiseptic, because as soon as he left the waters his legs started to sting away like nobody's business as if he'd eased under his skin with a razor and lifted a strip up, the way Jennifer Faulkner says it felt when he coaxed her to carve his name in her arm. So he just lay among whins down by the road, listening to their seed pods pop in the direct sunlight and the little trickling sound of their thrown spores falling through adjacent bushes. He was getting his puff back, grinning at leg pain, then chuckling, hearing vehicles whizzing past, north. He squeezed the shirt best he could and pink water from its cheap dye came out. His legs were killing with stungness. What he needed wasn't just a pair of breeks, he thought, but some blonde bint in suit and Porsche to take him north for a kiss per kilometre. Or better still, a safe house or bolt-hole himself. Stood with boxer shorts tugged that bit lower below the long shirt, and his big boots, he'd might just pass for some ridiculous Australian backpacker with normal shorts and here he began to think, in his moment of weakness (as, he must confess, he had done after imagining the Hole's anointed fingers, fixing the toilet seat), of Paulette Mahon, who lived a few mile up the road at Boomtown and who might, if he played his cards right, provide a safe house for recovery, and trousers!

So the Nephew lay there, near stung to death and half drowned, shirt spread out on whin-bush spikes, head on the squelchy bag of typewriter ribbon, thought of his young twenties, snout-faced Paulette's lispy vocabulary from a tongue-piercing she once swallowed. Paulette, with a burgundy and aqua tattoo of a weeping willow's downshower at the *very* bottom of her spine and those legs! She was using a tin of his shaving foam a week during his residency! Only let him bide two weeks, then posted him forward a package of oily socks: 'You forgot your socks,' wrote in a surprisingly precise hand!

Paulette spent so long in bed, her nail varnish matched her pyjamas. Paulette, mostly languid in a long, drained bath, always tuned to Aluminumville FM, playing 'Riders on the Storm', 'His brain is squirming like a toad,' her rendered half-decent through the always-open bathroom door, archipelagos of clung bubble bath on the strategic points all along her somehow tannedness, devouring cannabis resin through a pipe made from a Coca-Cola can. In the mornings, he had the brief privilege to learn, she only ever seemed to have one dream, about a chocolate Malteser being lodged in her belly button.

First thing Paulette ever said to the Nephew, at a crowded wedding table that he'd gatecrashed, was, 'Women stand stiller than men in the Ladies toilets, doing their make-up in the mirror,' she said, 'you become so still that the movement-sensitive monitor puts the light out on you and you smudge your make-up; it thinks there's nobody in there. Gives me the maximum creeps, makes me feel I don't exist,' she shivered.

'You know, I very much identify with your experience of existential dread there. I've felt a very similar feeling, I believe, when I've noticed, late at night, the low swaying bow of a tree setting off a movement-sensitive lamp outside a property.'

Ah, the poetry of love!

In those days Paulette's only nourishment ever seeming: sperm, Asti Spumante and forever nibbling on a snap-brittle stalk of unboiled spaghetti. Her famous flight to London on modelling trial for a swimsuit catalogue and picked up by some rich man on the train, her shouting from a pulled-down Hackney taxi window at King's Cross to first London prostitute she'd ever seen, 'I love your shoes, they're beautiful, where'd you get em?' After a week or so you imagine the rich boy realised he could not handle Paulette in her wildly scandalous girlhood, but when she came back here she'd a bobby-dazzler wardrobe of silk she was forever having dry-cleaned, so these wee blue number labels were always attached to her cuffs with a tiny safety pin. The Nephew thought, Oh Paulette! Sadness of wild spirits broke by their own excess which only kings should know.

Now she's part-time at the Sea Life Centre in a skin-tight wet-suit, kneeled in the Rock Pool Environment holding out starfish to wee kids, hitched to probably some ordinary boy who likes his footie, but he'd definitely heard worked shifts offshore. Two wee daughters that look just like her, the Nephew'd heard, when he cautiously enquired round the pubs, and mortgaged to the hilt on the new scheme at Boomtown, just a few mile up the road. What if that hubby was two week offshore? But the Nephew couldn't turn up looking like this . . . had to get a pair of trousers, at any rate, before calling on Paulette, yacuntya!?

He jumped to his feet and got that warmed, damp shirt over his shoulders. He chose his thumbing pitch on the long straight so's he could identify Fed cars at some distance. A white taxi going south made him duck briefly. Forty-seven northbound vehicles, private, heavy goods, utility and public service, passed him, most markedly accelerating. He hardly bothered thumbing latest reg, all company-car chancers. He could read no meanings from resultant registration plates, nothing at all; no combination of number plates communicated to him usual informations, nor did number plates spell out Man Who Walks or Paulette! That concatenation of letters and numerals seemed meaningless. When wee he used to demarcate all vehicles as either 'sad-faced' or 'happy' depending on the anthropomorphic design qualities of their headlights and radiator grilles, but now he couldn't decide if these modern, madly overpowered vehicles, clearly designed for other worlds than Argyllshire, had sad, happy or even angry faces.

Forty minutes later the Nephew came out of sun behind him, down into Boomtown from the megalithic burial grounds up above the Old Folk's home, through that place below Forestry Commission conifers where he once saw a pine cone big as a full-size chocolate Easter egg, one of the ones that he never got.

Blood-stained trousers not too noticeable, he stepped over a picket fence and walked up to Paulette's front door. Doorbell played the *Close Encounters* coda.

Leaf-pattern glass swung open and an adorable little miniature Paulette looked directly at him cause he was at the bottom of the steps and she says, 'Who the fuck're you?'

'Mummy or *Daddy* in?'

'You're not social services, are ya?'

'No. I'm an old pal of your Mummy's.'

'You mean an old *boyfriend*?'

'Well, goodness me,' the Nephew coughed.

'Don't tell anyone,' she whispered, 'I'm home alone! You can wait out there, I'm babysitting ma silly wee sister; Dad's away offshore, Mum's just down the shop and I've never *ever* to let anyone *in*.'

'Quite correct,' the Nephew nodded.

She did her size equivalent of slamming the door, sort of running, heaving at it so's you thought she'd come through that glass. She clicked the Yale, the Nephew thought, with that foul, confident possessiveness of Settled Community kids round their secure little houses.

He sat cross-legged, plucking daisies on that wee lawn; Mary Queen of Scots had her head chopped *off*. The lawn hadn't been cut for four or five days, so *at least* a week till hubby was home. He took out his Japanese address on that bloodstained piece of paper writ in a very, very shaky hand and put it safe in the shirt pocket. The wee daughters pulled over a chair to the front-room window: stared through dirty double-glazing and giggled towards him. He overheard a cheeky comment about his trousers being far too long.

That doorbell! Yes, the movies were not the Nephew's chosen art form. He recalled, once and once only, The Man Who Walks took him to the cinema, in the Port's flea pit, and paid for his seat in the stalls; there *were* only stalls. It was meant to be a scary film but the Nephew was scared enough by the time he got to his seat. 'I can't hear a fucking thing,' The Man Who Walks roared, and the woman seated in front of them jumped and her perm shook.

'No characters are talking yet,' the Nephew whispered.

The Nephew has never managed in picture houses though he's bought many tickets. The Nephew enters, armed with valid ticket, chocolate-chip tub, or the incredible yellow mustard on his hotdog, but he can see nothing in the gloom. To crash his way to even the nearest seat would be an embarrassment. So he tries waiting for a brightly-lit scene that may illuminate his way forwards, but no, all the films are so moody these days. The Nephew waits in vain, lurking, sinister-seeming to the back-row dwellers and their furtive ways, so he retreats, pretends he's making for the bogs but instead he leaves the picture house altogether with his valid ticket, escapes the melancholy of some moronic screenwriter's denouement and feels newly invigorated to step out so soon, back into evening airs again, with his copy of Seneca's *Consolation to Helvia* in his jacket pocket; he takes a shivering stance on the street, watching interlinked teenagers brace the thoroughfare in both directions, and lifts the ice-cream to his lips, eyes missing nothing. Alive!

When things don't go well for him, the Nephew turns his mind to what is written in wry Suetonius: vain Caesar staring at a bust of Alexander the Great, thinking, By the time he was the age I am now, he'd conquered the world. Or old Art Schopenhauer, his steady gaze being returned for hours by the orange orang-utan in Dresden Zoo which the old cynic grew so fond of, towards the end.

The Nephew stood abruptly when Paulette's head on its swan's neck sailed along top of a hedge, like it'd been severed. He groaned at how she *still* looked and he thought: whatever so mine eyes desired I kept not from them.

Neither smiled nor frowned when she saw the Nephew, but she put down the shopping and lifted a hankie to her nose. Front door came open and two daughters piled out screaming, running round Paulette's denim legs, way that wee dug Trafalgar had bothered me, he thought, till I flung the cunt by its back leg into a wheelie bin.

Paulette looked him up and down, in his conglomerations of clothing, her snozzle was all red and chapped and in nasally voice she says, 'Well, least I won't have to worry that I haven't done the hoovering. Don't! . . . come near me. Less you want a cold.'

'Well worth it!' he goes and pecked her on a cheek. Her daughters wolf-whistled. He'd forgot eyes were that colour; a few more lines at the side but that was from too much laughing for these lands. He tried to take the shopping bags off of her, but she shrugged negative. He says, 'What happened to the hotel?'

'Long gone, stranger, like you.'

'Boating accident.' He held out his arms, squeezed down on his feet: water fizzed and buzzed still, from top of his boot.

'Chucked off a trawler for too much wanking?' she goes.

'Nah, it's true, bit of canoeing.'

She laughed, took a hanky out her sleeve and blew a real grogger.

'I travelled for years, recently I work at Agricultural Supplies, heaving pony nuts for well-to-dos basically.'

'No get yur leg over they horsey women types among the alfalfa?'

'Stick to the horses.'

'Poor horses. I work at the Sea Life Centre these days.'

'I know. Saw you in the brochure, they had you everywhere, in the water, behind the till, in the cafeteria.'

'That's how it is.'

'Our Prince is in the heather once more,' he shrugged.

'Your mental Uncle's still doing the runners!' she sniffed. 'Why don't you just let him alone?'

The Nephew stopped at the front door, 'He's a danger to himself. I'm worried sick about his well-being.'

'Ever thought, it's you an yours' mentalness he's tried to get away from; you keep catching him like a stray dug and dragging him back?' She looked at the Nephew out corridors of shadows, one girl-child wrapped round a thigh. 'Colin's away, come in if you want, mind your boots on the carpets.'

Colin, was it! The Nephew says, 'Some cold you've got there.'

'Summer colds are aye worser and with these wee ones it's hard taking to your bed any more.' She blew that cute snout again.

Front room he goes, 'Nae telly!?'

'Against them. Bad influence on these two.'

'That a paper there?'

'All you're going to get is the relentless goal machine that is Oban Cammanacht,' Paulette flicked out yon dreaded local paper (est. 1861) from the shopping bag. 'Want a beer?'

Plonked on the armchair of the three-piece suite, a cold Heineken was therefore delivered unto him but with unfortunancy those wee daughters brought an endless series of toys for the Nephew's inspection, Barbies, unfamiliar alien creatures and a plastic baby that both vomited and pished itself. 'I had a cuddly elephant when I was wee called Markus,' the Nephew tried.

They were unmoved.

Finally the tallest child dropped a living, all-too-ratlike gerbil from two cupped hands onto his groin area. 'Johnstone,' she introduced.

'If we want peace, I suggest the washing-machine room,' Paulette jerked her head, so he shucked off the gerbil and followed her to the washing-machine room that was more a cupboard with a Bendix inside, doing a demented cha-cha. With his lower lip pushed out in cursory interest he re-read, for fourth .... fifth time, front page of the newspaper: the customary photo of a minor member of the Royal Family who had strayed within one hundred miles. Also:

STOP PRESS

TULLOCH FERRY SEX ATTACK ON OAP COUPLE AND DOG MISSING

... elderly couple ... wish to remain anonymous, managed to reach their phone and summon police ... embarrassing task of untying them ... stripped naked, bound with electric wire and exposed to a torrent of verbal abuse by a drug-crazed man *IN THEIR OWN HOME* ....

The Nephew looked down the page.

HEAVY GOODS ASSAULT
A lorry driver's nose was broken by an ungrateful hitch-
hiker . . .

As per usual he flapped the pages and smartly slapped them
back to the Personals at the rear, a new editorial innovation.

HE SHOOTS HE SCORES
Dougie, 29 yrs old, into hunting and shooting, looking for
a lady who shares those interests. If that's you then reply
BOX 436

YOU CAN TALK TO ME
Malky, 28, SINGLE, wants to meet girls. BOX 434

Ah these silver-tongued devils of my homeland! the Nephew
thought.

Door pushed in at him and Paulette squeezed through, yelled
above washing-machine spin, 'Awful car crash up the road, they
was saying in the shop, must be bad, took the boy away in an
ambulance just there.'
   'Oh!?' he went, quick-slapping yon rag into a folded square
and sliding it well in under the washing-machine. He noticed
these envelopes of silver foil beneath the machine's wheels, to
stop it running away or whatever.
   Paulette sighed, 'Aghhhh!' tiptoe reaching, her slimness
perfectly intact, to a shelf for the makings in a Golden Virginia
tin, lid clipped into the base and green paint worn silver, then
she did a long slide down, sat against the door bottom, legs
along the Nephew's, feet *really* close by his thigh, his boot by

hers, she got whole-hunkered forward, hair falling into her face with the jerks as those daughters shoved at other side of the door, shouting behind her like some proto-drug squad, but they soon wearied, way kids do these days with all food additives and video games in them, he thought. She went about blowing her nose and asks, 'Dinnae have any snot on my top lip, do I?'

He shook his head, mesmerised by her.

Paulette's experienced fingers were sprinkling an Rizla-ing up.

He goes, 'I know an old gypsy cure for the cold,' but she ignored so's he goes, 'What age is the biggest?'

'Niamh,' she went.

'Neeve,' he goes.

'Know how it's spelled?' she says.

'N - E - E - V - E,' he goes.

'Nut. N - I - A - M - H. It's Irish,' she went.

He didn't flinch, 'What age is she?' he says.

'Eight.'

He whistled, 'Jeez, yonks since I saw you.'

She lit up, inhaled, held down and passed to him. She blew smoke and goes, 'I must say, I'm impressed, I was expecting you to be jamp out bushes every night for months, or Colin to show up with his legs broke.'

'He's fairly clipped your wild wings, hope this is all paid for,' the Nephew sneered and toked deepest of deeps, nodded at the jiving washing-machine.

'Want me to straddle it?' she whispered, blew out smoke.

'Bet your daughters do while you're down the shop,' he finally says when he couldn't hold smoke in any longer.

She pointed at him, 'You will *not* stray within ten metres of my daughters without me being there.'

'Don't worry, Paulette, y'know fine they're too old for me. So how d'ye keep the old spark alive in married life then?'

'Who says we're married and at least he can get it up.'

'Your memories no frazzled then.'

'Hard to forget worst sex of your life.'

'I've been researching.'

'Aye, on yersel.'

'For the day we two would meet again,' he bowed, gesticulated.

She laughed, a sort of sneezy sound, and grabbed the toke off him.

He knew he shouldn't smoke dope. Could lead on to major relapse, buying cigarettes and voddy instead of beer, and once back on the spirits you're doomed, man. He'd get the urge for powders and Bob's your uncle! his wee castle would come tumbling down. He thought, Couldn't let myself go that way again. Last time on dope I minded looking at a goldfish bowl trying to decide if the water was behind the glass or surrounding it; I got drawn into a conversation regarding Carpaccio and the evolution of perspective in Venetian art, and I gave away too many juicy ideas of my own, yacuntya.

Paulette was talking, 'The older one, Niamh, worries me. One night when she was younger I had a girlfriend over, who was at high school with me. We're both eating tea and my wee Niamh put her chin on the table and says, "Mummy, there's a battery up my bottom." Well, panic stations broke out and, sure enough, one of the double AA's you put in a Walkman, a Duracell, was shoved in and stuck up there. She coulda been lectrocuted.'

'She's got an illustrious future.'

'Shut your gob. So I sit her down.'

'She could still sit?'

'And I says to her, "Now you shouldn't be putting things up your bottom."'

'Put it in Latin on the family coat of arms! Don't you want her to take after her mother though?'

'"And if you really want to, you must come and ask Mummy first!" "Oh," she says, "does that include food?" So I says, "Food's meant to be up there, darling," and she says, "Even the frozen peas I get out of the fridge and stuff up?" And she'd been getting the froze peas and putting those up too!'

'Ah, the joys of parenting, eh?' The Nephew just started talking, hearing his own voice, not caring that her children were already hopeless psychoanalytic cases, knowing if he looked in a mirror he could never focus on his own eyes. He says, 'Paulette; hey, Paulette! Up Bealach an Righ, past Pennyfuir through Tulloch Ferry, choose east or north to you here, I'm no fussed; I went away from old Dalriada, to the army, to a country, to somewhere proper, these lands would play on me at nights, like the shadows on the ceiling. Travel? Travel is for students; don't want to travel, I want to *arrive*, be elsewhere, like old Ovid, concerned with objects that transform themselves.'

He took another hit of spliff. 'Aye, Paulette; hey, Paulette! Have you ever had a place where things have gone down big time for you, just a place that's going in all directions?'

'You what?'

'Far as your eye can see. Out and lonely among the waters. Ranged somewhere among rock and you've say spent a dod of time there or something happened to you and then you go back to this very place that should mean so much to you and it just, ach, disappoints or something?'

Paulette drawled, with a smile on the sides of her mouth, 'I see you still cannie handle a smoke. What're you on about? You're way too deep for me as per usual; all those dictionaries

64

you swallowed burping up again.' She was getting fixed to roll another and the fat whopper they worked on was not near done.

'Nah, nah, this isn't book stuff, it's real! I've been to New York, I've been to Rome, seen a million birds circle St Peter's at dusk, the flocks go invisible until they wheel and flourish like a swarm, opening their wings above the Eternal City, heading west. You come back here and the place seems thinned out, nowhere near as real as it was in your fizzed-up brainbox. Nostalgia. You start to notice tricks time has played. Trees are taller, there's a new something over there that wasn't in your mind's picture, or you'd excluded, foolishly, the way Napoleon warned his generals not to make pictures in their heads but to trust only what their eyes could perceive. Jeez, you get back to home-town you believe you have strong feelings about, to find maybe certain buildings are a whole storey higher than you remembered but you kept those cherished memories so sacred! Memory is the mark of love. You find your vision, the product of your love, is grander than the reality. Memory is the mark of love, Paulette. To keep something in your mind and cherish it, what a miracle in this world.'

Paulette giggled at him, concentrating, rolleying away, smiling to herself: aroused by some briar she'da been tumbled over in long ago; dumbly superior as if he'd no done that stuff with McCallum sisters, gone and given them some *plein air* memories too; aye aye, a wee nest egg of sweet memories for him also, to take with him when he goes down slow with the cancer or the angina or the pneumonia or the linguistic area of his brain blacked out in a spreading aneurysm's fireworks.

He says, 'Aye, like time I had to fight Robert Sinclair when fourteen.'

'Here we go,' she whispered.

'Hardest guy around. Like some medieval joust, his gang had to meet my gang and it was in this place, way up on the pony-trek to Black Lochs. Fuck alone knows why we'd have chose to meet out there cause we was so knackered by the time we's reached it, on a scorching heatwave day, lucky we could lift our arms, or at least it seemed that way . . . *seemed* it was miles and miles to get there and I minded it as being this lush little plain meadow with all the ben sides seeming to dip down into real rich, long straps of fresh grass. A green basin surrounded by mountains curving away up to the turned-back summits and a full sky above black mounts. Now a few month ago I walked back up there, to find that meadow where I bested Sinclair; a stroll down memory lane sort of.'

'Aye, back to your glory days!' Her snigger turned into a mucus release and she darted her beautiful fingers up her cuff for yon hankie. She muttered, 'Near as a dosser like you'd get to a battlefield, since you gave away yur Action Man.'

'Listen, Minnehaha, course it wasn't miles at all; I was there in a jiffy.'

Fabric hanging, white and green in front her red lips, there was a giggle. Nodding.

'And it wasn't this grand amphitheatre of my mind at all, with embankments all soared away up on every side, it was just this totey wee *cabbage patch*, with some slopes over to wee, *wee* cliffs. See, it seemed so far cause I was all the way there psyching myself up. Hills seemed all round cause when me and Sinclair walked towards each other, the whole world shut out, huge mountains just flew away back with the bang of first punch. It enclosed us, cause there was no way you could escape that conflict, so I *felt* all mountains round us. Then when I'd triumphed, I recalled it as this, arcadia . . . that's sort of paradise like. What I'm saying is, it's where our head is at that prints our impression of the landscape! I realised early on, growing up in grandeur like this that you and me are surrounded by each day, I sussed that cause I was lonely I preferred landscapes to people, then I was reading Bertie Camus, as you do, and I read in his *Carnets*: "In our youth we attach ourselves more readily to a landscape than a man. It is because landscapes allow themselves to be interpreted." And of course they do, but differently depending on the state of your mind.'

'You were certainly nae good at attaching yourself to any woman.'

'The land is here, all round us, but each of us pulls from it or inserts into it what we want, we all see it different, like we could meet the ghosts of other folks' needs and dreams wandering the places at night.'

'Watch you don't meet your own,' Paulette curled her lip, a little uglily.

'Exactly. I believe we live in a semi-spirit world. Sometimes the deceased just forget they're dead for a moment or two. Like I knew soldiers, eyewitnesses, who can't agree on where they all were on the field of battle cause you have all these highly excited individual viewpoints jostling with each other. No just Gulf or Falklands or Normandy. Some battles with hundreds of thousands of men, it's been impossible to find the battlesite cause no one there could agree; only the burial pits grown over to show for real, like at Culloden. Some battlesites have gone missing, generals arguing it all happened over the next hill. Like the Romans in Scotland, the Ninth Legion marching north to relieve the Tay garrisons, they vanished and it's said at night you can still hear them marching. Aye, when you look at this earth we walk upon with adult eyes.'

Some of the conversations folk have in this life, eh? yacuntya.

'Hoi, you've nodded off, ya blethering lightweight.'

Right enough, his legs were stunged to billy-o, dope was crashing the Nephew out – knacked; he goes and says, 'Aye, look, gotta make a phone call, hardly slept last night.'

'Oh aye!?'

'Maybe I could have a quick wee nap of forty winks but you'd wake me later, aye?'

'More like forty wanks with you.'

He tried to get to his feet but the pins were wobbling. 'It's no the grass,' he defended, 'I can tak the pace, pal. Suppose I should have something to eat. When *did* I last eat?'

'It's no grass,' went Paulette.

'Eh? What is it?!'

'It's some New Drug. Look, I crush down the seeds under the washing-machine, that's why I've aye got it on Spin. There's nothing in the wash.'

Right enough, the Nephew leaned down and glared seriously in: the washing-machine was empty. The envelopes of tin foil under the runners were grinding the drug up. His mouth went all dry. He didn't want to tamper with things he didn't understand.

He followed Paulette out the washing-machine room, along a corridor of echoes to bottom of the stair. She was carrying his black backpack that he'd forgot existed, he noticed white, semenish stains on it, then salvaged a memory, Dried salt water, he thought. She had another New Drug joint in her other fingers.

'Conducted tour. Girls' rooms, out of bounds.'

He nodded, not paying attention, to his later detriment, goes, 'Aye aye,' he'd realised how hungry he was.

She pointed up the stair so's he led the way, disappointed,

sumley supposed she thought she'd grab him if he fell, but he'd been looking forward to watching as her tight behind went up. He ascended.

Top of the stairs she swung a door to a single bed in a wee room and tossed his backpack in on the duvet. Wallpaper was all bright colours; place looked like it was never used. 'Luxury,' he goes, and she kissed him, aside the cheek.

'Give us a call in a hour or so, I've got to make an urgent phone call. Business.'

'Okey-dokey,' she sniggered. 'It's sort of good to see you, ya lightweight,' she pulled the door tight.

He smiled in the true joy that only a woman can give and got the Buddhist snowboarder's breeks off, then sat on the side of the bed, fascinatingly poked at the wasp stings on his thighs that'd come up as hard little lumps. Off with the damp shirt and keks and he wormed under yon bright blue duvet, shivered at coldness, his toes came against something so he reached down. Pulled up a cold, rubbery hot-water bottle from the last guest. He let it slide with a collapsing blurble down on a bedside rug. Then the visions began.

Brand-new reg car stopped, raged into reverse. Above the reg the enamelled number plate read: WARP SPEED MR ZULU. The Nephew picked up his backpack. The Nephew didn't know if it was polite to let *him* lean over and open the passenger door or do it yourself, but the driver leaned and shoved it open.

'Are fifteen possums going to appear from the trees?'

'Sorry.'

'Australian?'

'Nut.'

'Are you jogging or do you just have no trousers on?'

The Nephew leaned down to smile and the driver looked

disappointed, as if he was about to drive on, so the Nephew clambered in and water poured out his backpack swinging over the gear stick. 'I had the old canoe accident this morning,' he says.

'Oh, white-watering, I see.' Disinterested, he looked in his mirror, accelerated impressively.

'I'm headed for Ballachulish.'

'Where's that, is this the right direction?'

'Aye, twenty mile north.' He'd got the seatbelt on and looked at the driver's face, realised, just then, immediately and intuitively by that face that they were going to crash in this car. Glued on dashboard top (he could still see a hardened run of Evo-stick down past the clock) was a little cup made of coloured glass squares, there was a real candle burning inside. The driver nodded at the candle, 'I'm a Buddhist.'

'Aye?'

'I'm a snowboarder. A Buddhist snowboarder.'

'Right.'

Music with a mechanical beat was playing very loudly. The Nephew knew this type of music was called 'gangster rap music'. It didn't have a patch on Roses or Lizzy. He'd seen it performed on televisions by men moving their arms violently in an effort to back up their articulation. Once, at some girl's house, he'd listened closely to the words; each song was a sort of narrative and, relevantly enough, he'd noticed each song, one after another, was set inside a car. It was the music of a car-bound planet. Often cars would draw opposite him when he was thumbing it at Give Way junctions and the low sound of that car music was actually rocking the vehicle on its low suspension. With a sinister, subtle motion.

The Buddhist snowboarder took the first corner with the needles on the speedo and revs pointed directly up, gearing in for curves. The Nephew glimpsed a lone sheep in a field with two magpies standing on its back, signifying God only knows what on the luck front. Cars were queued up in the petrol station at the caravan site and he glimpsed an old lady with the petrol nozzle stuck in a jerry can.

'It's summer,' announced the Nephew.

'Sure is glorious, eh?'

'There's no snow.'

'I thought you had mountains?'

'Aye, but no that high. Few patches lying through summer in the corries but you won't find more.'

'Well, shit. I drove all night. I need a cup of tea.'

Looking straight ahead the Nephew pondered this relationship between himself and the unknown body part inside him right then that would fail one day, lead to his death. He thought, If only we knew. Way when you look into someone's eyes you don't foresee both will be serrated in a future crash impact, unless you predict futures and bring out those lacerations there yourself. Often the Nephew would dream that all future injuries and fatal ailments on the bodies surrounding him, at a party, or in the street, or with the women he'd lay beside in quiet rooms, that those ailments all immediately manifested themselves simultaneously on the humans around him: tumours fruiting forth, faces tearing open, lungs as heavy as bags of seawater so all destiny was revealed in its sordidness. He believed it would be a mark of mercy to act immediately, invoke those destinies.

'You wouldn't know anywhere we can stop for a cup of tea, would you?'

He took his chance cause they were going to crash. Silvermines Hotel in Boomtown would give him a chance to case Paulette's place across the field on yonder new scheme; he could tell by the washing-line who was home, so he says, 'Aye, there's a sound farmers' pub up here, on the Moss Road, you couldn't lend a pair of breeks . . . trousers, could you? Most ma gear's . . . lost at sea.'

Speedo was at 110, one finger at midday on the steering wheel the driver went on, 'It's a nice cuppa I fancy, I gave up the drink.'

'Me too,' lied the Nephew.

'I used to have a great girlfriend, outdoor type,' he looked at the Nephew scornfully.

Obviously I don't qualify as the outdoor type though that fucker of my Uncle would be top of this cunt's class, no doubt, the Nephew thought.

The driver goes, '*She* liked canoeing. Yeah, classy smart lady.'

'Aye? Know what I saw yesterday? Lorry, from right here in the Highlands and the crazy driver had a "I Swerve for Kangaroos" sign on the back!'

'Never. You don't say!'

'Right enough.'

'I tell you, she had a thing about showers, getting men in the shower with her; that's my conclusion, with hindsight. She sends me letters from bloody Sweden, every month or so. In one she was up in the rainforests of the Northern Territories and she was mad for this fella. You're not Australian, are you?' He geared a corner at about 60.

'No. I already says. I'm from hereabout.'

'Right, well, she'd the eye for this chap who of all things used to sit in a bathtub of ice cubes, middle of the rainforest with a felt hat on, reading poetry. I get all the details.'

'What poetry?' the Nephew said, grimacing at another corner.

'Eh?'

'What poetry did the fella read? You can often get the handle on a fella if you know what poetry he reads.'

'You don't say? She never mentioned *those* details, she's in such a rush to get to the sex; *Australian* poetry, no doubt. He wore a felt hat, I know that, so never to be trusted.'

'Couldn't agree more, never.'

'So the chap has a house with a balcony at the back.'

'I see.'

'Yes,' he laughed. There was sweat on his upper lip. 'So in the pitch black of night she goes into the rainforest, she swims naked in the river and builds herself a bonfire, picks bags of this moss growing on the river bank, rolls herself saturated in river mud, then sticks this moss all over her body and stands in front of the fire. It's luminous moss, glows green phosphorescent when exposed to light, and she walks back to his house, climbs up on the balcony, pure alien, green and glowing, she knocks on this bloody guy's shutters and when he opened them she said, "May I use your shower?"' He yelped with laughter.

'That's some chat-up line!' the Nephew jerked both knees over as they burst out a dry verge and left a gritty cloud in the wing mirror.

'Isn't it! Isn't it just,' the driver laughed. 'Same thing in Africa few years later, she came bounding off the game reserve, up to this guy's compound covered in dust, he was an Australian too. They're bloody everywhere. "May I use your shower?" she'd said again. Volcanoes!' he yelled. 'That was another of her thangs. Dragged me to Pompeii to see all those stone people with their lungs liquefied by the heat. Erotic murals of buggery, bestiality, wanking and orgies; you name it, they were up to it then.'

'I agree.'

'Didn't get a minute's sleep in the motel. Then it was off to

Iceland. Anywhere there was volcanic activity there was no holding her back.'

They passed a man with no arms leaping up and down on the spot by the verge.

'I've seen it all now,' the driver giggled.

'That's Itchy Magellan, asking for a lift, a local'll get him; he danced the tango with an auto-thresher and walked calmly to the phone box, dialled 999 with his nose, knew if he'd ran he'd bled to death.'

'Sounds interesting, wish I'd picked up him instead of you. Why's he called Itchy?'

'Cannie scratch his own back.' The Nephew wished he could interrogate Itchy, a sometime imbiber with his Uncle, who'd lift the glass to Itchy's lips.

'I had this other girlfriend in Japan, where I became a Buddhist. This one went off with an Australian too. You can imagine what she got into there.'

'Escorts. I hear they're crazy for Western escort girls there.'

'Oh, sure she started at that, but that wasn't enough for this one. She got ten thousand American dollars in cash for one month and a night's work.'

The Nephew whistled, 'Jeez-o, ten thou. A *night's* work?'

'Oh yeah.'

'Must say, my curiosity is whetted.'

'She gets locked up in a room for a month.'

'Yes.'

'Ate nothing but sturgeon beluga caviare.'

'Mmm.'

'Drank nothing but Evian water. After a month she's looking something else. She sent me the polaroids. Then the night's work.'

'Yesss?'

'She gets taken to this private men's club, richest men in Tokyo, she does a striptease for them on a huge glass stage with the men all underneath, looking up. When she's stripped off, she crouches down and takes a crap on the glass with all the men's tongues pressed against the glass underneath her asshole.' He accelerated more. 'Then those men took it in turns to come up and eat her shit. They pay a fortune for it.'

'You wouldn't give me this girl's address, would you?'

'Ha!' he barked out, then grimaced in the mirror.

The Nephew looked aft in the wing mirror. A sleek Fed Mondeo was sat right on their butt. His stomach sank, he could see the driver was propped up high on cushions, mutt in the back, all windows wound down ruffling the Alsatian's coat. The Nephew shrunk lower through the safety belt. 'Shit, slow down,' he says.

'Can't do it, mate. Problem is,' he yawned, 'one of my brake lights isn't working. If I touch the brake pedal, this policeman is going to pull us over.'

The Nephew found himself shouting, 'Don't touch the brakes then!'

Boomtown's thirty-mile-an-hour limit was coming up fast.

'Why? What's in it for me?' Driver was smiling at him and he crunched down those gears to second, the revs almost went off the scale and a plume of smoke went backwards over the bonnet of the Fed, but they crossed the village speed limits spot on thirty.

'Only kidding,' the driver says, 'brake lights work fine. You have a fugitive feel about you, how come you're so nervous about the police?'

The Nephew glared out the window, then back at him, and snapped, 'Yon hotel's on the right.'

The car swung in careful onto the gravel and the Fed kept

going on through Boomtown without a backward glance. They pulled up, parked and the insane driver puffed out his candle so the smoke stung the Nephew's right eye. 'Sorry, don't *have* a spare pair of trousers,' he announced.

The Nephew led the way as the driver beeped central-locking behind him. Nephew glanced over at Paulette's. Refuge was there, he could only see wee lassies' gear hanging straight down in the drying green. He scoped the other washing lines but no a breek among them, yacuntya. There'd been stacks among the wash-line whirlies on the Old Fellie's estate night before.

The public bar was full of a spectacularly decrepit clientele and there was a dreary, humourless hush about it as the Nephew squelched up to that counter in his boxer shorts. Place had been refurbished, of course, and quite cosily. 'Pint lager and tea for one,' he says to the lassie in a white dress who looked down at his bare legs.

'Sorry?'

'Pint lager and a tea, please.'

'Earl Grey if you have it,' the driver chipped in.

'We don't have lager.'

'No lager! Call yerself a pub?'

'No. Actually. This a nursing home.'

Back outside, the driver says, 'Used to be a hotel, you say, hey man, you really know where the action is. What's wrong with your legs?' He was putting on an annoying Ozzie accent.

'My canoe had a dormant wasp's nest in it.'

'You're no lucky mascot, are you? C'mon, let's get you to Bala-who-who.'

He knew he should trust his instinct but he paced back to the car anyway, self-consciously adjusting his boxer shorts, fastening his seatbelt.

Sure as fate, half a mile on, yonder side of the village, they passed a man on a bicycle, the wing knifed so close the Nephew noticed the bicycle had no chain. In the mirror he saw the yellow wellies spreadeagle and the bike's back wheel rear up as the cyclist vanished into the ditch; then another mile on, the Buddhist snowboarder yelled, 'Streuth,' under-steered a corner, they crossed the road, the Nephew grimaced and, taking forty feet of barbed-wire and rotted fence posts with them, they stopped on the downward lee of a sloped rapeseed field, out of view of the road – two sickeningly-coloured snowboards almost took the Nephew's head off on their way out through the busted windscreen. The fucking candle was still burning.

'See that, my Buddha looks after me.'

The Nephew turned to his driver smiling, says, 'A car crash is the least excuse I need. Get your fucking trousers off.'

Wow! The Nephew jamp into woken-ness, thought himself still in Man Who Walks' dreadful den. It was pitch dark and him no reported in to Foreman, yacuntya! *Told* Paulette to wake me! He sat up with fiercest of fierce thirsts upon him. Jeezo, what drought! He had to drink. He swung his legs out, stood, thought he was on the New Drug still, cause he floated, then fell forward on the carpet and bit his tongue so's ornaments chinked out in that dark there. Jesus *Christ*, I musta woke the dead, he thought. He held his breath and listened out for dear life. Not a cheep. His legs weren't there, they'd got numbed.

'Itchy Magellan?' he says out loud.

His reached-down hand came on the bone hardness of swollen feet, like as all the wasp poison had sunk down to his toes. He couldn't stand up his feet were so numbed and invisibled too in such darkness. Where was the light? That hot-water bottle was beside him, so's he unscrewed the top and gobbled rubbery-tasted water out it, most gushing down cold onto his chest and as he gulp-gulped down out of the hot-water bottle he realised, *simultaneous*, he was furiously bursting for a pee too! Nothing for it, after he'd drained the water down his gullet, he got the end of Old Moody, the Marquis of Lorne, into the hot-water bottle end, trying to spill as little as possible as he pee'd back into it! Like this cow in a field he saw, drinking from the big trough his Uncle once had his eye on, a cow drinking and pishing at the same time, its tail canted out. 'In the fields of Abraham,' he moved lips to the words.

He screwed the hot-water bottle top on, realised how chilly it was, so he pulled himself back into bed and cuddled up, holding warmnesses of yon hot-water bottle filled with his own urine to his chest. He was famished hungry.

The Nephew nodded back off into delicious visions but then he was full awake, needed to pee! Yes, yet again, shamelessly unoriginal and repetitive but true, and most probably needing to evacuate the same volume of liquid he had ingested from within the hot-water bottle, now unlikely to receive a similar volume of urine again back into itself; even taking into account that absorbed by his dehydrations. For who can calculate the strange ministries of the body? And should he, say, commence the peeing and find the hot-water bottle, in simple mathematical terms, pushed to its volumic limits, well, imagine! How could he hold his head high again after peeing the overflow onto Paulette's spare-bedroom carpet, especially if she noticed! This would bring his already low standing, in her and the general eyes of the countryside, to a new low. In conclusion the Nephew's meditations were led towards one pulverising insight, in the manner of that written about by Leibniz or was it Santayana's essay on Lucretius? Who cares, the conclusion was: Get me to the pisser, yacuntya!

He got his arms down on carpet, then he lowered his numbed feet. He tried to find those boxer shorts, in case he run into one of Paulette's pesky daughters out there, him in the scud, and he'd be back in the newspaper for child molestings this time! It stung like billy-o getting the keks over the swole feet, they felt utterly ginormous to him, almost frightening, as if they may split, like when Hacker'd whispered to him, if you pulled back hard on your foreskin, the shaft of your knob would come shooting out like a banana, clunking to the floor and you'd never fit it back in again; in the days when it was rumoured, also by Hacker, that you could swallow your own Adam's apple!

Too painful to shuffle forward on knees so he'd to hunker self forward on elbows, pulling his dead legs behind him, like a slither of knapdallicks hanging, bloody, from the arse of a ruptured sheep, as his Gran used to intone, for a variety of situations. Even before the Nephew reached the door, the carpet had pulled off the boxer shorts to his ankles and his elbows were tingling. He could reach up easy to the handle of your average door without the use of legs. This was a very average door. He reached up to try sweep the emulsion, find a light switch, but it was so dark, he couldn't make a thing out till his eyes adjusted to the little leaked light from beyond the curtains. His reaching fingertips could just manage a light switch. He thought, Perhaps there's some EEC directive as to exactly what height light switches should be positioned at? Fuck alone knows, cause obviously Glasgow has to be taken into account, and you know what they say, Nay need to replace a light bulb at the Blind Home, yacuntya.

By pattering his fingers, the light burst on. His feet were so swollen with these little toes on the end. Like an orange when you stick it full o' cloves. He sort of panicked at the sight of his feet, maybe he needed a doctor; he didn't like abnormalities at the best of times though fascinated by them in other people, but these were substantially abnormal feet swellings.

Trying to be as quiet as a ghost, he crawled out onto the landing, pulling on the base of the banisters. He listened to the hermetic silence of the slept house and was sure he felt a commensurate arousal in his compressed penis.

There were two other doors. Dragged his poor Old Moody over that acrylic carpet; he too-clearly experienced the insensitive textures of a bargain at Landmark warehouses. The Nephew clicked the door handle and gingerly shoved the first door, perhaps this was the little girls' place and a chorus of wails would arise. Light from his room showed up this other room: he saw gym equipment, one of those torturous-looking weight-lifting mechanisms, and it seemed all other bodies were down the stair. He slithered, bit by bit, over to another door, but by the time he'd pulled it back it was just an airing cupboard with a breath of warm air from a dormant immerser tank, then some bloody towels fell on his head giving him the terrors but he yanked hold of them competitively (as if someone would beat him to it) and continued to crawl, throwing the towels ahead, clawing over them, easing that down the stair passage, planning to use the towels to shroud his nudiness should his crawl be intercepted. He was fair bursting to pee by then.

The stairs were awful steep-seeming in the darkness and blood ran to his head as he began his descent, testicles steadily compressed by each stair edging till he could lay his left cheek on the downstairs corridor carpet. No improvement in the man-made fibres department. Now there were more doors, up and down the infernal corridor. He wasn't even sure what was the washing-machine cupboard any more, never mind the locale of the cludgie. Sorta eeny meeny miney mo, he sumley surmised. Made him think of that Traffic song, 'House for Everyone', on the first album:

> On the door of one was: 'Truth'.
> On the other one was: 'Lies'.
> Which one should I enter through?
> I really must decide.

A Dave Mason composition. I do believe. Yacuntya.

He reached up, gently compressed one door handle, pushed the lightweight, hollow-feeling door in gently, and he was trying to check the walls for kiddies' posters, My Little Pony or Jason Donovan, whatever the fuck floated the boat for these queer nippers of nowadays. Why had he not suffered hisself to get the snowboarder's breeks on? Cause bastardising things wouldn't get over his blobby feet!

Another unoccupied room almost in darkness; and his people homeless! He noisily elbowed the way in, dragging his legs behind like a snake shucking its own skin. Even a bucket or flowerpot would have to suffice by now.

There was a strange, excited trundling sound in the blackness to his left.

A light went on.

Sitting up on a bed beside him, under a Lion King duvet, so close she could have leaned down and ruffled his hair, was one of Paulette's daughters, the Niamh one. To his left now, in his white cage, Johnstone the Gerbil was frantically galloping on his revolving wheel.

'I can see your hairy bum.'

'Hush!'

'Have you come here to have it off with me?'

'No! Shhh.'

'Have you come to have it off with Mum?'

'Nooooo, shhhhhhh, your Mummy'll hear,' he flicked the towel backwards, trying to shield his arse. Some of it got covered by a roping of towel along the crack, so he lay, splayed out, trying to wiggle his boxer shorts back up his shins.

'Why are you crawling? Are you drunk?'

'Look at my feet.'

'Yeuch, what's wrong with *them*?' she goggled, fascinated but smiling; she wasn't petrified at all.

'I'm looking for the toilet, darling, and I can't walk.'

'Don't call me darling less you want to be my boyfriend and I've two of those already and they'll burst ya if you try an two-time, *three*-time with me,' she tiptoed out bed, stepped over him and, to the Nephew's horror, carefully closed the bedroom door, shutting them both in.

'Niamh, now I've GOT to go for a piddle. I'm bursting!'

'Here then,' she pattered over to her wardrobe; helpless, his head followed her.

'It's Katia.' She was holding up that vomiting and peeing doll she'd waved in his face earlier.

'Eh?'

'You have to fill it up with water, so she pee-pees. A girl can't do it, I try and it goes everywhere!'

'You're joking.'

'If you don't, I'll call Mum.'

The Nephew looked at the doll's ooo-ing red plastic lips, the pale white of its descending oesophagus.

'Come on *then*.'

'You're mad; show me the toilet.'

'Fill Katia so she pees real pee.'

'What if I . . . spill. It's *dirty*.'

'Careful is what careful does.'

'Eh. Well, turn round then.'

Something squeaked, it was one of those anglepoise lamps she'd next to the bed and she'd twisted it so it glared in his face. 'I'd like to watch, please,' she says and folded up her legs.

Nothing for it. He coughed and rose to his knees.

Niamh giggled. 'It's true what Mum says! You have a tiny one.'

He grimaced, took the doll, rolled to the side, away from her so the flaccid, carpet-chaffed tip of Old Moody, the Marquis of Lorne, was placed into Katia's dead, outrageously accommodating lips. The daughter simply stood up on her bed to enjoy a full view, her brown eyes upon him, he sensed the jamming up of pee in his tubes as a massive case of Stage Fright descended, the need . . . the inability! 'I can't,' he hissed, 'with you *staring*.'

'Don't be shy.'

He looked away from her, tried to pretend the stupid-faced doll's lips were those of others, warm, living faces in the washing sea of lust.

'Go on, pee in her mouth,' Paulette's daughter whispered, then suddenly she groaned, all to herself, and it was the privacy of that groan which led to a terrible arousal lifting in the Nephew, not so much at the latest jailable offence but the narrative of this event and how he would be able to slur it in some woman's ear at the perfect moment, as a first few driblets came, then a rich stream, and by angling the plastic doll's head she took it all proudly. He could have written to the manufacturers with admiration, praise and relief!

The doll grew heavy and warm in his cold hands and, when

he was done, wisps of his desperate steam emerged from its lips as if the thing had taken up Marlboros. He was reminded of the drinking days he'd kneel to the chemical toilet in the dark, then light a match to check if there was any blood in there.

He looked at the young girl and licked his lips slowly.

'Men are so disgusting,' she said, stepping over him, then very gingerly cradling Katia. She placed the doll in a regimental row of imitation beings. 'Night, night, crawl quietly and don't wake Mum.'

He began to crawl out again; she made him struggle with the door and she switched off the light; all the way Katia stood in the corner of the girl's room with her dismal gang, watched the Nephew's painful progress with deadened contempt.

Halfway back up the bloody stairs all the lights came crashing on. Least by this time he'd re-hoisted the boxer shorts and perfected a stair-edge hop to prevent them working down. It was version two on the sprog front. The Nephew looked down, along the length of his leg at its reprimanding stare, then he pitifully attempted to accelerate his ascent when the child walked away, but moments later, pulling a dressing-gown around her and coughing, Paulette stood, shockingly tall at the bottom of the stairs.

'Why didn't you wake me?' the Nephew whined.

'I bloody tried, you were out the game, mumbling all kinds of stuff, and what are you doing crawling around nude in the house?'

'Excuse me, but could you direct me to the toilet?' he sighed in normal volume.

'What in the name of Christ is wrong with your *feet*?' she says and honked her nose.

'There was a wasp's nest in the nose of my canoe. I was chastised.'

She climbed the stairs and studied his swole feet, then let out a phlegmy chuckling, 'Only one cure for that. Along with a little anaesthetic of course.'

Paulette rolled him down beneath sodium tangerine street lamps on the stolen hospital trolley, as all the lights came on in the adjacent houses and the curtains moved. They stopped where the drive ended in an oval turning place.

'You got a tax disc on this?'

'Does for wheeling Colin in the house when he gets back from the pub pished mortal. Right. On your feet, son.'

With his arm around Paulette's towelling robe they made on into the Argyllshire Debatable Lands, the familiar tracts where new estates blunder into reedy fields with a pretence of civilisation; where cable TV and sewering runs out, abrupt, where telephone wires turn back on themselves while the lazy movements of drifting night beasts rustle against the thistles. Farm animals wander freely here with the same liberties as the holy cow in India. A patrol of blue keel marks on sheep flanks show just above the reeds of the ever-damp ground. A perfect gate stands alone, abandoned on each side by its fence.

As they laboured into so-called fields a particularly virile thistle banged against his thigh, a fat sappy nettle released its bubbles of poison along a shin while her terry-towelling threw the plants aside before her. With disappointment he could detect the frazzled end of censorious under-denim round her trainers.

They halted in unformed fields, deep in dark, the estate just mushrooms of streetlight vapour to their rear, the roofs shining. Paulette blundered him from left to right, almost toppling him a couple of shots till the dimensions were agreeable, his naked legs, gynaecologically splayed, both his swollen bare feet were deep sunk in two substantial fresh cowpats, hardened by daylight's sluggish encroach, the crusts digging into blond hairs on his upper feet.

'Best cure for swole feet is the good soak in the fresh cowpats,' she announced dubiously, darting out that right hand to his shoulder, steadying him as she lit up two more joints of the New Drug in her mouth and he relaxed but shivered as she popped the now familiar gear in his lips.

'It's great for pain, I took a good toke when I went into labour with Niamh fore they carted me away.'

Stood in shit was karmic revenge on him after the Fed, the Nephew thought, and says, 'Is there no risk of infection?'

'That what you say to all the girls?'

'When Mockit's old man got sunk on the convoys the men used to pee on their hands to keep the frost out them and they all got infected in their cracked knuckles and that.'

'Well, in an open wound, sure, but your own waste can be good, all the supermodels are drinking one another's pee these days. I find that sexy.'

'Mmm,' he kept quiet, then says, 'I feel, Paulette, you run a visceral household.'

'I never need vaseline.'

'You're sexy, Paulette, I recall you used to like a man to sing a song in your ear while . . .'

'Is that what you call it? Your singing was no better than your shagging.'

The women always have their wee thing, the Nephew thought, like that bint: showers and volcanoes! Yup, if you can find the wee button of their fetish and press it forever, they'll love you okay. Once I get The Man Who Walks' money, a wee trip to Japan might be in the offing, everyone's always on about the dump, and working up a lather with yon caviare whoor in the jacuzzi, chucking out the soap suds, mmm.

The Nephew, a symbol of his nation, shivered, stood square in the cow shit, musing under cloudy Scotch skies on better days ahead.

The Man Who Walks moved down those slopes with a camping pack on his back and his unlit pipe upside down in his mouth to stop it filling with the rain. On the end of each long arm dangled a carrier bag. Both bags were filled full of water, the plastic handles strained against his hands, and he had to hold the bags out to get them clear of his moving legs.

The bag he held with his left arm had a large dead salmon floating inside, curled around against the plastic; you could see its silver flank of scales. The other bag just had water in it that splashed out in response to his erratic walk.

It was still raining when he arrived outside the Hotel. In the Hotel carpark, next to two parked buses, he tipped out the water from the bags. He wrapped the salmon in one and laid it by his boot; then, using two fingers, he reached up to his left eye and removed it. It was a glass eye. After he'd taken out the glass eye he poked into the dark recess of the socket and from beneath the little flap of skin he removed a small tin-foil package of cannabis resin. He unwrapped it, used his thumbnail to split away more than half, then swallowed the lump of resin. He wrapped the remaining portion and put it back in the socket behind the eye, which he replaced. He picked up the salmon and crossed to the door of the lounge bar. Inside, the Hotel was busy with tourists from the buses who would have been staying there that night.

When he reached the bar he said, 'A score of nips.'

'A score? You want twenty whiskies for the bus party?' The barman slid out a tray, then started to count twenty shot glasses.

The Man Who Walks shouted, 'In one glass, man; in one glass!'

The barman looked at him, sighed, reached for a tankard and started filling it with repeated shots of whisky.

The Man Who Walks slapped the salmon on the bartop. 'Cash or fish?' he asked.

The barman said, 'Look, sir, barter went out with the Middle Ages, it'll have to be the legal tender.'

The Man Who Walks took a very large wad of wet one-pound notes from his greatcoat pocket and, with one eyebrow raised, peeled the paper notes; a few tore in half they were so sodden, but he stuck them down on the wooden bartop.

The barman collected over twenty of the soaked notes and half notes but didn't put them in the till, he laid them out to dry on a radiator by some beer crates. The barman rang up the till and put the change down beside the dead fish. 'Can you take that off the bar, please.'

The Man Who Walks took the fish off the bar and put it inside the plastic bag. 'What a beautiful big fish, is it a salmon?' a nearby tourist asked.

The Man Who Walks removed his glass eye again, grinned at the tourist, then said, 'Look into my mind.' The tourist moved sharply away.

The Man Who Walks took a small case from inside his overcoat. He opened it and removed his drinking eye. This glass eye was similar to his other but the white of the eye was specially rivered with reddened blood vessels designed to match with his living eye after the consumption of twenty whiskies. He fitted the red eye in.

An hour and three-quarters later it was after closing time and the lounge bar was deserted apart from The Man Who Walks; his tankard still had a good dose of whisky in the bottom.

The barman repeated, 'Come on now, sir. I'll have to ask you for your glass.'

The Man Who Walks picked up the carrier bag: the upside-down dead eye of the fish and its gaping mouth were inside, pressed against the greyish-looking plastic. He lifted the salmon out by its head, clamping the gills with his grip, he gently tipped the whisky from the tankard into the open mouth of the dead fish, careful not to spill a drop, then banged the emptied tankard down on the bartop. Good night! he yelled. He stepped out of the Hotel into the rainy darkness and held the big salmon's mouth up to his own, then tipped his head back and gulped all that whisky out from the insides of that fish. Then The Man Who Walks took the salmon's tail in both hands, swung back and gave the big bastard a good fling across the road. The fish went spinning through the night, then landed with a bump on the roof of one of the buses — no doubt leading to a lot of shitey speculation among the tourists in the morning concerning the feeding habits of the golden eagle, etc, etc, but meanwhile he was off, striding into the wet black of nightimeness with his thumbs under the straps of his camping pack. He moved along the backroads, across the Concession Lands, between the outlying homes he made his way through the darknesses until he came to a slight gradient in the road where he halted. He stepped into a flat field and strode into the blackness. There was a large crack and a blue explosion as he walked into an electric cattle fence cranked up to the max. He yowled, fell backwards into a puddle on his arse. He could not see a thing in front of him, behind him, to his left or to his right, so he did not know where the electric fences were, out there, in the dark, waiting for him.

The Man Who Walks sat still in the raining field and chuckled in the dark, then let out a sound more like a sob. He leaned forward and swung his backpack off. He pulled out a set of poles which clinked together and sounded like tent poles. But they were not. He was unfolding the plastic walls and roof of a child's Wendy House which he often used for his camping expeditions. He tried to get up on his feet to pitch the Wendy House, but he was mortal as a newt and slumped back on his arse each time. Eventually he unlaced his boots and removed them, then lay back and just pulled the Wendy House plastic up to his chin like a sheet.

He started snoring, water made bubbles in his upturned nostrils and there was also the sound, in the darkness, of big raindrops pattering down on the plastic. In the morning his boots were filled with water.

In the afternoon sun, carrying a new bag of water, The Man Who Walks came down off those hills. He entered Old Greyhead's General Store to get provisions. He placed purchases on the counter beside the till, spilling water from his bag all over the floor as he moved. He bought four cans of South Atlantic pilchards and one can of North Atlantic pilchards! He bought Clann tobacco, two copies of the Daily Telegraph, two copies of the Financial Times and two copies of The Times.

'It's brightened up a lot now, hasn't it?' said Old Greyhead.

'Shut your mouth and give us a carrier bag,' The Man Who Walks said, and he'd forgotten to change his drinking eye so he had one red eye and one clear one. Although he stinks, shouts, spills water and once shat pilchard skitters on the floor of the shop, then wiped his arsehole with a dead pigeon, Old Greyhead held The Man Who Walks in the highest regard because of the quality newspapers he reads.

'Good afternoon now, sir,' Greyhead said, following The Man Who Walks with a swishing mop.

The Man Who Walks moved up the paths to his one-storey house on the hill. He emptied the bag of water into a 45-gallon drum in the overgrown garden which the rain had already filled, so it poured down *the sides. He opened the front door to his house. Afternoon sun still shone over his shoulder but it was dark in there: pitch dark. He shut the door behind him, got down on all fours and dragged the carrier bag of provisions, crawling forwards though the network of filthy papier-mâché tunnels and igloos he had constructed inside the rooms and corridors of the house: the papier-mâché made from years and years of never-read quality newspapers.*

By the Bonnie, Bonnie Banks
of Loch Lomond

I was born on the bonnie, bonnie banks of Loch Lomond in the Sloy camp during 1944, where Ma (God rest her soul) and so-called-Father were interned. I interrupted the male nurses, also internees, as they tried to bolt a hot dinner.

'Oh, Petulia,' Doctor Schmidt sighed to Ma, snapping on his glove: five ghostly, pale prophylactics, luminescent as snowberries at dusk. 'You *promised* you wouldn't interfere with my lecture.' When I'd been dangled magnetic south and skelped on the arse, the good doctor sighed, '*The Sorrows of Young Werther*, it was to be tonight.'

Such words ushered me into the world.

Crouched, nine months before my birth (I have always been punctual), Ma gasped as a comet of fire went over her hair ribbons, up in the stars. She actually heard the invisible bits of metal thumping, gouging and shaking the pine trees ahead of her, seeming to be cantering over the hill chasing after the burning, up there in the sky!

Ma said she never heard it hit cause my so-called-Father was on her by then. She said it lit the clouds from under, in time with the climax of her passion: all purple, lashing light up into the cloud's bores, pumphels and droops, then everything went dark. Dad had floated down in front of her on his feet before she'd finished peeing; he must have seemed almost handsome in those confusions of lights.

What's to be expected in a world where girls of sixteen raise their skirts in the open country and semi-naked, vigorous young men float down from skies?

As for him, imagine it! Poised up there, cowled by inverted flame and spattered with oil, half his clothes torn away, then out the canopy, dropping and tumbling between silvered cloud tops of the dark, slightly lit by his burning plane below him, then darkness inside but angels' breath cupping his cheeks, clouds moistening his goggles and amazing silence of silk's pure floating. As the invisible field comes up at his toes to find himself faced with a half-nude teenage girl, her skin blue in the night; a celebration was called for. Call Ma unpatriotic if you wish. Many a man had passed through her hands since (and before) but she always was adamant it was the greatest fuck of her life, God rest her soul, and that was shouted at the local priest as an excuse.

Later, so-called-Father sewed her up new underwear out of his silk parachute. That's how I, in her belly, came to be living in a prison camp at the dam construction where they had all sorts: Jerries, conscientious objectors (poets to a man), lost Molotovs and Eyeties who built a church out of cardboard and painted it gold. Some with engineering skills remained in camp, others, navvies, were brought up and back in open coal wagons on the railway from the Royal Navy base each morning.

So-called-Father, till one day, up on the dam wall, he tumbled a John Deere tractor over the edge and two hundred feet down inside the dam wall's shell. Never bothered winching what was left of *him* back up, just retrieved the spark plugs from the tractor and poured the concrete in on top of him.

Each time I click on a kettle and the lights dim, I take joy in thinking so-called-Father contributes his wee bit to the hydro-electrification of the Scottish Highlands. Indeed I once penned a missive to the then Energy Minister expressing how our family really should get an electricity discount. Never received the common courtesy of a reply. Nuclear power, based on my mathematical researches, was to be the next swindle for the consumer. Who was my real father? Isn't that obvious? Colonel Bultitude of course! It was all a cover-up, which the Bultitudes denied when I tried to gain recognition for my uncredited scripts in Hollywood.

My winning smile and stunning resemblance to King Edward (or was it Georgie?) stood me in good stead at primary school on the island where we scratched our names on roof slates with chalk, wiped them off, then sneezed. When you had to go, you raised your hand politely to Miss Campbell, then went out into a swaying cornfield to pee or plop.

On the island one had to walk two miles to school each morning and when one returned you could tell by the blood or feathers on the caravan steps if it was to be the rabbit or the chicken for dinner that night. Once Ma showed me a rabbit's boiled heart – it was a grey little pebble. Mother was a dab hand with the old bow and arrow. A talent I've inherited.

We were pitched next a house: number 4. Why number 4? There were no other houses or buildings for two miles! Strange looking back on it, but the exact distance to everything on the island: the big house, the schoolhouse, the nearest crap house, the pier over to the mainland (to which you could almost throw a stone at low tide, over slick black waters and revealed kelp, lying unsupported, the erect heron precisely doubled in his own stoney reflection!) – the distances always seemed to be two miles. Later, when I became a trained mathematician, these calculations took up more of my time than Doormat's Theorem. If one were a dyed-in-the-wool Freudian biographer, conclusion would be made that the absence of houses 1, 2 and

3 on the island is what probably led my speculations onto the theoretical side when it came to physics, rather than the practical side.

At the age of ten Ma believed I had diphtheria (or was it scarlet fever?). She also believed fumes from the tarmacadaming would burn out all the badness in me, so, in our Sunday Best on a weekday of summer ascendant, I was made to shadow the Irishmen's slow progress up the big house driveway, downwind, inhaling deeply as they scattered the sticky gravel.

Ma left me alone as she was led away by all five Irishmen, to see where the fairies gathered, and I was standing on the tar tank, my face obediently hung over the open hatch, inhaling up-fumes. Black, shiny tar covered the tank flanks in layers of matt, solidified dribbles; where a knock from a metal stir rod or rake had chipped away a platelet there was a gloss sheen.

The tar pony, with his blinkers and nosebag of leaking water that steamed on the fresh asphalt, moved forward, despite my yells; his hooves had sunk in by the time the Irishmen raced back, panting, with my tousled-haired Ma; tar pony was stuck solid. When they extracted him, all week you heard the pony coming a mile off with those blocks of hard black tar still clunking round his front hooves.

Got leathered on my bare behind with the strap that night. Inevitably there was tar on my Sunday Best as well. I asked Ma if she seen any fairies and she called, Five, tiny wee ones. That following Sunday the tar pony died of fume inhalation. The venerable Colonel Bultitude had the horsey chopped up to feed to the tiger they said he kept in the big house.

I liked Padraig (pronounced Porick) best of the Irishmen. I used to carry them down their bucket of tea every day. It was Padraig who showed me a drainage pipe tunnel the Colonel's wife had insisted they lay under the driveway, so the fairies could use it and not get their ever-so-dainty little feet stuck crossing the wet tar.

Every Friday night, Padraig would collect Ma from beside number

4, in a brand-new suit, bought off the travelling Pakistani. Padraig would wear that suit all weekend as he emptied his wage packet on drink and tobacco in the pubs of mainland with Ma. Come Monday, wallets empty, Padraig and the other Irishmen with their brand-new Friday suits on, climbed back down into those ditches again and began shovelling, draining, chopping and road making. 'Best-dressed labourers in Scotland,' the Colonel would roar to house guests from the back of his Bentley, on a two-hundred-yard dash from the yacht mooring, as the Irishmen saluted from the ditches. Come Friday pay day, Padraig and the others'd duck head and shoulders in a water barrel and buy another brand-new suit for the weekend. Never troubled by laundry needs, they wore those new suits right through the weekend and next working week till the following Friday again when the garments were filthy, torn and hung in fatherings, then they would purchase yet another set of brand-new suits. A sartorial extravagance I have always tried to emulate, though the time gaps between dawning a new suit and discarding the faded tend to be more on the lengthy side.

So Ma tossed aside her German Grammar, went south to Burns' Country, near Darvel or was it Newmilns (?), and I dallied in the fields with Blueberry Bill who lived in a hay rick and planted in me (among other things) my love of rambling and wild ways, and that's when the Territorials taught Ma to drive a lorry up in Edinburgh there. The driving report (one of my prized possessions) states her Route Knowledge was 'unorthodox but effective' and 'her steering is confident and sure despite the fact she took away a businessman's umbrella on Princes Street', but she told me this was because the tester had his hand between her legs and all her wheels were stuck in the tram lines for most of the driving test!

One summer, ditches alive with crawberries hitting at your hubcaps and leaving their juice on, Ma was driving our old ex-army Bedford eight tonner, back-laden with wafted curves of sky-blue silk slabs, draped, in case of rain, by a canvas cover hanging on the framings. Taking it down to the milliners' warehouse at Darvel.

Blueberry Bill cadged a lift in the cab, one elbow boldly rested on the door and flicked his cigarette dowp out of the opened window. He climbed to the ground at Loudoun Hill to run loose on the battlefield. A mile beyond, Ma saw the first white smoke trembling in her wing mirror, blowing off across the fields. The back of the truck was hopelessly on fire. Ma knew the only chance to save the cargo was not to halt but to speed onwards, downhill, up the narrow main street with horn sounding and trying to skid to a halt outside Darvel Fire Station where the boys she was well acquainted with would douse her wagon with their big hose. But by taking this risk there was the real possibility it would lick round the diesel tank and put the whole thing up in an explosion, possibly right in the town square, but Ma knew how much that silk load was worth so she pressed down on the accelerator, scattering a group of pony trekkers, then, as the burning truck reached the hill bottom, the canvas cover came alight and ripped away in huge release, the cotton rope tethers of the load itself snapped, sheets of flaming silk, sky blue and orange flames began to peel backwards as Ma entered the small town, trailing a river of blue, like a tanker gushing paint, the very edges of silk crackling and smoking, until the front doors flew open and the ladies of the houses of Darvel stepped out into a blue river with scorch holes as if the street was again flooded but this time with the shimmering fabric rather than sewage water from the mill river. When Ma yanked on the handbrake outside the glass lattice doors of the fire station there was only twenty feet of silk left, burning in the back of the lorry, and she stepped aside as the vehicle burned up. The rest of the silk stretched two miles up the road, rippling in the verges, so pilots bringing Dakotas into Prestwick radioed to ask what was being celebrated and for twenty years the dresses of the débutantes of

Darvel were of the same distinct blue, often with a scorch mark deeply concealed, under the skirts, next to those modest, bare legs.

Well, two mile of silk winds out to a fair old price and when the factory found Ma'd never been able to afford any insurance, they dropped my mother the hair-raising bill for every single foot of that silk, spread from Loudon Hill to Darvel Main Street.

We had to break for the Highlands before first light, me crouched under her crocked elbow and her canvas bag, keeping the spotting rain off me, carrying all we owned, led cross-country, under cover of the night, by Blueberry Bill, to pick up the long-since lifted branch line at Drumclog where we rode in the guard van of the early goods. North to some marshalling yard south of Central Station where Ma sent me outside while she had a wee ceilidh with the guard in the van and I watched the big black fives steam by . . .

The Nephew's lips moved: COMPLETE AND UTTER UNTRUTHS! He shook his head. It was pure fiction, made up, using bits and pieces of family history, stories he's heard in pubs! Sheer nerves of shameless steel that Uncle of his has! And bloody disrespectful to his own mother, sired by a Luftwaffe fighter pilot! That'll be right, yacuntya!! And the snobbism of it! Man Who Walks always was snob without reason. Just the sort would claim aristocratic blood; the nearest The Man Who Walks has ever got to aristocracy is his arsehole fixed round the toecap of a gamekeeper's boot! And Christ knows, Gran never drove no trucks . . . never glamorous enough for that!

The Nephew's forehead-screwing efforts and intellectual medievalisms had gone on all day. The previous night, after their romantic sojourn together under starlight, well, under rain clouds, to stand in the cowpats, Paulette had, lovingly he thought, doused his wasp stings in iodine after a bracing hose down to clear off the kach: her elegant, ringed thumb jammed over the garden hose spout, and then she sent him to bed, permitting only another peck on the cheek.

Below the Nephew's bedroom window that morning (how strange it sounded: 'your bedroom') he'd heard click of clothes pegs and pulled himself up enough to gleer down at Paulette. Her cold seemed worse, with her mouth full of multi-coloured plastic pegs, that youngest daughter sat on a rug playing with Katia the doll, making it urinate a jet, tasting a sample. You had to laugh! What a touching domestic scene. Spoiled because the sight of humble clothes pegs reminded the Nephew yet again of the one there was to be no peace from, his Uncle, The Man Who Walks, clothes pegs always hung on his garments from when he'd recently liberated them from somebody's clothes line.

Paulette brought him spilled broth, balanced on a tray, and banned daughters from coming up the stair to torment him, but to all intents and purposes the Nephew had been confined to bed in a house with no telephone (a bad influence on the kids, Paulette had said). Despite anxieties of going AWOL and non-reporting in to the Foreman, despite the miles The Man Who Walks was putting between them, the Nephew had been bored out his skull by midday. He'd reached and dragged over the backpack with the miles of typewriter ribbon inside and begun examination of it.

It was electric typewriter ribbon that had been violently extracted from the casings, so towards each end the ribbon strained, corrugated, and ink flaked off the plastic into transparency and silence. But with coloured pencils from the drawer, in a children's drawing book, on the blank reverse pages, the nephew could while away the hours, transcribing the inconclusive literary efforts of, obviously, The Man Who Walks:

```
dnomoLhcoLfosknabeinnobeinnobehtnonrobsawI
```

Then transcribe from right to left:

```
IwasbornonthebonniebonniebanksofLochLomond
```

Then run your orange pencil lead along the words, inserting a dash to separate them, reading the appalling narrative of lies, outright hallucination and familial innuendo as you go:

```
I/was/born/on/the/bonnie/bonnie/banks/of/Loch/Lomond/
```

. . . and further to that I suffer from a rare condition. In fact I suffer from a great deal of rare conditions including a violent skin allergy to decapitated and stuffed steer heads mounted on the walls of our finest country homes, but among my conditions is a deformity of my cochlea and inner ear affecting balance. After consuming the slightest traces of alcohol – say, a 1942 after-dinner Armagnac for instance, even those traces contained in tomato ketchup, or the menthol in cough unctions (of which I am particular afficionado); or even trace elements of sorbitol found in chewing-gum, or, in the days before I lost all my teeth in an unfortunate dental accident, even toothpaste – an instant reaction will take place in my innerest of ears.

Exposed to alcohol (rather than just exposed), my balance is affected in a unique and particular manner. I find it impossible to ascend or descend the slightest *gradient* without crashing to the ground or spinning in navigational confusion!

As a soldier of the sauce, resident in one of the sparsely populated, mountainous regions of our United Kingdom, where scores of miles can exist, easily, between public houses, best served by owners of private cars heedless to Drink Driving Legislation, this disability had clearly exerted a huge influence over the years of my life. A mere trip from the Creagan Inn to the Ballachulish Hotel Ferry Bar, twenty miles at most, could take me the best part of a fortnight. And that's skipping the temptations of the Appin loop!

Imagine! Even as a child, after indulging in a Wrigley Juicy Fruit (if there was any), or later in my courting years (if there were any), when I donned the weekend suit, condescended to a quick wipe of Colgate squirt round my gnashers with a hankie, in order to manoeuvre with more confidence my once tooth-filled mouth towards the lipsticked cola hole of some seasonal wench! Then when I 'walked out' with her, I often had to take her home on a fifteen-mile detour from our initial trysting point. It tried the patience of many women who were meant to be endowed with that very faculty.

Or of course when I pursued the less innocent but far more obtainable recreation of taking my dram in peaceful, isolated taverns thousands of feet below ravaged peaks! Then I would immediately find it impossible to stroll up the slightest brae or to climb onto a public omnibus or even to manage the step (and many examples of this architectural trait do indeed exist), up into the Gentlemen's lavatory, necessitating relieving myself at the bar with always similar reactions from staff and clients.

As you can imagine in a tribe such as ours, where drinking forms a central totemic structure, my travels and goings forth have, inevitably, mainly involved making the most outlandish and extravagant of detours in order to reach a longed-for destination.

Where *you* could travel from, say, A to B as the crow flies, I can only find my way to the beloved B by that path where no gradient or decline lays before me, that is, until the effects of the alcohol leave my bloodstream, whereupon, refreshed by pure mountain streams, I stomp over and up and down mountains, upland slopes, braes and cliffs, sgnurrs and scree, hills and slopes and accumulative crap of the Silurian and all the other geological eras to reach my desired destination.

Or, of course, to effect an *escape*. For we are not always travelling *to* places, often we are escaping, fleeing from things terrible (the Macushla) or merely the squeeze of ennui. Anschluss and exodus are the common movements of our time and pursuance is a frequent malady best depicted in innumerable Hollywood movies I have written which copyright forbids me from quoting such as . . .

NB: typewriter ribbon ends here. New ribbon picked at random.

April 7th. Yesterday night, needing to urinate, I crossed to the telecom box along by the bus stop and put my hand on the door handle. The telephone-box door wouldn't budge open, then as I looked down I saw a large rope right next to the ground, wound once round the box, knotted and tensely stretched out into the darkness of the loch waters. Mockit the Psychotic, that mental trawler man, must've anchored his *Seaman Queen* out there in currents, a party of them shored in a dinghy on the scavenge for drink and the marijuana; slung this line round the phone box case it slips anchor.

That was a jinxed vessel if ever there was one. They had the nets down on it one day there, and they seemed to have a huge catch. When they winched in, all they'd caught was a dead horse. They anchored off the sands and winched the dead horse ashore to bury it. Took them days to dig the pit and they all got sunstroke. None of that crew were ever the same again! I suddenly developed the new-fangled notion the Macushla, who was one of their cronies, was out there in the darkness aboard that trawler, as Keyser Soze was, 'killing many people' on the boat, in the Hollywood motion picture *The Usual*

Suspects, which I both wrote and directed. The Macushla out there on that trawler; left in the dark on-deck, where they'd carried him, somehow coordinating dark and sinister operations, willingly harboured by the fisherman, many of them permanently scarred by brown jellyfish stings on the face from when their scallop winches have whipped the spineless ones up in out of the depths and they have slapped over the boom. All the fishermen wearing the distinctive 'stonewashed' denim, created by putting their Levis down on the scallop drag for a few days.

When I returned later, still needing to relieve myself, the entire British Telecom telephone box had been torn free of its mountings and dragged into the sea behind the boat, leaving only a square of urine-scented concrete. I imagined the telephone box: a transparent coffin, elegantly floating, like a wind sock, just above the sandbeds, trapping fish near its roof. As a shareholder I intend to notify central office about this.

April 10th. Imagine the old Yog Shoggoth or whatever was on its passport and other creatures of the pre-creation more terrible than anything Lovecraft or Arthur Machan thought up, even in their cruellest dyspepsia, and you cannot imagine how odious is the Macushla. Crowley, all that stuff we used to pull off the gander's head to back in the 60s while dreaming of Tangerine. Imagine ten times worse and it will still give you no idea of the Macushla and all the terrors he drags behind him; as Ma always used to say, like a ruptured sheep dragging home bloody knapdalicks out its arsehole.

Can there be any accounting for the Macushla's loathsomeness? His contention that penile warts are a positive thing, having the same stimulatory properties on the female genitalia as, say, a silver-studded piercing to the foreskin? Patting fake Chanel on his herpes sores. His revolting sectarianism. His cruelties to women innumerable. I quote: vaselining (stolen) mobile phones, programmed to their vibrate facility, pushing into vagina, then phoning the number from across the room and, I should add, this while he has a switched-on electric toothbrush (that he'd just polished his cheap gold rings with) shoved up her behind as she writhes in the bed before a digital video camera (stolen).

His known tastes: dosing up from the syrup o' figs bottle, then defecating into a durex (extra-strong), freezing the filled condom in the ice box next to lean mince (*and* McCain's respected family-favourite pizzas, an invention of mine), then inserting the frozen condom as a dildo, to the grave health risk of his participant. And all this vented upon his younger sister! I must take a brief break from writing.

Ah, the relief! Where was I, oh yes, and that *disgusting* family, what a dose of them. Talk about a high-density no-hope area! You've heard of dancing an eightsome reel? Well, an eightsome in that family was those eight children in their caravan sharing two beds and so few clothes and shoes they had to operate in a shift system, four out in the daylight while the others slept, the eldest four out, scavenging on the nightime backshift in the same clothes, up to all sorts. A rota system for the (stolen) Nike trainers tacked to the wall. What a sight! Aye, the girls wore the trousers in that family, literally. There were no skirts.

And the manners of them! Didn't know what a house was. Let alone a 'please' or a 'thank you'. When that Macushla was a teenager, he vomited on someone's carpet at Hogmanay, just knelt down, cut out the offending area with his switchblade knife and tossed the affected patch of carpet out the window, as if the hosts would not notice.

Whenever you saw the Macushla he'd have three-week-old blood splattered down his shirt; but always someone *else's* blood from a pub assault. He's a violent, violent, *violent* man, yon. Once I heard he'd got rushed to the chest hospital and I was glad he'd got his comeuppance. Turned out he'd been admitted just cause he'd to have another boy's tooth extracted from his own fist. The Macushla'd punched him so hard it'd come through the burst cheek. I remember the Macushla in them days with special grooves cut by his Stanley knife in the heels of his shoes so they would pick up cigarette butts off the pavements to scavenge tobacco for roll-ups . . .

The Nephew broke off transcription at this point, thinking, Is that meant to be some kind of smart-arse pun then: 'harboured by the fishermen'? Too clever by half to be intended by Man Who Walks, and yet more lies, fiction and, in fact, the Nephew noted, a dose of libel! Usual recurring delusions that he has been a famous 'scriptwriter' in Hollywood and has written songs with famous musicians (whom he barrages with abusive, scrawled letters written on old newspaper from the chippers, demanding royalties!). And the Macushla *he's* going on about? Honestly, if you knew The Man Who Walks, having the affrontery to criticise a family doing their best!

The Nephew pondered and flyted. Honest-to-goodness, this the man with pony nuts filling his coat pockets into which he'll thrust a dirty hand and toss them nuts to the back of his detestable mouth, most pony nuts missing, pittering onto his steel toecaps all over the pub carpet and after he's gulped down a whisky on top, you might be unfortunate enough (if he's travelling without falsers as per usual) to glimpse that dut of rotted molar right back in there where once a tomato seed took root and the plant was growing, shooting out of his tooth, so he'd chew it once a fortnight to get his greens, then when he was dragged forty mile (refusing to travel without his jackhammer) to the dentist in the kilt who tried to pull the tooth, the entire atrium of the jaw tore away while the nurse fainted. 'Don't panic,' his Uncle bubbled through blood, holding his cheek together, 'I was hit by a ship's anchor *years* ago!' which accounts for his twisted smile. When he came in a pub for a pint and his favourite jellied eels, he'd remove the ill-fitting false teeth. They were kept in place by chewing gum and he'd stick the blob to the side of his pint glass while he ate. He'd rest the teeth in the ashtray, then secure them back in with the chewing-gum, caked in cigarette ash.

Mentioned his beloved jackhammer, only true romance of The Man Who Walks' life. He managed to fool a navvy boss into letting him contract work for Lord Wimpey or Sir Bob MacAlpine down the pass when they was widening the main road by the power station, building out east onto pontoons and surfacing. They gave Man Who Walks a petrol jackhammer and he'd never be parted from it. Each and every night he took it on the work bus with him back to the house, into the paper tunnels of his sett to polish it, oil its bearings, stroke it with a cloth, then at dawn back again. He slept with the jackhammer by his side, arms thrown around it. On his weekend pub crawls he took it with him. The Man Who Walks got barred from the Tight Line once cause he started up the jackhammer in the fucking lounge bar to try and impress a bunch of wifies. All the ice in their gin and tonics started chinkling and one's wig flew off in the fumes! There was even a rumour The Man Who Walks was seen once, mortal drunk, the jackhammer aimed down the stank road, juddering homeward on a bright summer night, lashed to the machine.

The Nephew was weary of the lunatic and precise efforts to render forth The Man Who Walks' sub-literary ravings and elected instead to savour the joy of intercepting him, doing the procedure and getting that cash offof him. After all, there was The Procedure and there was The Cause.

The Nephew got out of bed and tested weight on his legs. Still tender, but the swelling had fallen and he was about ready for active duty and his travels again, so he hunched to glance out the window at the drawing-in dusk. Foolhardy to go bare-headed under such active skies with the ghost bags all along the crow roads, he thought.

Venturing down the stair into familial lairs, the two daughter things occupied the scullery, mixing up some baking concoction in a ginormous pyrex with reggae music thumbering from a ghetto blaster. The Nephew savoured his newly-recovered height above them and deliberately drew up.

'Mummy's ill in bed, hairy bum.'

The younger tittered.

'Is she?' he shouted.

He helped himself to two Heineken from the fridge, ignoring when it bleated, 'Did Mummy say you could have that?'

The Nephew swaggered along the corridor, drawn by Paulette's racking cough, pausing to take a dek around in the tallest one's bedroom, but the little besom hadn't matured into the mobile-phone stage yet.

'It's the prodigal son,' Paulette says, with her fevery eyes a bit teary.

'You look awful and shouldn't be smoking that.'

'Hoi!'

He grabbed and stubbed out her joint, sitting on the edge of the bed, gulping the lovely beer, looking down at her, reaching to push hair off her face, which she let him, then glancing round their Pumping Palace: the usual lace and ostentatious curtains, flowery wallpaper, chintz French dressing-table strewn with a harlot's works.

She blew her nose.

'Can't they no turn down that Paki music?' he mumbled.

'What're they doing?'

'Baking.'

'Fairy cakes. They won't burn themselves. Leave them alone,' she smiled.

Sickening sentimentality of parents, he thought, and shuffled a bit. 'Shouldn't they be in their beds?'

'Soon.'

He nodded. Paulette produced a pack of cards, ones of nuddy 1970s women. The two of them, the Nephew getting hornier, played Hunt the Cunt as she lay in bed, him sat on the edge dealing onto the coverlet. Paulette kept winning.

'You know,' she coughed, 'you have such anger still, all knotted up inside of you. You have this anger inside you that you need to make contact with. Even when you read you're angry. I used to watch you, way you bent back the spine and always broke it, thumbs rub-rubbing at the covers so it leaves two greasy prints and your eyes all goggled out, eating up the words.'

He nodded and says, 'Aye, suppose you're right; kind of resentment at others' eloquence.'

'Aye, what*ever*.'

'So?'

'Where do you think that anger comes from?'

'The moon and the stars, girl, and now I've to make a phone call. Lend us a quid coin, will you, and I'll pay you back in a matter of days?' He placed the cards, suit up, by her knee and gave it a squeeze, with her giggle he knew she was giving him permission for anything.

The Nephew walked whistling through a canyon of twitching curtains as he'd once strolled up Third Avenue under waterfalls of glass.

'It's me.'

'Where on Christ's earth have you *been*?'

'Accident. Crossed Loch Etive in a canoe that had a wasp's nest in the bow. Near fuckin drowned. Couldn't walk. I'm in Boomtown.'

'Where's my *phone*?'

'Deduct it from my share. Expenses. One hitchhike on the main road and I'll be in behind him. I think the bastard took my pal Hacker's boat. It's no engine but he could row it so he'd of long beat me.'

The Foreman says, 'He'll be in Ballachulish by now, so get your finger out your arsehole. I've reports he visited the inn at Portnacroish yesterday yelling, "Who will bring me the skin of the Red Fox?" Hear he fair wrecked the place. *Domhnal Sgrios* himself. There's the new bridge over Loch Creran now, God Bless the EU, so get up there; he'll be pilgrimming James of the Glen's grave at Keil. Get him at Ballachulish, hang Man Who Walks high, by the neck, when his flesh falls, string his skeleton with barbed-wire so his bones click in the wind. I don't care, just get me that fucking money.'

Foreman hung up and the phone didn't give the Nephew back the eighty pence he was due. He did what he estimated was eighty pence worth of damage, then sat on the old, closed station platform by the lifted track where the privatised buses turn and wait, with their mud-spattered flanks. He smoked out the pack of Embassy Regal stole from the eldest daughter's bedroom, one cig after the other, using her lighter, which was emblazoned with the word FILTH for some reason.

At least there was the new bridge at Loch Creran. The old structure was beloved of The Man Who Walks but dangerous with its square holes in the solid cast base, never adequately patched by farmers. Sheep and whole cows would drop right through into the loch sixty foot below.

Night once again came from behind the outcrops. Erect before the luminous skyline as if day were the negative and night the true state of this world – the positive. Golden constellations of gnats hung like spirits over the dried puddles of the turning place as the tobacco made the Nephew dizzy.

Thought of his past with Paulette, ribbons in her hair, they would hurry their lovemaking before sunset turned to darkness, one of her solitary pubic hairs left in her Mum's butter dish that they'd used as lubricant; he thought of that small-breasted girl of early May and how she would watch her own body as if it were a stranger's. Now the Nephew realised it was her own wonderful body alone she was celebrating in the things they did together, her eyes lowering and raising over the subtly pre-positioned mirrors.

Light festered to the south of Lorn, across the multiple lochs west to Appin and Lochaber; the night was a massive activity, working steadily, already the cigarette butt he'd flicked furthest away was invisible to him. The moon heaving up between a crack in the cloud, a travelling cumulus indented it, drawing sideways and diluting its milklight, but then moon burnt out through a slit with a wink of blue. It was like moving from sleep into true clarity. Like Nosferatu born up in Slane Castle, the Nephew felt his body was being returned to him. Vesper Adest, Juvenes.

Foliage barely moving behind him was turning silver. The moon lifted like an elevator in its new pulpit, created a second horizon above the true one: the bay began to tremble silver.

Under an entire bar of sky, stained white against dark purple shadow in the cloud, he returned to the kitchen to drink beers alone in the fridge-light, desperate to change his world. Those children had been bundled off to bed and he made his way back to Paulette's room, where she was smoking sleepily, to whisper, 'I know a gypsy cure for influenza.' She was wearing her husband's pyjamas as he took her fingers and rose her to full height and in through to the kitchen.

'You need to be able to pee,' he growled.

'Can pee *any* time.'

He opened cupboards to find the requisite big saucepan, slid it between her bare, nail-varnished toenails on the kitchen tiles.

'Prove it.'

She stared, almost invisibled in fridge-light, just muttered, 'Slam the fridge door then.'

Smoking, the Nephew squinted as she took her bottoms all the ways down, hooked the pyjamas in under the pan handle. His eyes, her eyes adjusted. She was enormously still, looked directly at him in the dark, then she was sudden ducked down almost to the pan, there was a silver dash, the softness of plonks, then the rich rush as the saucepan depth lushly deepened; a jetting, then sudden silence and she yanked up the pyjamas.

'C'mon, dress for outside,' he ordered. On the way Paulette leaned over to try kiss him, but he turned aside as she huffed and tried to cover up her move towards him by opening the fridge and taking out a beer bottle.

He lit up the endlessly mysterious blue flame of the gas cooker and began boiling Paulette's fresh piss. One large egg (free range) from the fridge and, so not to crack it, lowered with his own fingertips into her warm, disappointingly scentless, clear pee.

The egg was rattling about when she stepped back in. A black woolly sweater but a less-than-medium-length skirt and tall leather boots, 'What are you *doing*!' she giggled through lipstick.

To pass a double-egg-timer duration the Nephew then kissed Paulette long, with grabbing bites at her tongue, and when she turned her head aside she smacked her lips, shook hair and giggled, 'This is naughty, this is really quite . . . *bad*,' but there was the crushed sense, the Nephew was sure, that their infantile hedonism had been done three million times before and he pledged, more than anything, to transgress it.

He took the saucepan, and held it against the sink side to decant out her boiled piss, then he plucked the reward: the big hot egg, tossing and turning it in his palm. 'You need a needle, like a common pin.'

'A needle?'

'No, not a syringe. Like a needle, from a sewing kit.'

She muffled a laugh, came back from the living room with a pin cushion.

'The thinnest one. Right. Okey-dokey. Making little holes, write your initials on the egg.'

She got down on her knees at the kitchen table so the skirt fell like dark blood on the back of her calves and the Nephew could see the worn soles of the high-heeled boots as she concentrated. 'Oww, it's hot!' The first hole caused a wee crack and he could see she was making the 'P' too big.

'Not so big. That's it, make one hole a wee bit bigger by shoogling the needle. That's right.'

When Paulette'd poked her initials in the egg the Nephew, who'd been watching her fingers, murmured, 'Come on out into the night with me.'

'Shouldn't leave the girls.'

'C'mon. They're safe. I promise. I'll be with you. Just three hundred yard, come with me up into the tree-line,' he whispered, but helplessly thought, Up in the tree-line, Julian the Apostate will abolish Christianity and restore the ancient gods. He says aloud, 'I know what we need, saw them yesterday afternoon. Lock the door, take the keys.'

'What? What!?'

'Shush. My present to you.'

He stood by the door and when she squeezed by him he shivered, reached down and had full erection! but what a bloody rigmarole to get one! Still. Felt so alive, much like his old self again.

They stepped out, down past the slow-moving street lights above them, back to that turning place where the road ran out at the estate fringes. They didn't speak and the Nephew was sure he could feel it between them. Kinda stuff Paulette loved so much. He was still exciting her. Should have been him shacked up in yon quarter-bought house with her and two healthy sons, not those wee delinquent, precocious perverts.

Blackness as they climbed the forestry path into soft, ample conifers, so he took her hand ascending back up towards the megalithics.

'Where?' she mumbled.

'Here.' Their voices were so useless in all that night. All that darkness and mute hostility with animals listening out, waiting for them to crash to the ground, pounce and pick their bones clean. The sole thing that was real, the only thing that was valid to the Nephew, was Paulette's strong litheness, moving next to him through ancient, proper night forest, high-heeled boots buckling, heaving her side to side into the clearing where there was a rack of brush-fire brooms, then they crossed into a fire break that moved east. It hadn't been well maintained, so crisp windfall had clogged it. A forest blaze would easy have jumped across in tinder-dry weather, but he gave no a fuck. The grand canyon fire in general, let it come. He thought he'd noted them well, but even his nose was lost in such pure dark despite the fullish moon, so they'd to turn and go back a ways.

'Right; here. Stop. Turn round. Get down on your knees.' He kicked a branch aside with crisp, dead cones rattling like Christmas globes.

'What is it?'

'Got the egg.'

'It's here okay.'

'See this mound. Very careful, you have to protect the egg in your palm, so it's not crushed, but with your fingernails; don't start yet, listen. With your fingers you must dig in, slowly forward, into it. You need to get the egg way in, right into the heart of this mound, then leave the egg in there, planted in it, and even more slowly withdraw your arm back out. You'll need to go in deep, really in, past your elbow but protecting the egg in your palm, or the spell won't work.'

'Is it . . . What is it?'

He was kneeling by her left arm and with his right hand he moved fingers in up her leg, in, under the skirt, high enough on goosebumps to feel she'd nothing under as he knew she wouldn't. Her breathing changed. He flicked his fingers up and down, up and down too, so he could feel, get the stimulation of the top of those high leather boots almost up to where her knees bent. She breathered jumpily. He says, 'You slowly go in, Paulette, slowly, gently go in with your hand.'

Her short but black nail-polished finger-ends scraped aside a pine needle carpet on the mound and rustled. She gave a little grunt. She said, 'No, no. Off with the jumper.'

The Nephew flinched as she jerked back but she just heaved

the jersey up over her hair, which plashed back down on her mooned shoulder-blades, tits hanging a bit, like bats in the dark but not what you'd think after spitting out two children!

He reached to the buttons on the front of his trousers with one hand at the same time as he touched the firm muscle, but he couldn't get his trousers undone so he'd to remove the fingers of the right hand to pop his button. What was it in *Gulliver* as the miniature army marched between his legs? 'And to confess the truth, my breeches were at that time in so ill a condition, that they afforded some opportunities for laughter and admiration.' Admire this, he thought, and yanked the breeks down, but as they passed he felt his Bethlehem Steel just start to shrink. Quickly he repositioned himself between the two dead-cold leather boots and to revive his ardour, he hoisted her skirt, revealing the plenitude of Paulette's exposed buttocks, moonlight creaming the darkest sharp shadow along one of them. He neatly folded the skirt material around her waist so he would still see thin shoulder-blades working under him at her excavations, then he took his half-erection and placed it where he wanted it to be, trying to get some lub off its keratinised end and in there. There was none, so he moved in two fingers where she was saturated, and swept some back up, onto him. Paulette's body movements came from the thrusting forearm that already seemed to be buried well into the earth mound.

The Man Who Walks' Nephew moved fingers up and down on the coldness of Paulette, stroking at buoyant muscular properties and whispered, 'It's ants, Paulette.'

'Oh God, you're sick,' she whispered.

'It's an ant's nest and you're gonna push that egg boilt in your own pish, right deep way into it, far as the queen's chamber, they won't like it, you might feel some nippy bites, too bad! Then, lodged there, slave ants'll crawl into the egg through the holes of your name, Paul-*ette*, and they'll eat on through the egg white to the yellowness of the yolk.'

'Oh Jesus, this is perverted shit!'

'Ants will eat through egg white but bring out only that rich yellow yolk, shuttle it back out through your name's initials and feed the queen's fucking hungry mouth. That's where the magic comes from. It's an old tinker magic cure for the flu.'

'Put your cock in me then, you sick-inside-your-brain, sick man. In my bum hole. I'm almost there!'

'Go slow!'

'Yesss*sss*?'

He gave one them little, urgent mini-wanks, then there was a cold breeze across them that goosebumped up his thighs and shrank him further, yacuntya. He just *had* to get the old Marquis of Lorne into her butcher's window, into her furburger, into her fucking *central cut*, yacuntya! The Nephew whipped a briny finger into his mouth and, with its wet end, gently put the forefinger in Paulette's wee tight back passage, just up to half-moon of nail-end, like the Old Days! He sighed, nostalgically, dug in a fraction left to right to try get it all the deeper; when she squirmed she squirmed at waist, let out that long low sigh.

'I'm near there, I'm up to my elbow in ant's nest,' she burred, clearly aroused.

'Take your time, gentle,' he says, still going at himself with his left hand, stared down at those lunary curves under . . . but . . . but fuck. He tried thinking, P.a.u.l.e.t.t.e, almost a boy's name. She had a cheek against the pine needles and he could feel a jerking movement in the dark; with her other hand she was touching up herself. That was that. He went completely soft.

'It's there, the egg's in the middle. It's *in* the middle!' She was starting to withdraw that arm.

He remembered how singing to her could bring her off so he bent, awkward, to be near her ear, his lip touched it, lobe ice cold, in his trembly baritone.

Yoo Got to . . . !
AccenT—Tuate the Positive . . . and
Elim . . . in-ate the negative and . . .
Latch on, to the affirmative
But . . . don't mess . . . with Mr Inbetween . . . ah
You've got to spread your . . . AH! to the maximum
And bring Gloom down to the minimum
And have faith in pandemonium, liable to walk upon the
    scene!
To illustrate! my last remark: Jonah annn the Whale,
    Noah in the Ark
What did they do just when everything looked so dark??
MAN, THEY *SAID* . . . ALL TOGETHER NOW
ACK CENT CHEW Ate . . . THE POSITIVE

She grimaced, 'No HIV-positive, are you?'
He pushed the finger up more.
'Uhh.'
Old Moody was exhausted now. A frustrated rage rose up in the Nephew.
Suddenly Paulette exploded. 'Dirty queen ant, Colin, COLIN, COLIN! You can do anything to me . . . Ughhh. I came,' she says quick as her body shook. Disinterested in seconds.
The Nephew leaned back, hopeless, defeated, sunk in jungles of depression and inadequacy; immediate and considerate, he removed his finger.
As she withdrew that arm from the nest mound you saw

black tide-froth of ants round the long, pale white tube of her slim bicep. 'Eee yugs!' She swept her arm with her other hand, let the slave ants swarm freely and she began to turn her fingers, flick her hands to rid herself of them and desperately swished at those naked, white limbs. She sputtered, shook hair out of her eyes. 'Oh, that was rampant but I need a shower, uch, they're everywhere, eeeehhhh.' She was looking at him in the moonlight. 'Couldn't get it up, could you. No change in the leopard.'

He looked away, thought he would cry.

Paulette whispered, lay on her back now, skirt bunched up on her belly by fists, 'Piss on me then. Miss the boots in case they stain.'

He smiled and stood; this he could most devoutly commit. He took Old Moody, spread his legs and jettisoned the primer of piss onto her thigh, then aimed up, letting it batter across her flat stomach, glint in the belly button, then down, onto her vagina, directing the force onto the clear triangle of her hair. She murmured something. 'That looks like an open wound to me,' the Nephew growled.

'Arms, arms, wash these wee fuckers offof me.'

He directed the pee up her long, held-out arm as she watched, eyes slightly squinted against the spitterings.

'And the other. Quick. Then . . .'

He stumbled a little, stopped the jet with his thumb and forefinger, repositioned and urinated up her other arm. When his pee-line came to her ringed fingers, she clawed them and opened them into the flow.

'Mouth,' she dared, so he moved directly onto her face, which took her a little by surprise, but she quickly closed eyes and turned her cheeks from side to side in the still powerful jet, then opened her teeth wide as he filled it, till a few last droplets and the dying arc downed onto her glistened torso. She closed her mouth, hesitated, then swallowed it down just as the naughty dwarf had to drink the quart of cream he dropped tiny Gulliver into.

He sighed, amazed at her, trembling on his splayed legs. 'Paulette, girl, give up all this now and come with me, I can get you money beyond what you've ever imagined.'

He knew she wouldn't let him lay in the marriage bed with her that night, which he suddenly wanted more than anything in the world, to desecrate where she'd masturbate away for hours, focused on tons of filth, ignited by him but a million mile away from him. Like the Old Days. The Nephew hated to dwell on these facts but it is as in the *Travels*, Swift buckling to his scatological obsession yet again, Gulliver leaving the little girl's huge palm to shit between two leaves of sorrel: 'I hope the gentle reader will excuse me for dwelling on these and the like particulars; which however insignificant they might appear to grovelling vulgar minds, yet will certainly help a philosopher to enlarge his thoughts and imagination . . .'

Paulette shook herself, stood, began immediately to stride away downhill, probably remorseful already, shaking her hair; towards a solo shower, voice growing fainter, 'Oh, Macushla, *the* Macushla,' she laughed. 'You're gonna take me away from all this terribleness, are you?' she laughed, halted, then spat before stumbling on downhill, crashing through dead branches. 'Cure a cold! I'm fucking perishing. Just as well Colin'n me never bothered paying extra for the bidet to flush my fanny or arse, you hardly need one these days.'

Man Who Walks walks the lifted rail line. At the toes of his boots, silently glinting in moonlight, minute sections of flat, broken glass. He stoops, lifts a fragment, held between two fingers, he thrusts it out to the full moon: green. He squints. Or should that be, 'he squint'? examining the glass fragment with his one eye, the remaining one. He wipes the glass pristine on the rags of his coat. The glass colour is somewhere towards blue from green but not as far as aquamarine or turquoise. Other specks of glass are rich red, or even rarer, little bits with a colour between yellow and orange. The Man Who Walks has marked these locations with white stones, for there is always several miles of lifted track between the patches where the little scatterings can be found, like the remnants of stained glass from some ransacked church. But, in fact, this was the lens glass of the mechanical semaphore signals from the old, gone, Ballachulish railway.

The Man Who Walks takes the pieces of glass and fixes them into his eye, secure on the chewing-gum he has plugged his hollowed socket with. Behind the gum, inside the hollowness of his skull, he has jammed the miniature key-ring torch he got from a Christmas cracker, switched to the ON position. In the coldness of dark it generates a comforting heat deep in there. In the night's blackness, little fragments of red, yellow and green glass, which cluster like large fish eggs in his eye, glow incandescent with the ghostly light from behind.

Queen Victoria's Highland Journal

The Nephew'd mused on this land through which he'd go. Not just following the roads but knowing when to veer free of them, to miss out their meandering deviations and to take initiatives, cutting over green ridges and farmland, as the crow flies north, that is, if crows did fly, and were not squashed upon the road. So out in those boondocks, always nearly avoiding the freshest-seeming cowpats, the Nephew thought, Arva, Beata Petamus Arva! as Horace would have it, yacuntya.

Still in the forenoon, the Nephew came down a gradient that was studded with legions of raw, erect bracken, phalanxed like Spartans across the mountainsides. Anxiously he was lifting his head, now clean-shaved and fragrant, relatively, on Paulette's Ladyshave and from the ample collection of her man's greasy, dusted bottles of late 1970s aftershaves: a bit of Old Spice here, venerable Blue Stratos there; the Nephew'd mainly plumped for Pagan Man. 'There's a bit of the pagan in every man', the marketing legend on the packaging had declared; a tenet the Nephew was very willing to adhere to! The Nephew was also wearing more suitable trousers, new, double-upped socks (judiciously numbered with Tippex on their insides!), and he had obtained a reflective waterproof jacket from Paulette's man's North Sea Oil employers, bearing the extraction company's logo on the back. He'd fed on – the remainder of – the eggs from Paulette's fridge, he'd drunk from swift streams up above him on the hills, black specklets of peat twisting in his cupped palm! He didn't need any charity. For once.

His forward progress was challenged once more by a sturdy wall declaring the urgency of Private Property.

Let me state now, it is the experience of the Nephew that the accommodations of the rich hold nothing for him, aesthetically speaking. Their façades, their pretensions contain so many signals, it's all he can do not to explode in laughter when he sees the Mansions and the Big Houses, behind their shimmering monkey-puzzles and the burnished glisten of a copper-beech tree, several hundred yards hence. Aye, every great Highland house must have its venerable tree as it must have its thunderous Victorian toilet! No, as far as architecture goes, the Nephew mused, you can keep the imitation Balmorals of Victorian baronial; he'd rather stick with the pub stools, moulded beer-crate beds, perspiring sinks, mangers and mouse nests of The Man Who Walks' house or, far preferably, the endless erotic possibilities of some brutalist council estate, sweltering in a heatwave. Each bedroom window hiding innumerable secrets, especially glimpsed from a moving train as you leave the meadows on each side and enter the outskirts where generously-opened curtains reveal a whole world of privacy: a slim bed with the duvet thrown over, psychologically-revealing posters, or crossed elbows in a shirt, just lifted, her face invisible, a tautened torso under the functional bra, or just a pair of hands thrust into a sink ... this glorious democracy of *seeing*, everything the rich want to avoid where they exist, at the far end of lawns, behind trees, paged through intercom systems, tucked snug inside the airtight suck of a Jaguar's door, in their shame. There's a saying on the railway The Man Who Walks once taught him: 'Aye, son, even the first-class coach must pass through the worst parts of town.'

So, halted by a low wall with the big house beyond it, the façade, finely latticed by the tallest, thinnest French windows on the patio, closed to such a fine morning – the Nephew'd had the oil company jacket swung over his forearm it was so warm.

He glimpsed across the wall, just in case the perpetual gardener or the dowager herself was up against it, slicing verges in old dungarees. But no impressive garden at all, just rough, cloddy grass leading right up to the front of the house. Plenty enough acres though; could land a Chinook on this and, sure enough, the big cluster of ginormous sycamores right up the top.

There wasn't a soul about. The Nephew was going to be short-cutting across to their ribbon of drive that swerved round on its own self, fringed by the tilted amber tubes of withered daffodil stalks. The metalled track of the stank road would bring him down to the cattle grid and gatehouse, on the wrong side of the Private sign, but at least back onto the publicly-owned main road again.

He looked both ways, then hopped the wall, twisting his palm on the fresh concrete fluting between the stones. Stood very still on Private Property, the Nephew observed there was no sun on those French windows, concealing no curious faces watching, he just had to cross the rough clod and he was out of there. But the pioneering spirit knows no bounds. And Rottweilers aren't these nobbers' style, the Nephew concluded, hopefully.

He was drawn up the rucked grazing to the house rather than

across towards any driveway. A shallow stairway lifted him onto the patio, he noticed one of the tall French windows' frames needed painting. He checked the floor/roof lock rod: notoriously easy to jiggle free, only disadvantage is the noise. The second window down, loosely hung with red Virginia creeper, was held closed against any gusts of breeze by a mere wire hook and was half an inch open! In a long flowing movement that betrayed his commitment and complete lack of hesitation, the Nephew slid his finger through the gap, jiggled the wire up and jerked the window quickly towards him, then stepped in to enter the premises. A copper urn was by his foot, the polishy wood with the tuffety fringe of a fine big carpet by his boot toecaps.

What did it matter, he thought, he'd burned his bridges already. He wasn't going back to no agric supply warehouse to bait rats. No. This was make or break time, this time he was going to make good, get money due him off that Uncle. He didn't want to think about the Foreman this early in the day and put a shadow on such glorious weather.

What a room! An enormous tide of carpet islanded with graceful-legged antique tables, but the mirrors! Ornate gilt frames and huge! up to the cornice, throwing the either side of the room each at the other, forever. He was drawn to the middle to try and align his multiple reflections; dizzily, it reminded him of trying to organise Old Dear's satellite dish on the floor of their caravan. When he'd gathered himself in four mirrors, he had to take stock of how well he was in appearance despite his trials, his tribulations.

A young man leaned into the big room, put one foot forward onto the carpet, and lifted a pink palm to wave, 'Hi, sorry, knocked but there was no answer, so just thought I'd better come on in.'

Damn. It was Yank no less. The Nephew had almost dropped into assault position but since it seemed open house, the Nephew says, 'No problem, just *come* on in! I was admiring the mirrors here.'

'Well, yeah, they are really something now, pretty impressive. Yeah, they are something else. Bill, Bill Wright. Aunt Bethany calls me Raincheck, heh, heh.' Raincheck held out the hand. 'I don't usually visit but I'm in Scotland on business so . . .'

'Bultitude,' the Nephew yelped, then gave Raincheck a hand, thinking, Looks a wimp, no danger, 'Rodger Bultitude. Of the Bultitudes.'

'Huh,' the Yank nodded, smiling.

'It's, ah, lunch, is it . . . ? I wasn't too clear?' the Nephew asked.

'Yeah.'

The Nephew nodded, 'Yessss. What's your line of work then, Bill?'

'Aunt Bethany hasn't been driving you to distraction about me then! For once. Hollywood, tut, God.' He raised his eyes to the ceiling.

Self-deprecation. The Nephew could see he was secretly meant to be impressed, so just to spite the cunt he wheeled towards the mirror and went, 'Victorian?'

'Older than anything in LA is how I date things! What's your line of work, Rodger?'

The Nephew smiled, he wanted to say something like 'hit man' or 'pimp to underage girls'. 'Classics,' he snapped.

'Classic antiques?'

'No, no. Classics. Greek and Roman classical literature. Mainly.'

'Oh, you teach?'

'No. More . . . independent research. I'm just a poor scholar. As the old couplet beloved of millionaires goes,

Nihil Habentas
Omnia Possidentos.

"Those who have nothing own everything." ' He looked around scowling. Ready to make the exchange.

They had begun moving in opposite directions round the room, passing themselves repeatedly in each mirror.

'Have you read *The Hero with a Thousand Faces*?'

'Faeces?' the Nephew called, not looking over his shoulder.

'A study of mythic archetypes. I understand it was a great influence on Lucas.'

'Lucas? I haven't read him,' the Nephew frowned.

'No, no. The film-maker. He made *Star Wars*.' Raincheck laughed.

Oh, for fuck's sake, the Nephew thought.

'Ah,' the Yank was about to say something when an old lady who resembled a standard lamp stepped into the room too.

'Thought I recognised that cheeky-cheeky laugh! Raincheck. You look disgustingly healthy. Don't you ever do anything BAD among the smog of California?' she croaked.

'Aunt! Mr Bultitude was teaching me Greek.'

'Well, bully for you,' the old cunt shrieked and she hugged the Yank from Hollywood. What a fucking farce. Her beady eye was on the Nephew though.

The Nephew went into action right away, stepping towards her, timing it for the proffered hand he knew would rise to him and kissing it on the inner palm as in the old style, when this one would have done the society balls at Inverary Castle, that weren't without their debauched scandal; never think the aristos are missing out on a bean, that much he knew. 'Latin, actually. Pleasure to be here. Everybody must bore you with this, but we were just talking about the mirrors.'

'Oh Lord, they are Old Barrels' pride and joy. He gets up on Jemima's and Jacquelina's shoulders to polish them right to the top. Or at least he tells me that's what they're doing!'

'We were wondering. What period?'

'The *expensive* period, my dear. Since it's your first visit let's send you up to the company, Mr Bultitude.'

The lady of the house lead the Nephew and the American out and down a corridor with textured wallpaper. 'Jemima. Shirts and ties for Raincheck and Mr Bultitude. What shirt size are you, Mr Bultitude?'

'Eighteen for comfort, seventeen for formality.'

'Ah, Old Barrels' nineteens will do you then. Any preference in shirts?'

The Nephew replied, 'Well, I prefer good white cotton with a collar wide enough for a Windsor knot, dress cuffs,' in an oily way. He'd always mused on how he'd kit himself out when The Man Who Walks' house came his way and was sold off. An Italian suit, linen and silk mix, like cream on his legs – none of this bespoke nonsense – and a pair of shoes from Salvatore Ferragamo's as he had once stood outside their window on the Via Condotti in Rome, viewing the depth of shine in that leather with awe. What was it old Salvatore wrote in his fine autobiography, *Shoemaker of Dreams*? Ah yes: 'I discovered that the body, when standing, drops vertically on the arches of the feet. First you must have the feeling of support in the arch: that is paramount, fundamental, all-important. Next your toes should be free.' Some of the stuff you read in this life, yacuntya.

The old crone was looking down at the Nephew's cow-shit-encrusted boots. 'Are you the island Bultitudes or mainland Bultitudes?'

'Bit of both.'

'Aren't they all!'

'Ha ha ha ha ha.'

'Ha ha ha ha ha.'

They all stepped into the kitchen, there was a change of ambience on account of all the metallic work benches and massive hangings of brass and aluminium cooking utensils.

'Excuse us, chef,' the aunt smiled. 'We're sending another two up.'

A pot lid trembled like a blubbering lip letting out its last gasp and the chef grimaced sideways, stirring.

'How is the espagnole?'

'Clear as a bell.'

'Two days on the simmer. Read his book, Mr Bultitude. He's a worker of wonders.' The aunt smiled.

Jemima strode in with the shirts and ties draped over her arms.

'Trousers will just have to do, gentlemen, but please, no shoes allowed on the carpet upstairs, it's of museum quality.'

He and Raincheck kicked off their boots, unarmed and dropped their current shirts on the tiled floor among the burnished onion skins as the aunt looked on approvingly, unfurling the ties.

'Yorkshire cricket club, that should do you, Mr Bultitude.'

Name of Christ, the Nephew thought, starting to doubt he could go through with this, but he knotted up and shuckled to position a half-decent Windsor knot, using the particularly brilliant base of a hanging colander as a mirror.

'Squeeze in.'

They had crossed to the wall where there was a serving hatch, then the Nephew realised it was a dumb-waiter lift. By clambering up, lying on his jacket to keep the shirt clean, he fitted in a foetal position, presuming this was normal etiquette. The Nephew coughed lightly, murmured, 'I'm claustrophobic.'

'Wait till you get up *there*,' groaned chef as he snapped down the hatch and hit the switch.

In moments the dark ended as the hatch snapped open again and there was a big cheer. The Nephew clambered out.

The crazy aunt had beaten him upstairs to announce, 'Mr Bultitude of Broken Moan and also, coming up! my terrible nephew, Raincheck, from Hollywoodland.'

Our Nephew stumbled to the ground. There were at least twenty people round the egg-shaped table in a hugely long room; sure enough, none of them had shoes on.

'A Bultitude, a Bultitude, you're welcome,' roared the giant, surely Old Barrels himself, twisting in his chair and slapping the Nephew on the arse and into a seat beside him.

'Firm buttocks for one so old. Bultitudes are military. What are you: RAF, Navy, Army?'

'That's classified.'

There was laughter.

'At ease, soldier!' Suddenly, from beneath the cloth napkin on his lap, Old Barrels produced a shiny trumpet which he pointed in the Nephew's face and honked loudly. 'This is to curtail any speechifying when it gets too enthusiastic.'

Ranged round the table were a choice selection of some right weird-looking tickets. Nae wonder these fuckers keep locked up in their castles and great houses throughout this territory, thought the Nephew. And the clothes on them! It was like a collision between two trucks, one from the opera company and the truck going the other way from fucking Oxfam, yacuntya. All that fuss about clothes and here the standard was: shoeless, stranglers' ties, old codgers in worn tweeds, even orange tweed ties knotted too tight with threadbare ends, necks busting out of shirts, withered bosoms hanging within gaudy sequins, reflecting the candles.

There was another cheer and applause as Raincheck curled out the dumb waiter, holding a tray of scallops, some *gratin* sauce from which was stuck on the end of his nose.

'You're the image of your cousin George,' called some old busy.

'Hush,' went Old Barrels, 'wrong father.'

The scallops were served by Jemima.

Old Barrels stood and blew the trumpet. 'Let battle commence. Hand-dived king scallops fried with champagne, bloody eat them and shut up.'

The Nephew tried to ingratiate himself into the company, leaned over and whispered, 'I don't suppose amnesiac shellfish poisoning would make any difference here,' towards Old Barrels' hairy left ear, displaying stubble where it had been pruned back on the lobes.

He roared, 'Ha! Quite right, lad. If this lot's memories were wiped it'd be a blessing in disguise; a hundred scandals lost forever! You here with Raincheck and his damn movie shower?'

'Not exactly.'

'Cigar?' he yelled.

'Shouldn't we wait, till after?'

'Not in my house, boy . . . one between courses is just fine,' he flipped the humidor lid before him and helped the Nephew light up a foot-long Cuban, advising him to toss the second half out the window as the second half was always more bitter. 'Like marriage,' he grumbled, then the huge old man passed round a silver dish with Rennies indigestion tablets neatly laid out on it, garnished with parsley.

'Rennies between courses, anybody?' Old Barrels shouted, tossed a few in his mouth, inhaled cigar smoke and let it wander in, out, round his mouth and his grey wiry beard hairs. Droppers of viscousy sweat hit the tablecloth from his face then, rather than the trumpet. Suddenly Old Barrels lifted his finger to his lips to demand silence in a curious movement of tenderness and everyone did stop talking as the big man pointed to the windows.

There was a balcony behind the backs of other diners, through more tall French windows, which were open to let in air, the tips of birch trees and the dark blue loch showed. The Nephew noticed that a small bird, which, strangely, he couldn't identify, had entered the room and was positioned on a sheepskin rug. The bird was kneading out hairs from the mat and when it'd collected some in its beak, it twisted and flew off out the room.

Old Barrels raised his trumpet and blew a bent offnote. 'Eat, everyone.' The clamour re-established itself. He turned to the Nephew: 'They're using the sheepskin hairs to build their nest.'

After the scallops came firm, remarkable asparagus and oysters *au gratin*, then sorbet, which Old Barrels refused, announcing it would obscure his palate, before lighting up another twelve-inch Churchill. There were servings of beluga caviare, with lemon blinis; Barrels insisted everyone eat the caviare off the back of their hands. All this was served along with an iced crate of Bollinger RD from 1978 poured in stemless flutes with a diamond cut into the glass to excite the fine bubbles, hence they sped up in the formation of a perfect crucifix to the surface. When there was no champagne left the bottles were inverted in the silver buckets, then Dover sole à la meunière, off the bone, was brought up, accompanied by steamed potatoes, extra helpings of clarified butter in silver dishes and a crate of chilled 1973 Puligny Montrachet: 'Just cooking wine; afraid I'm saving the '75!' Old Barrels declared; then more sorbet, which was allowed to slump into vermilion puddles, after which came the organic sirloin steaks served medium rare without choice, along with creamed potatoes and a crate of 1982 Lafite that had aired since that morning in several non-matching decanters though Old Barrels teasingly showed off a crate of Reserve des Marechaux, a crate of Pichon Longueville, 1933, and one of Chateau Pavie, 1921, 'Should we have need of reinforcements!'

Old Barrels blew his trumpet and introduced the steaks. 'No mad cow's disease from this stuff, Raincheck, young Bultitude; had our own herds here for twenty years out front. All bloody lawns and tennis courts before. Nonsense. So we bred our own. Watch your shoes if you go for a wander later, it's a shame though.' Old Barrels separated a cube of meat using fork and the fierce-looking steak knives, surveyed the sirloin's glisten, then popped it in his mouth, chewing. 'This fellow here was called Big Mac, wonderful brown eyes and blond eyelashes.'

There was a cheer. He re-blew the trumpet to silence them, making gestures, spreading ash generously on the tablecloth and into both his neighbours' food. 'Acid rain falls, fungus fields roam, poisoning oysters, prawns, mussels, chemicals pour out of sunken boats, radiation pouring from power stations and sunken submarines, raw sewage into the sea, bloody Tampax rules the waves, all of it going into the fish. Genetically modified vegetables so your great-grandchildren'll be growing two cocks, pesticides in the vegetables, radiation from Chernobyl still moving through the watertable, double-headed lambs still being born up in Angus and the meat sold on, stands to reason if BSE is in the bovines it's in the milk and cheese too . . . all this and what are we told?' He raised the trumpet and honked a flatulent note. 'What are we told? Our society that has perfected the art of shitting in its own house, tells us to STOP SMOKING!' He roared with laughter, replaced the trumpet, bell down on the tablecloth before him, took an especially grand draw on the cigar. 'To our National Health!' Everyone toasted in support. 'Eat up, Bultitude, eat up and enjoy like a condemned man's last meal, you might be dead tomorrow.'

It was hard not to be impressed to see a man smoke a huge cigar while simultaneously devouring a juice-filled steak and quickly down glass after glass of first-growth red Bordeaux. The Nephew doffed his hedonistic cloth cap; had to admit these posh cunts could certainly go for it, but still, he looked along the table and thought, Must remember to re-read *The Communist Manifesto* again soon, yacuntya.

Then came forth a march of flambés galore, flames leaping up and more vertical burn-offs, followed by some cold soufflé. Despite the Nephew's libertarian speculations, he found it hard not to indulge and thus, of course, to be implicated. The apple in Eden has so many flavours, and so that garden fell out of reach once more as he guzzled, thought of Paulette in the moonlight and reached out for more soufflé, more huge halves of the largest cigars extravagantly discarded, thrown in a twirl out the open window and yet more lit.

Then came snappy green apples, baroquely sliced with caramel lacing, perfectly soft melon, fresh raspberries, so fat and cool they were dropleted by condensation, and then cheese: Gruyère, Camembert and stinking fresh Brie, but, the Nephew noted, a great fuss was made over the Tête de Moine and the Limburger. Some more lemon soufflé with fresh cream was specially sent up by Jemima for Old Barrels, then a 1935

Armagnac served for the ladies, 1893 Roffignac cognac for the men, liberally tipped out in pre-warmed snifters, the bottle left on display, then espresso coffees and . . . more cigars.

For the duration of this feasting, the Nephew observed, a great deal of luncheon conversation seemed to be directed over the bellies and towards the subject of the new Scottish Parliament, though the Nephew could not see, in any way whatsoever, how that venerable institution had affected or would ever affect the hegemony of this table. Doesn't change anything for the poor nor the rich, he thought. The phrase 'financial security' suddenly seemed to cover a multitude of possibilities, basically one's feet didn't touch the earth and he licked his lips at the thought of intercepting The Man Who Walks. Also, a remarkably incongruous obsession with social justice was expressed and the fate of the poor and the needy of the housing estates of Glasgow and Edinburgh was voiced, representatives of whom didn't seem too thick on the ground that afternoon. In Raincheck's area of the table, the to and fro of the electric conversation was exclusively limited to the love lives of various Hollywood celebrities always referred to in the diminutive by Raincheck. The Nephew himself was expected to maintain some degree of communication at his end of the table, despite trying to tuck away the continually arriving torrent of food.

'Do you like Fellini?' one woman leaned across at him.

'Only if it's washed,' the Nephew smiled and nodded. The Nephew was no denser, he knew in this environment the odd intellectual comment was required. No problem, he didn't have anti-social hang-ups. He cleared his throat and announced, 'Do you know, when he was Cosima and Richard Wagner's house guest, Nietzsche was estimated to be masturbating up to ten times a day?'

'A remarkable man in every way,' the bat across the table drawled.

Afterwards the Nephew announced, 'Lunch was wonderful. Like Aleister Crowley wrote, "I can go without anything, but when I have it, it may as well be the best."' He gave a small bow to cover up a belch.

Old Barrels' head swung round. 'Well, I'm sure we'd all be in agreement. That's the attitude, no thought of tomorrow, young man. Time to get started.'

There was a murmur of excitement. Two decrepit codgers in silly-coloured dicky-bows left the table, lifted and gingerly traversed a Victorian-style reading podium over the carpet to where Old Barrels waited. The podium seemed intended for one of those enormous, ancient household Bibles with the generational tree penned on the inside cover. It was moved to position and the guests, even Jemima, began to accumulate before the podium. Old Barrels stood up behind it and cast his latest cigar out the window. He then unlocked the cushioned desk top of the podium, which parted to left and right, and he removed something that resembled a huge, flaky cowpat. Jemima closed the podium desk for him as Old Barrels lifted the big object above his head.

Raincheck leaned over and whispered in the Nephew's ear. 'I've never seen it close up but they say it's bound in human skin.'

The Nephew was feeling dizzy after the gorging, a sweat seemed to be on his brow, but when he reached up nothing was there. What was all this mumbo-jumbo, yacuntya?

The old beardy man was sort of intoning, pompously, with a strange new gravity. 'Invocation. A wet wasp sting, sovereignty over all things. In the heart of these mountains are shining ones.

And we too, protectors of the secrets of the Black Book of Badenoch. A matutinal invocation on the Black Book of Badenoch,' Old Barrels announced, and the assembled diners all muttered something.

Raincheck leaned over and whispered in the Nephew's ear, 'It's a witch's book, said to date from the sixteenth century; been in this family for generations since: cures, spells, invocations, strange tales. Creepy stuff.'

Old Barrels reading this dreary, weird shit was really doing his head in, the Nephew could feel the sweat under his shirt now, and the fumes of this cognac rising into his face and the shirt collar chaffing it away, not being used to shirt and tie, these days. Or *any* days. Yet more tales put down in writing! In his drunken mind the Nephew was getting this old tale mixed up with the voice of The Man Who Walks from the typewriter ribbon and now, absurd as it seemed, the two voices seemed to run parallel to his voice in his own head, measuredly defining this series of indignities he was being exposed to, in pursuit of his rotten Uncle, for didn't we all have a voice in our head, running parallel with us, like the way the train will run beside the bus down Glen Lochy and, if it's Angie or young Si driving, you can actually wave at them up in their cab for a few minutes . . . as the train runs parallel to the bus, so a voice runs parallel in our heads, demurely recounting our thoughts and, perhaps, the state of our soul as the telegraph poles zip by.

Of course to hear anything deciphered from hieroglyphics and rendered into the King's English could only remind the Nephew, who moved slightly sideways and held out a hand to support himself on the back of a chair, of The Man Who Walks' nightmarish narratives as he had deciphered them, bed-ridden at

Paulette's house. Everything was becoming a confluence of narratives.

Raincheck leaned forward again and the Nephew almost shushed him, cause his whisper was of the American variety, but before he could, Raincheck said, 'Sotheby's claimed it could fetch half a million in New York with private collectors of occult books bidding against antiquarians and museums, but they won't hear of it, of course. Half a mil *sterling*.'

The Nephew stared at the shabby book below the booming old man, he looked over at the French windows and took a big breath. Yacuntya!

He was just about to say something when there was such an almighty crash down the stairs that even the Nephew jumped. Old Barrels stopped reading some spell involving crushed bluebells, looked up over his bifocals, and murmured, 'What on earth? You young ones. Downstairs and check that.'

Mournfully, the Nephew cast an eye to the podium, then turned and sped to the door.

With Raincheck, who took the wide stairway two at a time, the Nephew raced down the ornamental staircase and the grand paintings of ancestors galore spun past their shoulders with endless prints and gravures of military last stands with titles like *The Guns, Thank God the Guns!* or *The Last Man*. With a quick right they returned to the big mirrored room where the Nephew had first gained entrance to the house.

As they entered a huge, brown, long-haired Highland cow glared through its parted, ginger fringe and charged its precise reflection; it impacted the mirror with a shudder, tasselled tail whipped sideways and a wall of mirror glass collapsed down onto its shoulders as it reversed severely, splitting and scattering a small antique table, then stampeded another insulting reflection.

It was also hard to avoid noticing several large splattered cow turds and discs of skitters, diminishing in size, trailing all over the carpet.

The Nephew turned to a dumbfounded-looking Raincheck and said, 'Relations are breaking down between us and the animal kingdom.'

'Oh Christ Almighty.' Old Barrels had arrived and the entire luncheon party cowered, perceptively to his rear. 'Thatcher! Thatcher, you bastard, how did you get in here? It's *you* for luncheon next week!' he pointed vindictively.

'Don't reckon that's wise, Unc'. He's full of broken glass,' Raincheck insensitively announced.

'Who left that fucking French window open?' Old Barrels roared.

The Nephew had surreptitiously slid along the outer edge of the crowd, stepped into his boots back in the kitchen, then sprinted back upstairs, laces slapping, to discover Jemima, standing guard beside the Black Book of Badenoch. He slowed his pace, moving towards her, took a breath, then, to his utter surprise, the Nephew vomited hugely onto the museum-quality carpet.

Jemima watched the Nephew's hung head with her arms crossed on her powerful bosom, unmoved. The Nephew leaned over to the table and spat his final spit into somebody's empty coffee cup. 'I'll just go downstairs and get something to clean this up.'

'Just you get out of here,' she growled.

All was pandemonium downstairs, the varnished floorboards vibrated along the corridor as, with multifarious sounds of further destruction, Auntie Bethany, the two old biddies in the dicky bows and Old Barrels struggled to herd the cow out the French window. A crowd had gathered on the outside patio cooing strange theories of what cows might be attracted to. One of the biddies was wag enough from lunch still to yelp 'Ole!' as the cow veered past him, destroying some urns, one hoof shooting sideways, tearing through the carpet.

The Nephew was out the front door by this time and down towards the curved driveway. P.G. Wodehouse, yacuntya, he muttered. As he dashed across the wide turning place, boot laces clicking, he noticed a handsome silver car, Nissan Primera 2 litre, its bonnet scattered with giant cigar-halves that had burned down their duration, scarring the paintwork forever.

I woke to explosions. It had been somewhere near Guy Fawkes' Night when I started drinking. I could judge I had not been asleep too many days because the dregs of vodka and cranberry juice had not congealed into a hard, dark disc in the bottom of the glass still beside my hand. I felt the growth of my beard: 3 days. I shouted, 'Pub!'

I walked to the Ferry Bar. My scheduling was confirmed. Under exploding and contracting irises, the pink, strewn snow crystals of firework explosions were just melancholy fallings, a turning debris of gold. Bonfires seemed to roam across the upper escarpments as they did in celebration of Royal occasions, like the betrothal of Prince Charles and Lady Diana Spencer, my distant relatives.

The pub was heaving. It's called the Ferry Hotel but my definition of a Hotel is a Pub with beds above it, as I often told my vile nephew . . . I stood at the crowded bar. 'Excuse me, is this stool free?' a polite young man asked me.

'Yes, yes, you take it,' I said. It *was* my eldest nephew, the Macushla, and he had pretended not to recognise me, again.

'Thank you very much,' he said, lifted the stool above his head and threw it across the pool table at some other young men. I went . . .

Ribbon ends.
   New typewriter ribbon.

Then I came unto what I later, after several weeks, identified as: Dublin. Fascinating city – or at least it *sounded* fascinating. My pitch, along with the Man from Cavan and the Man from Navan (or was it the other way round?), was at the side of Clery's department store on venerable O'Connell Street.

The Man from Navan (or was it Cavan?) proudly removed a moulded lump of stone from his gaberdine one day. 'And would you ever guess what that is?'

I took the stone pudenda in my palm, the better to weigh it up for cracking over the back of his skull later should his horse come up. Cavan, or Navan, Man sayeth, 'It's the nose of that damn Britisher, Nelson, we blew him up in '66 from the top of his column just over there.' He nodded. 'We nippers fought one another on the street to pick up the best scattered bits. This was a souvenir for my Mam, and sat on her mantelpiece to the end of her days, God bless her.'

'That's not Nelson's *nose*, you stupid fucker,' was my reply.

Each and every morning, we were roused, me holding Nelson's bollock in my fist, by cheerful, enthusiastic talk of Brian Boru and King Sitric Silkenbeard from the summit of the open-topped tourist double-decker, which set forth daily at some hour of vomit-inducing earliness. The Man from Cavan (or was it Navan?) proclaimed that the commentator was 'a bloody Englishman'. Worse, he was specific . . . 'a Norfolk man!' no less. Anyway, I still find a warmness in my cooled heart for the King *and* his silken beard.

Both Cavan and Navan Man were Out Patients from St John of God's Hospital. (Should you be in any doubt who St John belongs to. And the hospital too for that matter.) They (Navan and Cavan Man, not St John. Or God) had both made the long pilgrimage from Ranelagh via the Appian Way to The Joy. Many times. They were recovering alcoholics. Or they soon would be again, once they stopped drinking.

Still prone to hallucinations, when they got some fortified cider, it was my amusement at nights to takes these Out-of-Towners up to the Phoenix Park where, though they didn't know it, the zoo was positioned. I knew they were trying to deny rhino, giraffe and hippopotamus drifting into their peripheral vision, but they would politely twitch, ignore and never dare comment.

Of course, being the son of an English colonel, I often kept to better parts of the fair city. The Grand Hotel, Malahide, where Smithy spent the nights before his transatlantic take-off in 1931 from the sands, for instance; or at least the wheelie bin behind its kitchens was a particularly favourite residence as the Eurasian chef tipped the goulash dregs in on top of me – both a source of warmth and nourishment.

But what clemency of climate for a hardy Scot! It's as my friend, Monsieur Camus (1913–1960), wrote, 'There are many injustices in the world but one that is never mentioned is that of climate' (my translation). If you prefer in the original: Je Boucoup de le injustice de le monde pour un non arbblement est dat de climat.'

Even in bleak midwinter as the frost glistened on my goulash-encrusted greatcoat (hand-tailored by Forsyths of Edinburgh; a gift from my father with a knowing wink at the servant's entrance!), I was a torrent of sweat within. By God, if I wrote back to the greater island mentioning that I was surrounded by palm trees they would take me for insane. Or worse, a poseur!

Then I would walk the tidal flats, pausing in the moonlit shadow of Phil Lynott's pink house to shout much more propitious chord progressions across his lawn before the Guards carried me down onto the sands. As they proceeded to kick my cunt in I would yell . . . 'Ahh . . . savages, check my pockets, I'm a famous screenwriter! For the films!' (I elaborated for their benefit, you understand.) 'Fallen on a creative slump. You will find matchboxes, even cutlery, a mustard spoon for instance, from some of the finest hotels in Europe' (kick to the ear).

'Pilferer as well as a Peeping Tom,' the third policeman grunted, booting out, harder.

'Ouch! Matches from the Hotel Eden on the Via Ludovisi in Rome' (sharp boot to the balls).

'A yah bampots. Hotel Meurice, Paris' (punch in the gut).

'Called us "savages" and "bampots",' murmured the second policeman (counting from the left), touching his pencil to his tongue and making a notebook entry before resuming his kicking.

'Look! A cocktail stirrer from the Connaught in Mayfair,' I groaned, but to no avail. I was like poor old Boris Pastoukhoff, who had to leave his paintings in hock at the Lancaster Hotel in the rue de Berri, in lieu of his bills, and they hang on the bedroom walls to this day.

Afterwards they left me lying there, my matches sodden and my cocktail stirrer snapped, waiting for the tide to come in.

Phil was the toast of the town (mainly due to my uncredited compositions such as 'The Cowboy Song', 'Warriors' and 'Jailbreak'). The town was full of Americans; why, even the graffiti showed a precise US influence: when at my Sackville Place residence, by my dreaming cheek was, hastily scrawled in magic marker, FUCK OFF TO RUSSIA ALL COMMY BEGGARS. A curious and tough line of poetry that has tugged at my metaphysical and political meditations ever since. I would have been more impressed had the author rendered it in the Irish. Or as I prefer it called: the Erse. As in the traditional Scottish air 'Four and Twenty Virgins Came Down from Inverness': 'Singing Balls to your partner and Erse against the wall, if you canny get fucked on Saturday night you canny get fucked at all.'

The town was hospitable for drinkers of beer. Sometimes the Man from Cavan would point out a reputedly famous poet in the Sackville Lounge, when our finances, or more significantly our appearances, permitted entrance. The Man from Cavan would add, ominously, 'Look, it's Terry, from Derry, who thinks he's from Donegal' (or somesuch). 'But he's still owed royalties,' in whispers, and this would lead directly to hints, despite the months of effort earning our entrance, that it was time indeed for our brisk egress. It was this pattern of events that led me to suspect the Man from Cavan, or perhaps I'm confused and it was the Man from Navan, or possibly both, had backgrounds in the publishing industry. I noted down their address, c/o Clery's department store, as a future contact regards these memoirs.

Though I am wholly formal, and detest the use of the familiar 'tu' in conversation, one day, after more confusion, I asked the Man from Cavan and the Man from Navan their Christian names. After hours of interrogation, including reference to an almanac in the library of the I.L.A.C. shopping centre, we came to the conclusion they were called Shane and Sean, or was it Sean and Shane?

The public transport system was second to none, as far as our requirements went. If weather became unstable, a modestly priced ticket could often be found lying on the ground outside a station, which allowed a person to ride on the heated trains all day, back and forth, to and from the line's farthest reaches, playing Spot the Nazi War Criminal or brushing up on international politics by reading the wide variety of newspapers and magazines so carelessly abandoned. If we couldn't join a train on a cold windy day, this was just another opportunity to play Spot the Erect Nipple on Grafton Street. Taking bets, would it be both or just the one! Happy days, in short.

As for high culture, just beyond the awning of the Gaiety Theatre, from where we were moved on, we could sample the most delicate Andantes by standing outside the music college, just below a window, though we were often shouted down at to move along, by the girl who played the Canzonetta from Tchaikovsky's violin concerto in D, so swooningly. As well as our rising odour, she yelled, it was our helpless weeping that distracted her so. 'Feck off and hurry up dying,' was her phrase.

As far as opportunities for capital went, there was quite a wide selection of portfolios available for myself and my two friends from the counties, to spread our risk among.

They themselves held a share in a syndicate horse that would run at Fairyhouse and The Curragh down in darkest Kildare, as they referred to it. Often they would begin walking to The Curragh days before a race commenced, snow stopping racing before they reached there. Eventually I learned their share in the horse was less than a shilling and they'd lost the deed which they were sold by a one-armed man in a pub. No sense keeping my legs crossed there.

One of the most just aspects of the civilised and forward-looking bus service in that city was this: if passengers did not have the correct change on them, the driver would issue a refund stub. I will illustrate: if your fare was 40p and you were fortunate enough only to have a 50p piece, the conductor would issue a 40p ticket with a small stub, worth 10p, attached!

By taking these stubs to the learned sages of the bus office in O'Connell Street, goodly Dubliners could receive *cash* back, right over the counter. If only every European city could be so enlightened in matters of excess fares it would surely encourage enterprise on a European-wide scale? 'Is this why Dublin is referred to as the Fair City?' I once yelled at the refund queue. They beat me up.

Therefore our main profession, as you can imagine, consisted of patrolling the streets, diving on any bus ticket that looked as if it had been discarded with a valid excess reclaim. Tourist season was the real harvest. Often tourists would be carrying extremely large denominations – a whole punt for instance – and the refund stubs would amount to the most outlandish amounts, credited on their ticket but which they would haplessly, not understanding the culture, discard – always in the bins which stand at the bus stops all the way up O'Connell Street. How we used to plunge in among the bins, almost embracing them with familiarity: 'bruscar' is the word for trash, in the Erse. Scattering the wasps who plundered the Coca-Cola cans, rooting among the lesser of the many evils in search of bus tickets. Ah, those days in the fair city, for it was a metropolis teeming with potential; we only had to stand on the Ha'penny Bridge, the River Liffey flowing seaward beneath us, to witness millions of gallons of potential Guinness.

And once, when I was flush with refund stubs: a woman! Is it not a truth that even a single encounter with the opposite sex always casts a positive halo on some distant city? I risked it lower and my nose, a section of which was currently missing, crossed the down, no! the *fur*, that seemed to connect between her belly button and Venus mound, then at last I found it. 'So here's the *craic* every bastard can't help bellyaching on about,' says I ('arsa mise' in the Erse).

Oh, but we were not alone in our wheelie bin behind Eircom headquarters and the Romanian refugee insisted on watching; he repeatedly struck matches which made shadows leap on the flip lid of the bin, only adding to my nausea, showing the tears streaming down his leathery cheeks till the match burned his fingertips. Due to years of communal sleeping I was weary with troilism and longed for a simple one-to-one. You get like that. Believe me. Besides, the refugee was hopelessly impotent despite his advances towards me. I'd have swapped places anytime. Nights like that made me long for my vibrating jackhammer.

The Man Who Walks was afraid of swallowing wasps. True, he wandered beneath the mountain tops with that decay-ridden, halitosis-haunted cave drooling, wide open, and what self-respecting wasp would ever have entered? Regardless, he rigged up a gauze wire mouth-guard around his jaw which, combined with the variety of objects he'd fix in his eye socket, terrified village street urchins at one hundred yards. Then he took to wearing a cardboard box on his head with eyeholes. This was some protest against him losing his driving licence and various anti-police slogans were painted on the sides and rear of the box, and the NATO star insignia on the top, in case of aerial attack. He eventually found a compromise by strapping his mother's old canary cage over his head, opening the little door when he wanted to pass in a beer can to his lips or toss some pony nuts to the back of his throat.

In those days he was living at the seamen's hostel by the pier but was soon enough ejected after he sawed his bed in two and threw it out the window at night for the high tide to take away. He'd passed himself off as a seaman since he'd rowed into the bay with a dinghy stole from somewhere. With the loss of the bed at sea he was forced to take accommodation elsewhere. He lived in a cave down Gallanach. It was around this time the mountain-rescue mascot, a St Bernard who they'd take with them on the helicopter, went missing. Legend always had it, when The Man Who Walks vacated his cave, a perfectly skinned St

Bernard's fleece was hung from the wall with two glass eyes stuck in the appropriate gaps. There was a violently broken-open brandy barrel too.

With mysterious funds, The Man Who Walks'd row across the bay to the Dinghy Supply Shop twice a day for different coloured distress flares to light the unthinkable goings-on in his cave.

Bonnie Prince Charlie's Flight
in the Heather

Hazy shower clouds hung in the distance over Loch Linnhe and the swerving gulls before them were being highlighted by sun from behind the mountains, so the birds' whiteness appeared spectral, brilliant and quite unreal. A seagull dropped a bright orange starfish down onto the grey tarmac of the road before him. The Nephew, thumbing it, top button undone and tie shoogled loose, wanted to step out, pick up its hard skin and frisbee the starfish back to the loch's water, which was just behind him, but a car's front wheel instantly crushed the starfish into a pink smear.

He retched dry air, took a few steps onward, then re-halted. He stuck out his thumb again, lacking in confidence that his stomach was ready yet for the sickly smooth ride bestowed by high-tech suspension regimes, then he swiftly dropped the thumb again when he noted the distinctive burn marks on the bonnet and roof of the approaching silver car but too late, always too late! The car began to brake. Behind the windscreen was the nodding, ever-affable face of Bill 'Raincheck' Wright.

'Rodger!' said Raincheck. 'Why the hell didn't you say you had no car?'

'Lost my licence. Drunk driving. Little embarrassed. I'd the car picking me up later, but I have to confess something.'

'Confess? Whaaaaat?' Bill smiled, struggling with the gear stick. 'Damned manual shift. I mean, you had a throw-up, I heard, that's understandable, man. Jemima cleaned up. The booze! They lay on that food too rich, man. Me, I don't drink. I know people in LA would have a heart attack just looking at that table!' He got the gearstick up into that shy and elusive fifth.

'It's not the being sick!' the Nephew lowered his voice in penitence. 'It was *me* who left the French window open! Can you believe that? See, I thought it might be non-smoking, so I stepped out there for a quick little puff before I went upstairs and I must have left the window off the latch. Feel terrible about it all. Absolutely terrible.' The Nephew used the electric window switch to shuffle down a half inch of space. 'I should really offer to pay for the damage. And, of course,' the Nephew indicated down his front, 'return this shirt and tie!'

'For God's sake, Rodger, don't go back there and offer to pay. Use money on important things, like the Free Willy Foundation. Y'know? To set the whale from the movie free? They can never pin the mirrors on you,' the American chuckled. 'Guess you weren't to know it was a cattle ranch out there! Don't worry, Old Barrels is insured for cow attack.'

The Nephew began to chuckle. 'Shame about the damage to your car here too.'

'The studio will pay,' he stated, confident and disinterested. Bill looked at the Nephew. 'Don't offer to pay. I remember the fuss around those mirrors from when I was a kid, they must be worth a *lot* of money.'

The Nephew turned to look at the Yankee and said, 'Suppose they could always auction the Black Book!'

'Yeah. Huh.'

'Is it worth all that money? Shouldn't they have it in a safe? Don't they lock it up at all?'

'Well, it's mainly just family that know about it and, you know, the country-dance set and that. That's why Aunt Bethany organises these bizarre readings. That lot are past it now, but back in the 70s they were quite wild, car-key parties and the lot. She's not my real aunt, you know, my parents knew her from Oxford.'

'Do you know, in the old days, the Clearances days up here, when they'd loot a house they would tear the pages from the books. Know why?'

'Why?'

'Well, they weren't particularly anxious to broaden their education. It was just because you could use the page of a good book to make a perfect musket cartridge from gunpowder. The musket ball that sunk into your thigh might have passed through a page of the Bible or a Latin primer or even a page of *Robinson Crusoe*!'

'You know about Highland history? You could have helped us out here with this movie.'

'How come? What's it about?' the Nephew smiled, politely.

'Well, it might interest you, Rodger, historic romance.'

'Oh reeeeally, my favourite!'

'Its called *Kidnapped*.'

'The *Kidnapped*?'

'Well, yeah. I guess. We got Darryl Simpson as Alan Breck.'

'Thought he was a black actor!'

'He is, but we see Breck more as an exotic, pirate figure.'

'Well, that's just fantastic, Bill. What is it you do in this picture?' asked the Nephew.

'Done a great deal of production back in lala land, but this is a big studio production. I'm just a freelance location scout and exec producer.'

'Location scout. So you would locate all the places where scenes are going to take place in the movie?'

'That's right. Battlesites, close to good communications, of course, especially outstanding scenery the characters can stand against as scenes are played out: castles, old drove roads, but it's hard finding places that haven't been used in movies before and, you know, trying to avoid those goddam electric pylons you guys have strung over the slopes. And our damned mobile phones won't work with these mountains.' He laughed, good-naturedly.

'Must admit, the movies are not my chosen art form,' the Nephew declared solemnly. Except for *I Know Where I'm Going*. How good is that! Utterly psychedelic. Unintentionally psychedelic. Only ever saw it once . . . never forgotten it.'

'I'm afraid I haven't caught it.'

'One of the strangest movies. My Uncle knows a lot about the films, but not me. How is trying to make a movie in Scotland?'

'I'll be honest with you. The line producer and I are thinking of writing a book about it, called "You'll Never Eat Deep Fried Pizza in This Town Again".'

The Nephew suddenly laughed, thinking, after all, he might *not* use this Yank as an unwitting getaway driver, after stealing the Black Book of Badenoch, then tie him to the back of the car with the tow rope and drag him up a lonely forestry track of stone chippings at fifty miles an hour. 'That's funny,' the Nephew admitted.

'Now it looks like the bloody place may run out of petrol. Can you imagine what that'll mean for our production? We really will be using horses. Man, everyone wants to be in Hollywood but they don't like dealing with reality.'

'An accurate summation of the contemporary Scottish character, Bill. It's the curse of Connery, old man gave us ideas well above our station. Where are you headed, by the way?' the Nephew suddenly asked.

'Checking into somewhere now called Cona Castle.'

'*Nice.*' The Nephew had tried to rob it once.

'Where are you headed? Is your parents' island near here?'

'No. I can get a taxi back this evening. Business. Up the road here. Ballachulish. Have to nip into the hotel and the local shop. And to be honest with you, Bill, I'm much obliged for the lift, but would you mind if we stopped to get a breather? My stomach's still a little tender. Just not used to all that rich food. Up here, say, on the left, I'll show you where. Interesting. The grave site of James of the Glen?'

'Sure, I'll pull over.'

'You know about James of the Glen? You might say, in Hollywood, it was a great story. That's what Stevenson's *Kidnapped* is based around.'

'Yeah, I think I read a li'l bit about that when we were researching this, yeah, yeah. Well, I'm here to look at locations, it'd be a pleasure to get a conducted tour by an expert.' The location scout smiled.

'Just here.'

Raincheck pulled the car over.

'It's my Uncle who's the expert. Used to tell me about it when I was a nipper, each night before I dropped off to sleep. Fitful sleep and nightmares. James of the Glen was hung, 1752, by the Hanoverian regime for a murder, which he didn't commit, up in the woods there. He, or his skeleton, is buried right here, come and see. You might want to use it as a location.' The Nephew climbed out and there was a large, long stick in the ditch by the gate. He picked it up and checked its strength, patting it onto his palm.

'Reckon the car is okay here, sorta blocking the gate?'

'Don't you worry. They'll peep if they want by. Come along now.' The Nephew climbed over the gate and strode on ahead, holding the stick in both fists. He crossed the farmyard. A dog barked and a rickety wooden door on an outhouse vibrated, held by a bolt; the muzzle of a collie showed, rummaging and snarling in the dust of the space beneath the bottom of the gnawed door. The Nephew moved onwards across the yard to the shore in the vicinity of the lifted railway.

Through swaying birches, loch shallows sparked. The Nephew stepped into the cemetery and turned to the remains' final resting place. He crouched down on his haunches. Placed on the grave was the dry cawl of an evaporated jellyfish, the crisp, emptied corpse of a flattened crow, surrounded by a delicate ring of plucked rowan berries, a drooping, stinging nettle in a drained Hennesey bottle and the fresh, human, *all* too human curlicue of a coiled, glistening shite.

'Looks like Uncle's gone over to the Hanoverians again,' the Nephew mumbled.

'Pleasant enough spot.' The location scout coughed, and an expensive camera shutter birled, slightly to the Nephew's rear.

'Yup,' the Nephew muttered. 'As Beckett wrote, "I have no bone to pick with graveyards."'

'Oh dear,' Raincheck had come up behind the Nephew. 'That looks like . . .'

'Yesss . . .'

'Rather disrespectful.'

'All kinds of allegiances up in these mountains, Bill. Shift with the seasons. Could be a Campbell shite. Could be one of the

Protestant falange.' He leaned forward and sniffed. 'Certainly too hearty for an Englishman's. The degree of droop on that nettle means he's only a hour ahead of us!' The Nephew stood, rubbed his palms and looked around.

'But, Rodger,' said Bill, 'mightn't the culprit not be heading south?'

'The "culprit". I like that. Couldn't have put it better myself. No, I can tell he's been eating the delicate dishes of *southern* Argyll. There's a chance he might be leaving his calling card, just north of here, up at the assassination site.'

'Assassination site?'

'You have your grassy knoll, we have our forestry commission sign.'

'Eh?'

'Assassination site, up in the woods of Lettermore here. The murder that James's rattlers here was hung for.'

'Ah.'

'Scene of the crime. C'mon, tell you in the car.'

They moved up the side of the loch, through the gears, northwards a mile or so. 'What happened here was, after the 1745 uprising, and the Jacobites' rout at Culloden, Stuart of Ardshiel's house oe'r the hill there was fired by the redcoats and he was exiled to France for his role in Prince Charlie's rising.'

The American nodded respectfully.

'Wife and kids were flung out, died in poverty down in England far from these hills. His half-brother James Stuart was pardoned and lived just up Glen Duror there. In '52, the factor from down at Faisnacloich at Loch Creran's head was Colin Campbell, an evictor know'd as the Red Fox cause of his red hair. Some say he killed a woman back at Benderloch, used his local knowledge to give up local men after Culloden. Pull over to the right there.'

They turned onto a rough forestry track up behind some houses.

'Okay, on up here.'

'Ah, might be a bit much for this car.'

'Don't be timid, give it some welly, but put it down into first.'

The car rounded the first corner and spat some stones out from its rear wheels. But around the next corner there was a yellow, high-visibility tape over the track and a painted sign read: TREE FELLING NO ENTRY.

'Ach, fucking Forestry. We'll need to go forward on foot. Maybe we'll surprise him.'

'The Culprit.'

'A Red Fox himself. C'mon.' The Nephew clambered from the car and eased out the long staff of wood which he'd stored, slid in through the headrest towards the rear window, shedding bark on the upholstery.

The Nephew ducked under the tape, as if he was entering a crime scene, which he was. The location scout struggled: coordination of leaving the car in gear with the handbrake on, beeping the car locked with the remote control.

The American followed the Nephew uphill, orange matting of last winter's pine needles still ribboned in wind-lain coils across the track. A series of lobbed tree trunks had metallic arrows tacked onto their angled faces, cut by the diagonal sweep from a buzz saw. One of the signs had metallic lettering that read:

MURDER SITE THIS WAY

but the first two words had been smeared out with what looked
like excrement and in black magic marker the words

MERCY KILLING

~~MURDER SITE~~ THIS WAY

had been inserted.

The ground was uneven and spongy; a narrow track, where two
people could barely pass, led away into the mature pines,
claustrophobias of fleshy, deciduous leaves breaking sunlight like
limp fingers, the slight sweetness of decaying humus dominating
that shade.

An erratic series of planks, hammered into the ground on
their edges, contained pilings of pink gravel, the brilliant
emerald efflorescence of moss mounds, and winter-brown ant
heaps tumbled fallen branches on each side among the old
boughs. Another arrow indicated that the assassination site was
some distance ahead, but suddenly the location scout jumped as,
in the forest hush, the Nephew's serious voice sounded,
ominously at low level, just off to the American's right. He
hadn't seen him, lurking there silently.

'The cairn's in up there, no one about. He's not here less he's
watching us, say from the true assassination site. There's an old
cairn in ruins under the new one the commission built, but
perhaps that was put there in the nineteenth century. It's like a
battlefield, Bill. Do you know some battlefields have gone
missing, the soldiers unable to make up their mind where they
were on the actual field where they were so afraid? Fourteen
hours stood in the cannons at Waterloo, Bill, relieving yourself
where you stood. That makes a battlesite like a field of dreams, a
shitty one. Has so much praying ever been done in one place as

a battlefield? More than in any medieval cathedral. Have so many souls ever been taken? It's a supernatural spot, imagine that mad exodus of spirits. Think of Waterloo, or Culloden in your case, the Macdonalds bursting apart under Belford's grapeshot, all those spirits rattling upwards so quickly they would need air-traffic control to organise them. You don't just choose a battlesite for your films there, Bill, you need someone like me to sniff out the bloodied ground for you, reconnoitre that specific degree of haziness on the horizon which is required: the proverbial stream that gets a gruesome nickname, the precise geography of a place where fate is going to close in on thousands. You know, when the Romans were in Scotland, Bill, Ninth Legion was marching north and vanished. Gran used to tell me if you listened close at bedtime you could just hear them, marching away in the distances. Many's the night I dropped off to sleep shivering as I heard them get closer and closer.'

The Nephew turned around and suddenly pointed upwards. Through the full leaves, hanging like some kind of torn green leather, there was a remarkable high cliff face of solid black rock glinting with water.

The location scout raised his camera and started shooting off film as the Nephew spoke.

'Some reports of the shooting of the Red Fox mention that the assassin or assassins were by a black rock. Now just as they have at Culloden, the Forestry Commission has buggered up this place. This track here's been bulldozed through, probably sometime in the 50s, must've altered lie of the land. If I was going to shoot someone coming along the old bridle path, where *you* are now, I'd do it from up there, good long aim down, with a musket and quick getaway uphill, probably without even being seen. Don't forget there'd be nae pine in those days, just sweepings of birch when the world was still pure and had a chance. All this,' he gestured, 'put in this century. You must feel that, Bill . . . all one big potential movie set.'

'Well, we could do a beautiful shot from down here, Alan Breck and Cluny MacPheeerson just where you are.'

The Nephew smiled. 'Hey, Billy-boy, that's not the kind of shooting we're talking about here.' He walked down towards him, imagining he swung out with the stick, no! waiting till they go along by the cairn, then whacking him from behind, using one of the tumbled boulders from the old National Trust cairn to stove his brains in, then drag the corpse into the woods. But it's all forensics these days, boy. The legacy of Dr Joseph Bell, who Sherlock Holmes was based on. That's your murders ruined for this generation. And he was stuck with the car and all *sorts* of circumstantials. And this one, he'd be more laden with the credit cards than the cash, and in the long run he was a direct link back to the Black Book. Don't want to mess up his chance there. The Nephew smiled and says, 'C'mon, let's go.'

'We're not going along to the cairn?'

'That's for tourists, the shooting took place here, right? Come along, Bill.'

The Nephew led the way back down to the car. 'They arrested James, took him down to Inverary where he was tried by Campbells on the jury and condemned on no evidence at all. He was hanged along here at Ballachulish, way up on a rock you can see from miles around. Orders were for him to hang there and rot on the gallows as an example of King George's justice, so for years under military guard he rotted away, swinging up there, crowded by an escort of crows and seagulls, and when his bones fell they were tethered together again with wire, to hang clicking in the wind. Whenever James's wife looked west to a sunset, it was through her husband's scrappy rib-cage, and when his sister over at Callerton, the other side of the loch, saw the sunrise, it was through the same bones.'

When they reached the car, swarms of black flies, in their unfathomable ways, were clung to the surfaces and blipped against their faces as they lifted together when the door was opened.

'So who shot him then?'

'Sixty-four-thousand-dollar question, Bill. But put it this way: I know people, loonies, who have the gun.'

'You gotta be kidding me?'

'True, the very Spanish musket that shot the Red Fox. Bit like the Turin Shroud or shavings of the Cross, or the Holy Grail, after all, every cave in the west ends up called Prince Charlie's cave; so there's quite a lot of fakes circulating, but the real one has been passed down through the families, they had it buried in a grave over on the island there.'

'Hey, we'd love to use it in the film. Accurate-looking period pieces are hard to get.'

At the bottom of the track, with a burst of power, the hired car jumped across the road and on round the lochside to Ballachulish, dominated by the large modern bridge which replaced the leisurely, flat-bottomed ferries the Nephew remembers from his youth.

They parked in front of the old Victorian hotel. 'Up there, you have Cnap a' Chaolais, where the rotted body hung. Up *you* go. You should go take a look for yourself, get a sniff of the atmosphere. They knew how to pick a spot okay!'

The location scout thighed up to the flank of the bridge, two steps at a time, his camera, the eye of the new world, held at the ready.

The plaque on the monument up there read:

In memory of James Stewart of Acharn, who was executed on this spot 8th November 1752 for a crime of which he was not guilty.

Erected by the Stuart Society 1911.

The location scout silently spelled out the words as he decided he would take the principal actors and no doubt the director here, to show off the depth of his local knowledge and research. He could just hear the actress's voice now: 'Did Rod Stewart pay for thaaaat?'

Sixty foot below, down in the over-cool, almost cold of the Ferry Bar, the Nephew nodded to the barman and says, 'Has The Man Who Walks been in?'

'I'm sorry?'

'Has The Man Who Walks been in here today. Or in the last few days?'

'I'm sorry but aren't *you* The Man Who Walks?'

'No. No. Certainly not. Fuck no, man. I'm his Nephew. He's my Uncle, I'm afraid.'

'Ah sorry, mate. I'm new here. They showed me a photograph. He's barred from here. They said he wasn't to be let in at all. He always has dead animals with him. Scaring bus parties!'

'Yeah. That's the cunt. Nobody's seen him about though?'

The barman was fucking Australian. Could you believe what the world was coming to? There was an unnecessary pause of play on the pool table behind him, so the Nephew turned and immediately the two boys, who obviously should've been at school, continued to play.

'Get you anything?'

'Pint Coca-Cola then, with ice, and a packet of prawn cocktail crisps.'

'Sorry, mate. No prawn cocktail.'

'Any beef?'

'Smokey bacon.'

Smokey bacon, thought the Nephew. Jesus, what a life. 'That'll do. Pass the Lea & Perrins too.'

'Is that Diet Coke or Classic?'

The Nephew turned his ear down onto his shoulder, as if peering into a darkest recess, trying to detect any hint of mockery, but the guy was genuinely serious, hesitating, pint glass loosely in hand.

'Classsic,' the Nephew almost whispered.

The barman nonchalantly poured out the drink, no hint of a sneer on his lips.

'Hey. I want to ask you something?' said the Nephew.

'Yeah?'

'See budgerigars, in Australia, out in the territories. Is it true all the wild ones are green? It's only the ones that have been caught and bred that are other colours?'

'Budgerigars? I don't know, mate. I'm from New Zealand.'

'Oh. Pity. Needed to ask about Ned Kelly too.'

'Sorry.'

The Nephew turned to glare at the two teenage boys. Youth of today, nay sense of tradition whatsoever. What tradition? Dunno, I've forgotten, thought the Nephew. One of them was extremely girlish, incredible really, but they carried on as if they hadn't heard a thing. The Nephew paid for the drink and crisps with the loose change, piles of two- and one-pound coins he'd taken from the compartment in front of the gearstick. 'Give us some twenties for the phone.' He coughed, then said, 'Keep asking Australians that and they don't know. Never seen flocks of them in the wild.'

The barman nodded.

'So, even though he's barred you haven't heard about the Uncle being around, you know, up at the monument there, or whatever?'

'No, mate.'

The Nephew looked at the crisps torn open and their inners doused with dark Worcestershire sauce and at the spatting, busy top of the Coca-Cola and realised he'd just been sick and had no appetite for them at all.

The Nephew took up his crisps and pint, then moved towards the toilets where the phone was. Ariseth, taketh up your pint and fuckin go! Ooo, Marlboro Lights, he thought, placed the pint on the CD jukebox and called over to one the boys, the girly poof. 'Hoy, son, blag a cig offof yous?' Far as he minded, this CD jukebox had nae Lizzy or Roses on it, yacuntya.

'Aye,' the kid croaked in that shaky, breaking voice. God, the burdensome awkwardness of adolescents. The Nephew shivered.

The boy lifted the lighter near the Nephew's mouth. The child's face was of real beauty, perhaps there was something provocative about the little scamp, personally lifting the light so near the Nephew's mouth? The Nephew flickered his eyes through the rising smoke but the kid just looked solemn, as if he was tightening a washer on a tap, chin pushed down into his anorak collar that was zipped right up. The way when you're that age you can just seem as cool as fuck without even trying!

'Cheers.' The Nephew crossed back to the phone and dialled the Foreman's top-of-the-range mobile.

'Yes.'

Speaking low, the Nephew said, 'I'm in Ballachulish and nae sign of him. Still to try the village and the signal at the manse, but I have my doubts. So. I'll try and get back to you the day.'

'Listen here: where exactly have you been?'

'Had to hide up for a night or so. So what? What are you worried about? What's he going to spend the money on up here?'

'Have I got news for you.'

'What!'

'He was up in the Black Garrison.'

'Never. Who telt you this shite?'

'Contacts. Prepare yourself for this. I think he's gone north of Ballachulish.'

'North of here!'

'Telling you, son, I think he's o'er the bridge and away, into unknown territory, into inhabited country.'

'He's never gone north of Ballachulish before. He doesn't have Ordnance Survey maps. There's no lifted line for him to follow!'

'Pursue him on up there, boy, see if you can find him.'

'Hold on now, I've no money. I can't go on some expedition up north, away on some wild goose chase, and what with this petrol blockade I might get no lifts. He'll be making his way back by now. He never goes beyond here. Terrifies him.'

'Get on up there and see if he's lurked in Aluminumville.'

'It makes no sense, why would he?'

'Knows he's been a really bad boy this time. Might be smarter than we think. Now, have you been in trouble with the polis?'

'Me. Nut. Why! Have they been sniffing round the caravan again?'

'Ach, you hear rumours.'

'Fuck them. They've nothing on me.'

'Just you keep well clear of them and out of trouble. Okay. Saw your Old Dear recent.'

'Oh really.' Once again he could sense the second presence of someone listening.

'She's a letter for you from the computer hacker. Your wee pal in prison.' The Foreman openly sniggered.

'Aye. Well, I'll get it when I'm back. Another thing,' he lowered his voice so the barman couldn't hear, he didn't want him, and those young laddies, 'specially the pretty one, to think he had some kind of budgie fixation. He whispered, 'Don't let the Old Dear take the budgie cage to the pawn shop. I'll get some more when I'm home and I've sorted out this cunt.'

'Then we'll have to watch we don't kill your new budgies with the bloody champagne corks when we catch that Uncle of yours. Get yourself up that road, son, and please, check in more often so's I know exactly where you are half the time. Don't go murdering that nutter now, just sting him good. Enough to let him know who's boss. Like last time.'

'Fucking right. I'll take his other fucking eye this time. From now on we'll just need to follow the tapping of his fucking white stick.'

'Ha! That's the spirit, son, you geld him good. Listening to me nice and proper now? We'll both end up hunky dory out of this one.'

'I'm fit as a fiddle.' In a foolish flush of confidence, the Nephew ignored logic and planned working with the Foreman again. He blurted out, 'I've another something worked out.'

'Oh aye? Tell us more.'

The eagerness of the Foreman cautioned the Nephew ever so slightly. 'A job. Easy peasy, don't want to talk on the phone. Put it this way, near us here lies a wee nest egg. You know I've always been a *book* lover.'

'Well, tell us about it?'

'I'll say no more.'

'Mmmm. Phone in tonight, okay.'

'Okay. Watch out for Old Dear.'

The phone went dead.

The Nephew left the Coke and crisps on top of the jukebox and sauntered outside, casting a last look at the pretty boy, to sit on the car bonnet, smoking the limits of the butt, pincering it with two fingers and flinging it distant, watching the fast current across the old ferry straits, seeing it move out under the big bridge, the oily look to the water with its swirling patches of smooth areas and its slicks of disturbed surfacing.

A Safeway juggernaut moved past, heaving round like a huge screen, reflecting the girders and superstructure on its polished flanks and away under the bridge. Minutes later the sound of the juggernaut, labouring up the slip and onto the bridge, could be heard high above him, up where James of the Glen had hung, and he could see the roof rim of the lorry heading away off over the bridge. He looked across yonder to Onich and thought of his one-eyed Uncle's last eye and how he would squeeze out the vile jelly okay, and here came that American, jaunting down the stairs from the monument.

'Hi. Just like you said. That's a *macabre* tale.'

'C'mon. Want to show you another sight.'

The American drove on under the bridge and passed a road sign with Glencoe posted on it.

'Hey there. One time! I know about the massacre of Glencoe. I read a bit about that. The Macdonalds got their throats cut after giving those soldiers shelter, real bad call.'

'Piper Alpha, Ibrox, Lockerbie, Dunblane. You know, for

such a small country, I feel we're very well represented by massacres. We take a great pride in our every distinction! Okay, we're pulling over here.'

'What's this?'

'Just pull over there in their driveway.'

The car U-turned into the driveway of a handsome Victorian villa set back from the road. In the garden of the villa, gallantly rising from the cropped lawn to the same height as the fringe of pine trees, was a well-maintained, lattice-framed, distant railway signal with a yellow arm, fish-tail end and black chevron. The arm was set at the horizontal position. A short length of wiring bordered the lawn to a lever system where the signal could still be set to the up or down position, signalling to the ghost trains.

'It's a signal from the old railway days. This owner in here, he's a train enthusiast. A railway used to run up here to the quarries. Shut down in the 60s. He can still set the signal,' the Nephew pointed.

'Ah.' The location scout nodded.

The Nephew swung out the door, ducked and rose up.

At the railway signal, at the sky, squinting, the Nephew was checking the coloured glass in the eye pieces was still intact. He sheltered his eyes with his hand. The Man Who Walks had been caught once before, in the small hours of the morning, having ascended the signal ladder with a hammer and bucket to collect the prized green and yellow glass to shove into his lost eye socket.

They drove up towards the village loop, passing a muscly-thighed female hitch-hiker thumbing it north. The Nephew coughed, uncomfortable that the location scout, in some Jeffersonian generosity of spirit, might actually brake to a halt, but hurrah! self-interest ruled the day. They checked the Spar where The Man Who Walks had not been seen. On their way back, they were distressed to see the hitch-hiker had crossed the road and was now hitch-hiking in the southerly direction.

'You know, Bill, my Uncle has a lot of ideas for movies that you may or may not be interested in.'

'Your Uncle?' Greedy as ever, Raincheck was actually interested, helpless for his holy grail, the Nephew thought.

'Oh yeah. I've actually got some of his notes right here, if you're buying, heh, heh.' The Nephew leaned back to his pack, pulled out the children's colouring book, from among the coiled typewriter ribbon. He turned some pages and read:

To be filmed by Werner Herzog. 1691, Goodwin Wharton, confidant of King William, 17th-century Lord of the Admiralty, believed he received communication from angels. We follow the expedition of two ships to Tobermory Bay under Wharton's command, to dive upon sunken Spanish Armada galleon, using dangerously primitive equipment, a 'magical mouthpiece' the angels designed, and a diving bell made from cow skins, heated with burning brandy that asphyxiated many divers. Perfect Herzog vehicle. Many drownings and fervent praying.

The location scout was looking a bit punch drunk. 'Historical drama, Rodger, like this one here, it really pushes that budget *way* up there, and gee ... when you need boats! Boats are trouble, big trouble, Rodge.'

'No boats. Quite right. I hate them. How about this:

Pitch faxed to Jake Eberts who likes his projects based on fact. True story: 'James' Barry, the first female doctor who graduated from Edinburgh University in 1812 but DISGUISED AS A MAN. Entire career conducted as a male impersonator! Women not permitted to study medicine then, but she is first doctor recorded carrying out a caesarian section. Fought a duel. Had an affair with a man!! Many dramatic possibilities here! Secretly gave birth to a child she either lost or had adopted. Sexual comedy. Lib/feminist *Guardian* appeal.

'I reckon *Tootsie* covered it all there, Rodger.'
'Never mind.

Dashiell Hammett-type private detective movie but set in Edinburgh after Darnley and Riccio's murders in 1582, round the taverns of the old town swaggers the world-weary, hard-drinking Bogart character, a private investigator hired by her enemies to get to the facts. Has access to femme fatale, Mary Queen of Scots herself. She's attracted to him and . . .

'Oh, what a load of balls. Here, this is better:

Film pitch: *Don Quixote* as a spaghetti western. Set in the Highlands of Scotland. Rosinante is a tractor. Sancho Panza played by Danny DeVito, Donald Sutherland as the Don. To be filmed in black and white. In the Gaelic. Lottery funding.'

'Mmm.' The American nodded solemnly. 'In Gaelic,' he ruminated, concerned.
'Don't worry, there's more, *lots* more here!'

In 1966, when the Ballachulish branch closed, I was twenty-one and I had an interview with the English water authority. Sewage works. South of London. I'd never left Argyll before. Using my railway pass I went to visit my Uncle Robert in Edinburgh.

Ah, how naïve I seemed in those days! Dear Uncle Robert wasn't so much an uncle as a former inamorato of my mother's; a brilliant sunset had brought them together on the esplanade one Glasgow Fair, down near the sewage outflow and the dead seagulls. Uncle Robert had an actual flat in Edinburgh, modest and situated above a well-stocked, exotic-smelling fishmongers, but a flat nonetheless. He worked for the civil service. He also had a good spare suit, worn at the elbows, but suitable for any interview, he thoroughly believed. We removed the black bun mother had baked for him from the brown paper and we wrapped the suit. Then Uncle Robert showed me the sights of Edinburgh, for sights are always free: the castle with its one o'clock gun which made Uncle Robert leap into the gutter of Princes Street, on account of his war experience, he explained to me, though he smelled of drink. Princes Street itself, where Mother had triumphed so well in her driving test for Heavy Goods Vehicles. The enormous clock tower of the North British Hotel, always running a few minutes fast to spur rail travellers promptly to their trains! Waverley Station, all covered in with glass but not as gracious as our own station at home,

I argued, over a shared half pint of the 80 shilling in the old Talisman bar. Then it was up to the Heart of Midlothian cobbles which Uncle Robert taught me to spit upon, which brought us back to his neighbourhood for a fish tea and to bed. Uncle Robert insisted on climbing in with me as there was only one bed.

Limping to catch the London train in the morning, my expression was rapt on the face of the North British clock, my suit neatly folded under my arm, though, I had to admit, slightly redolent of fish. A big Deltic diesel drew from the station, all 3,300 hp of it. Cor!! Away beneath the Observatory we went (which they had to close, and cart away the telescope somewhere else because of the rising smoke from the steam trains which obscured the heavens). Ah, but those days were the twilight of the steam engine, Great Britain was changing.

How could I have been prepared for the glory that was London laying in wait for me, beyond the great, luminous arch of King's Cross Station? It was a beautiful day. With my excellent map reading I soon reached Soho where I was promptly robbed by a young man with hair so long at first I had taken him for an attractive girl; well, that was why I removed my trousers anyway, up the alleyway, and he ran off with them. But nothing could dampen my spirits. Ever prepared, I simply donned the fish-tainted trousers of Uncle Robert's suit to which a few crumbs of my dear mother's black bun still clung; with an outpouring of nationalist feeling I almost shed a tear for my homeland. But what did a pair of worn breeks matter? I had my railway pass, I was young, healthy, alive in a vibrant London.

I wandered to Hyde Park where I asked the young people about Churchill's funeral the previous year but none of them seemed to wish to discuss it. 'Here, smoke this,' was their refrain. I began to feel wonderful.

I spent that night beneath an interesting construction of deckchairs in a starlit Hyde Park with some young people. They chattered and dozed all night, telling me of wonderful things. The next day I continued my journey to Uncle Laurence's house at an address in South London, after having exchanged some money for the smoking material the young people introduced me to. He wasn't really my Uncle Laurence but an inamorato of my mother's. He was a gruff and curt man, who worked for the defence ministry on what he claimed were top-secret researches and he didn't seem impressed by my forthcoming interview scheduled for the following morning. He told me he had to leave for work early and I would need to see myself out. 'You'll be missing your porridge,' he'd kept repeating, his hand on my thigh. His disregard for my interview didn't seem to stop him joining me in my bed that night, so he could make sure I awoke in time, he told me, and he persuaded me it was customary in England to perform a variety of outrageous acts.

Come the morning, I took advantage of the stewed tea, bread and jam Uncle Laurence had set out for me.

It was another beautiful day and, anxious to impress my future employers with my punctuality, I set forth early for my interview, changing trains several times in stations with unfamiliar names. The track condition was immaculate. When I reached the town that was my destination, I held out the letter of interview proudly to the policeman by a flower stand, asking him the quickest route to Main Street where the Water Board headquarters were based. The police-man looked at the address disapprovingly.

'This says Farnham,' the policeman said.

'Yes,' I smiled.

'You're in Fareham. You've come to the wrong town for your interview, my lad.'

I rapidly boarded another train. After several awkward changes I at last, now over an hour and a half late, arrived at the station of my destination. I raced to the first local shop and showed them the letter, pleading for the quickest possible dispatch to Main Street and the Water Board headquarters.

'This says Farnham,' the shopkeeper announced

'Yes!' I shouted, anxiously.

'This is Feltham.'

Back at the railway station I compared the place name on the letterhead to the blue and white station sign. No doubt about it.

It was late evening by the time I reached the Water Board headquarters at Farnham. The offices were in darkness. I decided I would sleep on the steps, despite the pressure this would bring to bear on my suit, then explain my mistake to the Area Manager in the morning. I rolled myself another of the expensive cigarettes the young people in Hyde Park had sold me. When a friendly bobby strolled over, dashing his torch at me, enquiring why I was sprawled on the steps, I asked him for a light. Once I'd got it going he chased me for several streets until I escaped into a railway marshalling yard. I doubled-back through rear gardens and allotments, smoking my cigarette, and would you credit what I came upon, glinting in the flux of moon and the glow from the fireboxes of the shunting engines? A pear tree, but each pear fruit flourishing within a glass bottle, dozens of them supported by a structure. To make a special liqueur, I believe! London was one helluva town, I decided.

I managed to reach Uncle Laurence's door very late that night and he was unimpressed by my nonchalance. I kept laughing as I explained what had happened. Words were nothing so much as olive stones in my mouth while Laurence seemed to issue forth an electric procession of questions. It would be fair to say he beat me. Then insisted on making up. Deep in the night, during his acts, he muttered a very strange thing to me that I still remember to this day. 'The Americans' (he said) 'plan to carve aircraft carriers out of gigantic icebergs.' It crossed my mind Uncle Laurence might be on drugs, like I was. The following day, I confess, I spent lounging alone in his bed trying to work out the facts of my situation. My postulation led to the hypotheses that perhaps I was shafted, or perhaps things would come up rosy for me. Like old Aschenbach, I was 'inclined to the former hypothesis'.

What would have become of me if I hadn't met Tangerine? She found me, that day, beneath a tree in Hyde Park reading a paperback the young men had given me called *Steppenwolf*. She asked me if I was inspired by the book. I entered into conversation with her, explaining the book greatly interested me, quoting to her lines that I still like to quote today, such as: 'man is an onion', or 'the hair on my brush grows grey'. She seemed to be impressed by my trenchant interpretations and explained to me how the book, in her mind, was a 'gateway to transformation' concerning a man's personal journey, from 'squareness' to 'hipness', as she put it. Then she asked if I'd any bread, by which she meant money, then she sold me a pill, and selected an identical one for herself. We swallowed each and we went, hand in hand already, as little children do, to the Rialto to goggle at *Morgan: A Suitable Case for Treatment*, which, under the circumstances, was a glorious motion picture. I vowed there and then to work in the motion picture business, which I have done, to great success.

Then I took Tangerine with me back to Uncle Laurence's, both to discourage his interfering with me and also, confusedly, to show off Tangerine. I didn't think Uncle Laurence's house would impress Tangerine, but despite her non-materialistic beliefs she expressed a great deal of admiration for the building's handsome proportions as we approached, hand in hand, up the street that day. When we arrived there, however, the large house was crowded with strangers and neighbours who immediately went silent at my sight. 'This is Laurence's nephew who has been staying for a few days,' announced a neighbour (who I'd never seen before in my life) to a formally-dressed man with short hair. I was led along into a private room and told he had the sad duty of informing me as the only next of kin that Laurence (he referred to him by his surname) had been in a terrible accident at the Atomic Research Station where he had been working. The details of his research were covered by the Official Secrets Act so he could tell me no more.

'I understand, I'm a Churchill man,' I said, winking. Laurence had met his death due to a terrible radiation leak.

I was stunned and Tangerine helped me through those difficult hours, regularly taking me to a private place to smoke from the substantial variety of apparatus she kept concealed on her lithe figure. She came with me to the hospital where I was to sign some forms allowing the Ministry of Defence to handle the burial at their expense. The acid pills we had also taken that day made this experience all the more bizarre, especially when we arrived at the hospital and found that poor Laurence's body was so radioactive it had burned through the hospital table and thumped to the floor. They put him in a wooden coffin, but he burned through that also.

Laurence's internment was a sad affair. He had to be buried in a huge lead coffin that was lowered into the grave by thick chain hung from a huge crane which was parked far down on the main road. I noticed none of the Ministry of Defence mourners were standing within thirty feet of the coffin. The few neighbours who had attended stood back also, so only Tangerine and I stood near enough the grave to kick in a few clouds of dusty soil, then the men in big silver suits and helmets rapidly rushed over with long shovels to sweep in the debris on top of the coffin and consign Laurence to his buzzing afterworld. Just as well Tangerine and I were cauterised by smoking joints and ingesting acid tablets back at the house.

Laurence's house seemed to have passed into my hands without question while his greater estate was pored over sluggishly by distant solicitors, so it was here Tangerine and I came to be living with one another, as man and wife (and a good deal more). Tangerine had so many young, intelligent, lively friends who she slowly moved in – and who we came to call the Colony. Almost all men, I noticed, apart from a frail, slim girl they called Hot Water Bottle who seemed to move from mattress to mattress and often joined Tangerine and I as they both instructed me in the mysteries of lovemaking. Believe me, those acts were a *complete* mystery.

We all lived for free, and since one or two members of the Colony actually worked, writing pieces for various journals and newspapers, they contributed to the electricity and rates bills so we could live in peace, playing the record-player section on the radiogram, which was switched on at all times, with 'Flowers' and John Mayall's 'Blues-breakers', despite the objections of the neighbours. I am not at liberty to pass on the names of all the other members of the Colony, for many of them in the early 70s, like myself, went on to be members of outlawed organisations and extreme political factions. Some of them were to go on and join Red Faction and affiliated groups in Germany, France and the RAF in Italy and some even graduated to liberation groups in Wales and Scotland, ho, ho. I, for instance, became a member of the Screenwriters' Guild.

How to describe the wonder of that summer and indeed the next two years as we lived as a commune in Laurence's large and charming old house? Tangerine allowed me to share and learn from so many things: records, books, visits to the theatre to see the plays of Joe Orton, concerts of rock music, drugs and, more dubiously, the communal soup. I grew my hair and began to wear the clothes that Tangerine chose for me rather than my sober suits. The old year passed and a new one came and I was in love with Tangerine and she was in love with me, but she said I had to learn not to be possessive, as when members of minor rock bands took her to foreign countries, sometimes for two weeks, or when she made love to another member of the Colony. I knew I was lucky, but it was true. I wanted nobody but her. And if that isn't love, what the fuck is? But Tangerine was enchanted by my Scotchness. Her favourite poem, rather bizarrely, I believe it would be fair still to say, was that absurd wonder, 'The Bothie of Tober-na-Vuolich', by Emerson's friend, Arthur Clough.

Oh, those evenings on the hard, rough floorboards covered in colourful mats, the waning sun streaming in through unwashed windows when Tangerine and I would read aloud those wonderful verses to each other as candlelight took hold:

There is it? there? Or there we shall find our wandering hero?
Here in Badenoch, here, in Lochaber anon, in Lochiel, in Knoydart,
   Moydart, Morar, Ardgower, and Ardnamurchan,
Here I see him and here: I see him; anon I lose him!
Even as cloud passing subtly unseen from mountain to mountain.

We used to visualise how we might withdraw from the class struggle for a few years to live in the Highlands. A few frolicking lambs, fresh eggs from the scratching chickens. For Tangerine and I it evoked Clough's immortal line

There shall he, smit by the charm of a lovely potato-uprooter,
Study the question of sex in the Bothie of *What-did-he-call-it*.

I described to them my humble upbringing, my years as a plateman walking the railway line to the quarry village of Ballachulish. I was a member of the proletariat they were so anxious to save with their Bakunin, Marcuse, McLuhan and Fanon and their *Pedagogy of the Oppressed* and Sartre and Jung and worst of all torturous Tolkien, which we would read aloud in the candlelight to one another.

It's my opinion 1967 was a fine year for the long-playing record of popular music, *Their Satanic Majesties Request, Days of Future Passed, Tim Hardin 1, Disraeli Gears, Piper at the Gates of Dawn, Are You Experienced?, Ptoof!, Kinks Live at the Kelvin Hall, The Grateful Dead, The Who Sell Out, Spirit, The Doors, Safe as Milk* and that silly Beatles one with Stockhausen and Crowley on the cover.

As our love of music grew, so our wish to transform society. A group vote was taken, as they so often were, on remedial action for the injustice of the circumstances surrounding Laurence's demise. Inspired by Morgan, we hired gorilla suits from a fancy-dress shop, hoping they would afford us both some measure of disguise and some small protection against any gamma rays; then, clustered on a JCB (much as Clint Eastwood, Telly Savalas and Donald Sutherland were to cling to the sides of a Sherman tank in the movie I later wrote and directed: *Kelly's Heroes*), we breached the graveyard in the early hours one morning; in a swift swoop, the mechanical shovel of the JCB excavated and swept up poor Uncle Laurence's coffin out of the ground, in fact we scooped up another one as well, which fell off the shovel in the High Street and burst open, showing a still impressively clad skull of burnished red hair.

Completely unopposed by 'Fuzz', towards dawn we deposited Laurence close to Aldershot barracks with these symbols painted roughly on the coffin, side by side:

The Empty Quarter

It was so hot. Their elbows out of all-the-way-down windows. Beside a river some guy in a Black Sabbath T-shirt and his girl, just in bra and knickers, sunbathing. Sculpted into the skyline, two other distant peaks in the clarity of a brilliant distance, through a windscreen, swept clean of insect spats by an arc of wiper over the sud spray.

But a receding wall revealed the two distant mountains to be the hairy, twin humps of a camel! Its tail flicked flies. Another two camels grazed far down the clodded meadow.

An angled, varnished sign elevated in a field's corner:

> Resurrection Apostle Church
> Vineyard of Comfort and
> International Miracle Centre!!!

'The magi's camels,' the Nephew almost whispered, nodding. 'March them through the villages with the wise men at Christmas, looking for converts.'

Raincheck fidgeted. 'You know, Rodger, I have to bring up a subject here you might object to.'

'What's the subject, Bill?'

'I'll be to the point, Rodger. The subject is . . . pot.'

'Pot? Pol Pot?'

'Nah. Pot, Rodger. I was wondering where you stood with people who have the odd puff of pot?'

'Well. Why? Is this a bust?'

'I'd like to know.'

'On this matter I'm a liberal. It should be legalised.'

'Really?'

'Yes, along with intelligence, pot should also be legalised in Britain.'

'And at the moment, what's your attitude to users?'

'My attitude to users? Generally to try and get some off them.'

The American chuckled. 'Let's pull over, this is the most lovely weather and there's something I want to show you in the trunk.'

'In the trunk?' said the Nephew.

'Yeah. Is there a good place to stop down here? A nice, secluded place to stop?'

In four minutes the bonnet-scorched Primera crunched to the end of a forestry access track, giving view onto the loch side. Bill 'Raincheck' Wright pulled up the handbrake and shut down the engine with a delicate turn of the key. He got out the car with a look towards the Nephew who immediately opened his door and followed him.

At the boot of the car Raincheck gave a proud smile and lifted it up.

There was a machine, a small machine with blinking lights that seemed to be some kind of medical aid with tubes and a face mask.

'What the hell is it?' asked the Nephew.

'We had to get it up to the set for the principal actors and actresses. We had to get it over from Amsterdam.'

'Right.'

'It enables the user to inhale only the key ingredient of cannabis, the THC.'

'R*iiii*ght.'

'The principals won't use anything else because of the cancer-causing agents.'

'Of course. With you. California.'

'Right. This is basically standard issue in California now for these health-freak smokers. It delivers three times the efficiency of a reefer.'

'Three times the efficiency,' the Nephew whispered.

A quarter of an hour later, stretched on the bonnet, the Nephew hammered on: 'Oh, I've known happy travellers too, Bill. It's not all gloom. I've known the gypsies moving up and round from Budapest to Spain for the festivals. Tree dwellers, some of them! Tattoos are all the fashion nowadays, but some of their grandmothers have those neat little Teutonic ones. It makes the mind race to see them, Bill, and I've seen those old ladies who made tea for me up in their tree houses. I've seen their grandchildren in small towns, at the Fiestas de Fallas, at the Catafalques, dancing all night, and leaping through the bonfires with crowns of jasmine.' The Nephew paused, remembered how the confetti came down in pointillist swoons from those wrought-iron balconies that are all curves, like women bending in lace dresses. 'Even the tough guys have pink and rose confetti jammed in the back pockets of their jeans next to their switchblades. As their girlfriends lower themselves they will release confetti until the café toilets of the villages are circled with horseshoe mounds of it – their brown cleavages are cluttered with it; it's in all the beds as they make love.

'Another time I knew an estate agent's clerk who lived by

Lake Kariba with two suits, one hidden on each bank, he'd swim in his trunks between the hippos and crocodiles, brush down the work suit, tighten the tie on the far side, swim back over again at sunset and appear home in his weekend suit, his damp trunks swung over one shoulder.

'My God, do you think The Man Who Walks is the only traveller walking under these purple, then dark skies?'

'I'm sorry? Who?'

'Never mind. But there's the others, Bill, all the others who crossed the Empty Quarter with a dream of Europe in their heads, slept all night in a tree because they thought a lion was slowly following, waiting for the weak to drop behind, and truly something did pass beneath the tree while they slept. The universities might have been destroyed but they knew a thing or two about the Empty Quarter. They knew to lie still when the rain came, even if the water almost reached your mouth as you slept, because if you stood and began shivering, the cold would kill you before dawn. All that water would be gone in the dawn, but they knew how to plug any small holes in their water-filled goatskins with thorns when the day got hot. They knew that sheepskin sweats when filled with water, and how to use threads from their worn clothes and headdresses as tinder, so they became more ragged but warmer. They could predict the movements of locusts and knew to lay still on the ground as a swarm passed. Crossing the Empty Quarter they had lain down in a swarm so thick a branch from a tree broke under the weight of so many locusts.

'They had tasted the saltiness of camel's milk. The girls, hair dyed gold with cow urine, knew how to blow into the vagina of a poor cow so it would lower milk down into its udders. I was told these girls once slaughtered a herd of goats they found and just lay on the ground beside the corpses and sucked the warm milk out of them. Oh yes, on their way to Europe, each of these men and women have squat to piss a hundred times facing the correct stars.

'The route is always to Bamako, capital of Mali, where the Nigerians really think of themselves as "Englishmen" and the Sierra Leoneans, all seamsters, are identifiable by the old hand-turned Singer sewing-machines, built in Glasgow all those years ago, balanced high on their shoulders – always ready for simple tailoring jobs. Next, they have to cross the Empty Quarter. What one? Who cares, there are so many. There are even trucks available for the better off, but the poorest must walk, a change of T-shirt, a hat, somehow always a mobile telephone and a petrol canister filled with water. There are bandits and rapists on the fringes of this Empty Quarter, they'll rob men and kill them for fun, and rape the young women who try the crossing.

'At the edge of the Quarter is a little pile of scrap, a small, baroque pile of metal twists; a little pile of Singer sewing-machines the weeping men from Sierra Leone had to throw down there before they could begin to cross a desert. You travel light or you die.'

They slid from the bonnet, returned, the Nephew crawling, to the trunk of the car to energise the blinking lights of the inhaler. The location scout had his camera on the back seat and the rear doors of the car were swung open, like a bird cooling itself with its wings hunched out. The Nephew reached, took the camera and pushed it into his salt-stained backpack.

'Ach, all the travelling and all the sicknesses of it,' he went on. 'Sea, air, travel sickness. We should *all* be sick of it. Always moving from A to B. Only a legacy of worn boots. The longing just for stillness. Eyes rest on nothing long enough for meditation upon it. We go through those gateways of transformation: airports; and we come back unchanged. When did travel last change someone? In what century? Aeroplanes get faster and faster and the journeys take longer and longer. We should despise and distrust travel. It's disgusting and insulting to think a changing landscape will change us inside. What will a new landscape change inside of me? Are we really just such chameleons? But travel has to be a fetish and mystified and sold and finally trivialised. All these travellers and no one prays for them any more, Bill! Jesus, even St Christopher was demoted. All those amulets, which touched against the collarbones round the world, are no longer valid for travel! No one prays for the little ones out on the roads with no destination and hell hounds on their tail. Christ's sake, I could describe them to you now with my eyes closed. They have legs, neglected of razors for days now – there is not enough water. They could easily shave them on their slidey, oily sweat but they don't want to. They might not make it across the Empty Quarter after all (another Empty Quarter, but believe me, their nature is identical and, for sure, they all have to be crossed!). So why not let a little down gather on their inner thighs and be there when the Israeli pathologist lifts back the unclean white sheet. Their knees are bruised from the jeeps. From climbing in and out the trucks. They came from high-rises, they came from villages and they don't have words for these new places on the fringes of the Quarter. Like those movies you see. Bedouin guides really do lead them through the deserts, on foot at night under the clearest stars they've ever seen. One, a seventeen-year-old, lifts her cheap rings and tries to touch the stars, she feels the blood drain from her hand and now she's cold and its iciness digs at her bare thighs the way the two men will grip them apart six weeks later in the parlour. The barrel salute of a tank wreck frightens her as it appears to their left, one from the '67 war, when her own mother was only six.

'Nine girls, one almost a woman, flown in Aeroflot the usual way on a noisy Tupolev to Cairo with three-week visas: dressed like tourists, *worse* than tourists; they cling to photocopied brochures of the pyramids at the airport. The contact gathers the photocopies to use again.

'The travellers stay in a roadside motel sixty miles from Cairo, four to a room, imagine the air conditioning!: ineffectual, clanking. One, the prettiest, has to share with the contact who cajoles her up off the floor and closer and closer in the passing headlights that spin her head and make her submit all through the night. The next day a truck takes them up to the villages of the Sinai. They'll get nothing there but dried meat and a bar of chocolate for two days, and they piss with the Bedouin women who laugh at them and don't let them near their own daughters. The Russian girls keep the big empty Coca-Cola bottles like they've been told.

'The Israeli border isn't secure, too long to patrol, too much broken wire and it's out here at night the Bedouin walk them. They never have sensible shoes and they always walk barefoot, holding some vaguely Italian high heels. There are old minefields out there or scorpions in the old tank shells. A year ago one girl with her leg gone from halfway down the shin, clean as if it'd been snapped, had one of the stilettos driven into her and two fingers missing as she died, calling for her mother in Russian. They buried her out there. They made the girls dig.

'The 4×4s, the Jeeps and Range Rovers, wait just on the other side of the border. The guys who own the Eilat saunas drive them. Barrel chests, ski sunglasses, big watches, balding with a skull of sweat, even at night. They exchange cash with the contact there and then. They even make a show of the girls standing in the headlights, touch up their tits (none are ever silicone), even look at their teeth; all the classic moves to make them grateful for not being sent back over the desert with the silent Bedouin and deportation to Russia. But the sauna owners have the exact money. These girls are bargains and no one is being sent back. These girls will have been fucked enough to pay their value in a week and they won't be leaving after having crossed the Empty Quarter. They're slaves to their owners. You can own a girl for $2,400 down in Eilat; the Czar, serfdom, rules again, Bill.'

The Nephew began calculating how many girls for £27,000.

The Nephew was a guest in the papier-mâché tunnels one bitter cold Christmas. By way of the social niceties, The Man Who Walks went off to carry home some stolen coal from the rear of the hotel. He carried the sack on his back the two mile from the village, but there was a hole in the bottom of the sack and lumps of coal were being left in a black trail on the white snow of pavement across which heavy snowflakes were blowing. The flakes seemed to move faster under each blush of sodium street light his hunched figure hurriedly passed. Then the street lights ran out where the backroad began. Safely in darkness The Man Who Walks halted and turned the bag the other way round, but then it developed another tear and the coal fell out that end. Now The Man Who Walks tried carrying the coal sack in his arms, as you would carry a sleeping child, if anyone would ever let him carry a sleeping child. A better simile: the Frankenstein of movies, uncomprehendingly carrying the limp corpse of a dead little girl, into the village where he will meet his lynch mob. Anyway, the coal still tumbled from each end of the sack.

When he arrived at his house The Man Who Walks had a pile of snow on his head, two large lumps of coal in his trouser pockets, two lumps of coal in his greatcoat pockets, two in each frozen hand, one small piece of coal was lodged in his eye socket, and he knocked by repeatedly banging his forehead against the door because he also held a large lump of coal in his mouth.

In the Black Garrison

The town lay, like a can washed up on some shore, spread along the lochside facing the blank exclamation of steep woodlands on the opposite bank. The shore was a strip of one-night, US-style motels and modern detached houses, each offering Bed & Breakfast and bearing appellations like 'Buenas Noches', 'Driftwood' and 'Acapulco'. Beyond, the town all clotted up in a mess of new architecture, and the loch suddenly veered west – as if it had recognised what the town had to offer.

There was a sprint of dual carriageway, known locally as the South Circular, leading to a carpark, which was Beneath the Golden Arches of a new 'Target Settlements Over 5,000' McDonald's, and beyond was an operating railway station.

Over to the west were the hidden-away council houses, satellite dishes bolted up in the trees, never sure if they are gardening or the front green is being dug up in search of bodies, traditional gate signs, 'Never Mind the Dog, Beware the Children', and the vast warehouse of the pulp mill. To the north the giant pipes were ziggered up the hill flank from the aluminium smelter where the ingots were trained out south on double-headed flatbeds moving slow and deeply in the a.m. hours and looming over it all the highest and surely the ugliest mountain in all the United Kingdom.

Back at the loch side, the location scout had been abandoned, head protruding from one rear door, feet from the other, relieved of his cash and camera. Stumbling in the dying day, through the gold leaf and flake of moths or gnats made brilliant by falling sun, the Nephew walked into the Garrison. He passed Poppadom Preach, the Indian restaurant, and he glimpsed the tug of war in a travel agent's window: should the big model of Concorde be taken out or left in?

In the Throbs Theme Bar and Disco at the centre of the Black Garrison, curious light of late afternoon was transforming into the even stranger hues of evening. The Nephew was never too sure what the 'theme' was. Who could be? Burnished, antique brass helmets of deep-sea diving suits hung here, a famous fiddler's splayed bow there. Most disturbingly, already a smattering of young fellows dressed as eighteenth-century redcoats manned the drinkers' side of the bar, tricorn hats jauntily tipped at unorthodox angles, grenadiers' peaks almost touching the fishermen's dusty nets hanging from the ceiling, cradling scallop shells.

Obviously the Hollywood production of *Kidnapped* had begun shooting, using local extras. The Nephew felt aggrieved the location scout hadn't informed him of this. Seemed to put everything on a far more official footing, the Nephew thought. Judging from the way they were drinking – beer with whisky chasers – Hollywood was paying generously as per usual and he had to confess he wouldn't have minded a shot at being an extra himself. That's what you get for pretending to be a member of the upper class. Nae cunt offers you a job. After all, that's why official charities exist, cause middle-class folk have never actually met face to face with anyone who is poor, they prefer to use their credit cards to keep guilt and redemption at arm's length.

Like how they are always making out street beggars are earning five hundred a day. Yup, how come the homeless aren't queued up in high-street banks getting mortgages? Same way most of these crime writers have burglar alarm systems on their apartments and never met a real criminal in their puff. Be warned, I have your addresses, the Nephew thought, and supped his pint of lager that was slipping down a treat and he wished he could afford another. Keep your *haute cuisine*, mate. Funny how the body rallies, even still.

Another reason the Nephew felt justifiably aggrieved was, without doubt, the price of local Bed & Breakfast would have skyrocketed in traditional welcome of the large, affluent film crew.

The Nephew's position, in a far corner of the Throbs, gave fearsome vantage across the dance-floor and onto the huge television screens. Surprisingly free of sport, a terrestrial station had broadcast a list of One Hundred Favourite TV Lists. 'Celebrities Behaving Badly' had been deemed the King of TV Lists. The Nephew nodded, as Oliver Reed gyrated wildly, hoisting a carafe of vodka and orange aloft in Bacchic supremacy. A new programme began, entitled *Get 'Em Off*, and its intellectual position was thus: an attractive young man and woman enter various night clubs in various cities of the British Isles. They persuade members of both sexes to remove their underwear.

That reminds me, the Nephew thought. Must re-read T.S. Eliot's *Notes Towards a Definition of Culture*, yacuntya, as he supped a gush more lager. Ahead, curled, forlorn sticking plasters were scattered all across the dance-floor from girls' heels; those slow shuffles, to avoid breaking sweat, had worked those plasters out, over the back of the hard, cheap stilettos.

There was only one girl on the floor now, dancing with a

group of seven or eight men. The men were part of some stag party, repeatedly exposed to dispersal, regrouping and further scattering under the day's alcoholic artillery. All were dressed identically, in white trousers, white T-shirts, regulation haircuts and dark sunglasses. The Nephew had noticed how the girl was so drunk that she kept returning to her drink, dancing back towards her partner and kissing him. But the identical-looking gentlemen kept pushing another partner into the previous occupant's place, so the girl continued kissing, and rubbing against someone she thought was the same man, completely unaware she was being passed around the entire company.

Across the floor, in the mirror-image booth to his, the Nephew spied a man alone and smoking. The Nephew began the rising and crossing what looked like an unperilous distance to blag a fag offof the guy, but halfway there – strange how the safest passage can turn sinister; and so quickly! – the Nephew noticed the man he was helplessly approaching was talking away to himself, in fact the geezer was fairly jabbering away, turning from side to side as if flanked by a host of compadres rather than just the phantoms of his storm-tossed mind! Christ, he's got ALL his mates in the night, thought the Nephew, grimacing, but it seemed far too conspicuous by that stage simply to twist upon his heels and return to his seat. Probably half the locals in the place were watching the Nephew, sniggering cause this figure he was hopelessly advancing upon was such a well-known fixture on the indigenous freak scene, yacuntya! But the Nephew continued onward, for it would seem sheer cowardice now to turn back if local eyes were held upon him, and he didn't want to draw any more attention to himself. He had to remain professional, he was here to do a job: to sniff out the spoor of The Man Who Walks.

The Foreman and his mother! Why should he finance *them* to have a bloody cider festival in bed for three weeks and briefly move up the social register by changing from cartons of Lambert and Butler to Regal Kingsize? Fuck it.

'Excuse me, blag a fag offof you, pal?'

'What?'

'Could I lend a fag offof you?'

'I'm on the air!'

'You're on something.'

'There's a commercial break just coming up.' The seated man put his finger to his lips, turned away and began talking again, looking straight ahead, 'And before *Evening Conversation* here is the news. Meetings today about BSE payments will take place in Brussels between Agriculture Spokesman, Brain Cowan, and EEC representatives. Lochaber's Roman Catholic population will later this month welcome the Bishop of the Philippines, Cardinal Sin, to the area. Police profits for the Lochaber area have halved in the last quarter, so the number of speed cameras fitted has been doubled.' The man paused for a moment, shook his head to a mellifluous jingle that, sadly, rang only within the good acoustics of his own cranium.

'News on Aluminumville FM. Now our hourly ski forecast . . . well, there is no snow. None expected for seven months. But the ski-lift restaurant at the summit is open for snacks and coffee with beautiful views. Back after this: Why compromise with injectables when jet suppositories will do? For all cattle ailments, including liverfluke! Use Lowry's lactic jet suppositories: www.lacticaresehole.co.uk.'

It was now, beneath that traditional lifted parka hood, the Nephew spied the big yellow earphones, clearly not plugged into anything, and he suddenly recalled this man and the circumstances of his misfortune. This man was the ex-main investor and radio presenter at Aluminumville FM! When that radio station first came on the air they made a right old song and dance about it in the Black Garrison: some imported girl in a mini-skirt strutted on the high street (she caught pneumonia) distributing helium-filled balloons, which shell-suiters emptied into their mouths, and she was swiping away prying hands. As the weeks passed, Aluminumville FM tried to build a relationship with its listeners and host community but could only get two adverts and both of those were for lost cats. Three weeks after broadcasting began, the main presenter really wasn't getting the feedback he'd dreamed of from the receiving hinterlands. Then he discovered some engineer hadn't put a plug in and, for three weeks, he'd actually been broadcasting to no one! The Nephew had heard it all: subsequent bankruptcy, nervous breakdown, excessive intake of whisky and fried food: here was the result before him, a man humiliated, broken and disturbed.

'And our chat guest for the evening has just come into the studio. Before that here's Roky Erickson and the Aliens, with "It's a Cold Night for Alligators".' His voice changed timbre from smeary professionalism to a breathless request: 'You can have a cigarette if you'll appear on my chat show.'

The Nephew looked around. Sequestered as they were across the dance-floor, no one seemed to be paying them any special attention or at least no more than was normal.

'Fair enough.' The Nephew slumped down.

'Little time to kill before the record finishes.' The radio presenter fumbled with his Marlboros, lifted one towards the Nephew's mouth and cupped the flame to the tip as if there was the likelihood of some wake turbulence emanating from the passing dancers. Glimpsing a closer peek now, the Nephew identified that they weren't even real earphones at all: industrial ear muffs! One ear-piece professionally slid back.

'How do you want the interview to go, want me to introduce you, or will you talk about yourself a little first?'

The Nephew inhaled, then blew out smoke. 'Oh, you introduce me.'

The radio presenter nodded, held up his fingers and silently mouthed, Three, Two, One. 'Always bringing you the big names on *Evening Conversation*, our guest tonight is legendary, feared and admired – the Macushla! Good evening, Macushla!'

'Hello, music lovers,' the Nephew mumbled, looked round embarrassed, and he took a drag on the cigarette.

'Grrrreat you're in town. When were you last here?'

'Here? I was here about ten months ago.'

'Oh, you've been in the Garrison since you returned to the area.'

'Yes. Sat over there . . .'

'We're live, folks. Live from Grovers Mill. Only joking! Live from the Throbs Theme Bar and Disco, sponsors of tonight's programme. Did you have a great time, Macushla?' the radio presenter panted.

'Ought to have. Won the pub quiz. Against five teams. On my fucking own! Prize was two eight-pint carafes of lager. Cunt came over and asked me for a pint. "Git tae fuck," I says and drank both carafes myself. Blootered. Two cunts tried to set on me up the road, couldna been fourteen years of age but I fair scattered *them*!'

'Yup, family entertainment always to be had at the Throbs, all year round.' He leaned towards the Nephew and dropped his voice, 'Just cause we're no the BBC, Christ sake, watch the language.'

The Nephew nodded curtly, biting his lip.

Pushing the cigarette pack across the table, the radio presenter said, 'So, Macushla, what are your feelings about the petrol blockades and their implications for rural areas?'

'It's Scotland's oil.' The Nephew smirked, helped himself to another cigarette and used the radio presenter's lighter.

'Your . . . involvement with extreme . . . factions.'

'What would you know about that?'

'Is that a cause to which you're still attached?'

'No.'

'Groups connected with . . . mmm . . . explosive packages. Holiday homes torched.'

'That is all hearsay, no proof of that came out in any court.'

'You would describe yourself as a gradualist now.'

'Wouldn't put words in my mouth, would you?'

'Are you? A gradualist?'

'I've withdrawn from the struggle, from all struggles for that matter. I'd call myself an individualist: that old scrap heap radicals end up on. It's a lot more fun.' The Nephew sighed. 'We have our history, an old tart, we don't know when to chuck her out of bed or when to roll over and shag her for a last time, and we have her pimp, our own wee parliament, big hotel in the sky for our representatives, faced with granite all the way from China, I hear. The most expensive they could find, like the grandest of old Parisian brothels. Keep the kilty liberals happy. You know you gotta keep the liberals happy, listeners.'

'Guess you're a good old Tory, Macushla, so you'd be for the death sentence in the new Scotland?!'

'Rather be a screwed-up conservative than a hypocritical liberal. Sure, I believe in corporal and capital punishment. What do you imagine they would have done with this Alan Breck they're making this daft movie about if they had caught him? Chopped his block off. Incidentally, do you know about our very own Doctor Livingstone? In Africa, he came across this charming tradition. You know that Cartesian physiologist, sent to the guillotine, who told his pals to watch his eyes as his head popped into the basket and he would try to keep blinking?'

'Eh, family show, Macushla, family show.'

'How about that for generosity towards the scientific spirit?! But centuries before the guillotine, Livingstone's African friends were experienced in the arts of decapitation; they knew consciousness isn't lost for a few seconds after you get the chop, so they did the most beautiful thing: bent a springy sapling and tied cords under the ears of the condemned man, so, as the head came away, his last few moments of consciousness would be of, miraculously, flying through the air!'

The radio presenter chuckled, a little uneasily. 'So you're not for independence then?'

'Sure! Imagine the joy of it all. Late parliament sittings to decide on the stewardesses' uniform for Scottish National Airlines.' He sighed. 'The glory of it all, after centuries of struggle. Always careful with the taxpayer in mind, we could dispense with the stewardesses' knickers at least. By the time you actually grasp it, if you'll forgive the pun, freedom doesn't amount to much these days. It was packaged long ago.'

'What do you think freedom is then?'

'Cash. Twenty-seven grand.'

'You were involved in travellers' rights as well.'

'*Traditional* travellers, aye. No rich kid hippies. There's none of us left though. All ... intermarried with the Settled Community. Taken the King's shilling. You need to go to Ireland to still experience the real traveller's world, the ghost stories they have! Been after a house myself. A particular house. For some time now.'

'You've served in the British Army.'

'Is that a question? That's always been a rumour.'

'Are you linked with any of these reports in the paper of a violent marauder being abroad?'

'Marauder.'

'A prowler. Violent attacks. No fatalities. Yet. A prowler upon the land as in the dark days.'

'Only prowler round here would be my Uncle, The Man Who Walks, out on his midnight creeps.'

'Yes. He was the guest on the programme just two days ago.'

'WHAT!' The Nephew whipped round and took an interest in the recesses of the parka hood. 'He *was*, was he? I'm actually very, very anxious to make contact with him. He's forgot his medicine and he shouldn't travel without his medicine. Where is he?'

'Well, I'm not sure, but he certainly seemed to need his medicine! In a medical emergency like this let's put out a request now over the whole of our broadcast area.' He bounced up and started screaming, 'Does anyone know the whereabouts of The Man Who Walks; guest on *Evening Conversation* two nights ago? If you have any information, phone in on . . .'

The Nephew had leaped to his feet and violently tugged the radio presenter back down onto his seat. Some bar staff looked over. 'Listen here, loony tunes, where IS he?'

'He was right here on the programme, talking about his days as the Christmas Tree Man; he used to collect all the used Christmas trees after the fifth of January for a pound charge.'

'I know.'

'Collected the dead Christmas trees from door to door for miles around.'

'I know, I know, I know; "seasonal employment", the spazz called it.'

'He'd a car in them days.'

The Nephew shook his head mournfully, submitting to the memory. 'We all learned to drive that first banger with no doors or windows, going round and round in a field, mud caked up your thigh. It should never have been allowed. You'd see the second banger, hatchback Lada, veered all over the road, twenty dead Christmas trees crammed in, tips pushing out the windows, the hatchback barely tied down with this blue rope, the same blue rope you could see swung under the engine, holding it in; clutch and brake pedals completely buried somewhere down beneath twelve inches of dead pine needles!'

'Man Who Walks, driving a car. Ironic, isn't it.'

'It was soon enough took off him by the Feds. He was back where he belongs, on the hoof, on Shanks' pony. I remember when he had that car he'd rustled up a disabled parking permit from somewhere, on account of the eye, so he just painted a wheelchair symbol and the wording from the permit on the bonnet and parked anywhere when he went round the town scavenging Christmas trees. Once he carried one out a window before Christmas was over, hoiked it off with the decorations still on it and the angel swinging on the top, flying along out the passenger window.'

'Then, I understand, he blocked himself into his house with sheer volume of dead Christmas trees.'

The Nephew was rustling among typewriter ribbon in his backpack. 'That's right, he had surrounded the house near high as the bedrooms, could barely see the house for them. You wouldn't think there was that many Christian homes in the hinterland! Environmental Health had to get them all took away and burned, up on the hill behind his house. Some bonfire that, kids came from miles around.'

'What's this?'

'Sort of a bloody diary or cheesy autobiography of The Man

Who Walks which I've been, eh, deciphering from. You tell me what The Man Who Walks' plans were, where he was headed and your . . . listeners may be interested in hearing this sort of stuff.'

'Oh, wonderful. Course my listeners would just love to hear exclusive extracts from The Man Who Walks' diaries! Unique to Aluminumville FM.'

'There was a wee bit here that he wrote when he had yon bloody car. Aye. Here you have it.' The Nephew crouched forward to read aloud:

I was on LSD most of those days. Since my . . .

The Nephew coughed, then read on:

Since my eye had been . . . removed . . . and strange antiseptics placed in its socket by the hospital, my mucus pickings extracted from my nostrils were of the most garish, hair-raising colours. I was collecting dead Christmas trees using the small car I'd lost the keys to. Shame, as all four doors couldn't be unlocked without the keys. Ignition was achieved by burning fingertips as you touched some wires under the steering column. I gained entrance and egress from the vehicle by using its hatchback rear door, which did not look so impressive when stopped by the local constabulary. I was frequently stopped by the local constabulary. But my papers were always in order.

'Mmm, there's more, but he veers off the subject. Want to hear it?' the Nephew asked.

'Please go on, fascinating.'

'It says:

that Pindar quote was my favourite, something like 'Oh my soul, do not aspire to immortal life, but exhaust the limits of the possible', or at least that is what I would rasp down the phone to the schoolgirls after I stole the register from Our Lady of Perpetual Succour, with all their mobile phone numbers. If I'd ended up in court I could hardly be imprisoned for broadening their classical education. Reminds me of how each morning I'd wake from the dream: an ocean below, an optimistically huge sun rebounding up into an unfeasibly cloudless sky as I whispered utterly filthy confessions into the young nun's ear; shoeless, her habit pulled up well above the knees. Reliably predicting Good Friday, Easter Monday, Sundays and Scottish bank holidays, the nun in the dream was always scrupulously replaced by a schoolgirl.

The Pindar quote is used as an epigraph to my friend Camus' meditation on suicide. I used to own a handsome (but pricey) edition of that strange little book, but I loaned it to the fair young nun I'd befriended in the Ember days when I used to seek alms up at the convent by the Tower. She left for the colonies to teach the heathens truths of the Catholic faith, but her plane went down off Madagascar. No survivors. Knew the book was wasted on her.

'Huh.' The Nephew sliced aside the children's colouring book he was quoting from, with impatience. 'Kind of nonsense you have to put up with from the spazz.'

'Revealing stuff though, Macushla. Now I'm sorry to put this to you straight, live on the air, we have the Macushla with us tonight, Nephew to The Man Who Walks, our previous guest on *Evening Conversation*, but, Macushla, the rumour, well, the *legend*, I just have to ask it so bluntly. What substance is there in the myth that you yourself took out The Man Who Walks' missing eye?'

'What! Paranoid fantasy in its own mind. Feels he deserves that cause of all the crazy shit he put me through as a kid. How did I pop it? Tip of a hunting knife, force it out with my fingers? This isn't *King Lear* and I'm not capable of that. How would I have got away with the Feds and that?'

'You have a reputation.'

'We all have a reputation.'

'Claims he was tortured. For days. You and an accomplice trying to get him to pass over house deeds of his mother's property which he inherited.'

'Preposterous. He injured his eye breenging around mentally in woodlands, as is his wont, and they said it couldn't never ever be repaired. I have the eye hospital appointment cards. He was out his mind with the drink, and licking rare fungus off trees as per usual. Now, his plans.'

'He had plans all right.'

'Like what?' he sighed. 'Look, admit I missed your programme. I always listen, but I missed that particular programme. That night. Where were his plans taking him?'

'Headed north.'

'North!'

'Talk to Nessie.'

'Nessie!' The Nephew yelled, but it was partially obscured as the deafening PA system leapt into life and the evening's Tina Turner impersonator muscled across the floor to a huge skirl of appreciation, her wig grazing the scallop shells.

'SIMPLY THE . . .'

'Jesus Christ, fancy an outside broadcast?' the Nephew yelled.

Twenty minutes later the radio presenter intoned, 'Here we are, live down by the piers. For those of you who are from out of town that's adjacent to Shore Street . . .'

'Hoi,' chirped the Nephew. 'Change frequency a minute, will you?' and he passed the bottle of cider to the radio presenter, who'd been cajoled into the off-licence. Then came a quick feature about the newly imported chip-making-and-vending machine, which had recently burst into flames. This was recorded for use on a later programme. The radio presenter then wished to dine Beneath the Golden Arches. He tried to interview a few passengers at the Drive-Thru, tapping on their car windows and thrusting the invisible microphone; shaking their heads in the negative, they refused to wind down.

Beneath the Golden Arches, an adolescent audience, who gathered nightly in the carpark in their small cars with alloy wheels, lounged in reclined driving and passenger seats, pulled up in a line, shouting through the open tunnel of windows on four vehicles drawn adjacent; this audience watched the radio presenter's activities closely, but the Nephew observed he was prudent enough not to approach *them* for any comment.

Inside Beneath the Golden Arches was just too much for the Nephew: garish-coloured, cross-eyed dinosaurs swung from the ceilings, dump bins threatened to topple as children, electric on sugar and additives, scattered drained milkshake cartons and clicked into place assembled toys, which seemed to come with the food, then sped them across the floor. The Nephew waited outside and the presenter boasted he had obtained a cheeseburger for ninety-nine pence.

'Anywhere I can sell this?' From under his jacket, cradling it as if it were a two-day-old puppy, the Nephew produced an expensive-looking camera.

'After one myself, supplement my interviews with photos.'

'How much you got?'

'Back at the digs? Let's see. About twenty-five pound.'

'You've digs?'

'Down the South Circular. Fantastic broadcasting properties because of the hill behind where my aerial is.'

'Mmm, wouldn't mind coming back there. Let me crash, you can have the camera for twenty.'

'Fine, aye. Follow me. I've the arts programme to present anyway, you could listen to that, it's always very interesting.'

'Mmm.'

They began to walk along the side of the dual carriageway. Rains came tumbling down as was wont to happen when Atlantic-crossed clouds were punctured by the gash of the nation's highest mountain, like guts pishing from the scythe-slashed belly of a pregnant cow.

The radio presenter walked ahead of the Nephew, emitting tuning dial sounds into his cupped hands for effect. To the Nephew's dismay the presenter seemed able, not only to do his own programmes, but to broadcast a whole range of others also, with passable accents, in between hearty back-swigs of the fortified cider which he would hurriedly pass aft to the Nephew.

The Nephew let his face fall back skyward in resignation and growled up at the looming mountain, invisible above him; he lifted knarled fingers to push the sodden hair out his face.

If there had been lightning, it would have flashed then; if there had been thunder, there would have been thunder – like stones being turned out of a cart – if there had been a pretty girl, there would have been a golden earring; and if there had been a golden earring, it would have glinted in the lightning. But there were none of those things: lightning, thunder, girl (pretty), earring, ad infinitum; there was just rain, rain, dark night, poverty and an insane radio presenter raising and lowering his measured voice, and the Nephew, who scraped his fingers up his forehead, letting the nails scratch into his drizzle-itched skull and shove back wet hair, but as his eyes looked sideways, his crow's-feet wrinkles pulled back, and in a feral instant, his throat moved like a sleeping eel, cheekbones darted and reappeared. He bore stunning resemblance to The Man Who Walks then. Just as quick the resemblance was gone because the Nephew spotted a Fed van slow-moving up behind them. There was conspicuously little traffic on the roads now, he'd noticed . . . something to do with this petrol blockade, yacuntya, he thought.

They had crossed from the loch fringes to the other side by this time and were ambling past house after house, so the Nephew simply stepped into some hen-pecked husband's perfect garden and stood against the dripping hydrangeas as the slow-motoring police car swished by, water sucking at the rear wheels, not even slowing to pass the landmark figure of radio presenter, arms raised, praising glorious properties of the ionosphere.

At the instant the car passed, the presenter did a perfect impersonation of momentary police interference over a radio, then continued, 'That was "Dark Magnus" by Niles Davies! A Welshman, I believe,' he yelled into that darkness, all sleered up with tail-light-on-wet-road ahead. 'This evening on *Artistic People* we'll be discussing Scottish publisher Carronaid's latest, highly original publishing project: yet more tastefully produced, budget-priced pocket editions, and of course, each introduced by a well-known writer or celebrity. This time it is Carronaid's lovingly produced pocket editions of the Highway Code which are exciting comment in the most sophisticated of publishing circles . . .'

'Hoi. Much further?'

'This classic British text, consistently a bestseller, almost part of the way of life in Britain today, is, thanks to Carronaid's vision, at last being given the literary respectability it has always deserved and its hidden, subversive qualities are being brought to light. Read *Motorway Driving*, introduced by *Crash* author J.G. Ballard. Read *Speed Limits and Their Meaning*, introduced by the Princess Royal . . .'

On the nutter yapped, then he pointed and said, 'Oh, that's my dog. That's *my* dog. I painted the white strip round him to identify him from all the other mongrel curs up the estate.' Right enough, a black mongrel approached and nosed lovingly around their knees, its wet hair spiked but laying flat where a healthy dose of white emulsion paint had been lolloped in a splashy circle round, across its back and under his belly in a complete hoop.

'What happened to your radio show?' the Nephew grunted and fully buttoned up Old Barrels' shirt against the rain.

'Everyone turned it off.'

The dog followed them uphill off the main drag into terracing driveways of even more detached Bed & Breakfast houses.

Nazareth Heights, the house name sign read.

'Home.' The radio presenter tried the front door, the nearly empty bottle of cider, which he stowed under his armpit, swishing and fizzing the reaming dregs round the base as he struggled with the lock. They made their way to the back and the door was unlocked. The radio presenter felt both sides of the wall for a light switch, then got it. The dog pushed on through.

'You don't live here, do you.' More of a statement than a question.

'Course I do. But, ssshhhh.'

'What's wrong?'

'Keep your voice down.'

'Where's the bog? I need to pish.'

'Second on the left.'

The Nephew felt his way along a corridor, opened a door and fingers touched the tick of a string-pull light. Bog right enough. An extractor fan began swirling in the ceiling. He put up the seat and pished, then used the towel to dry off his face then hair, and by the time he got to the back of his neck the towel was sodden. He looked at the curtain and considered a warm shower and its joys, but he needed to recce the area first and make sure this loon was on the up and up about the place.

There was light along the corridor, so he pulled the toilet door shut behind him and went in the door. The small bedroom was high-stacked on every wall with electronic equipment covered in switches and dials, beside coils of cables. There was a single poster on the wall of a young Orson Welles, talking into a radio mike with two flying saucers orbiting his quiff.

'Sometimes I pick up the most *incredible* things; sound like old ship messages from long times ago! You know radio waves go out into infinity, they travel forever into space? They only bounce back if they hit something metallic. There's something metal out there, maaaan!' The radio operator's mumbling face was up above him. He was lying flat in the low space before the ceiling. He slept up top, pressed to the ceiling on the summit of all the piled electric gear. He jiggled his foot. 'Once, I burned my bloody big toe on the light bulb there.'

The Nephew scoped around, but there seemed nary a place to sit, never mind trying to get down for a spot of kippage. Another night, and there were so many, where anaesthesia was going to be the only answer. As a visible token of his economic muscle, the Nephew lay down the location scout's camera in a prominent place on top of some kind of mixing desk that seemed to be waxed in the dribblings of crusted soup. 'Anything to bevvy, would you imagine?' the Nephew grumbled.

'You'd need to wait till they're back. They drain everything.'

'They?' The Nephew twitched.

'Heathens I share with.'

'Who are they? What do they do for a living? Not policemen?'

'Christ, no. Not tall enough.'

'Not underage kids, are they!'

'Nay, nay, nay, engineers. Contract engineers installing these mobile phone aerials that are going up all over the land.'

'Fair enough.'

'Couple of bastards.'

'How come?'

'Down at the Throbs there one night, in between shows, and I'm talking to two pretty nurse ladies, trainees from the Belford trying desperately to get a place to share out of the dreary nursing accommodation. "What kind of places have you seen?" I ask them. "Oh, some right scary old dumps," they tell me. "All of them awful, one of the worst rooms going in some place was at real knock-down price, to try and wheedle us in, but it was full of all this electric equipment and wires and junk, like an old second-hand telly shop, empty whisky bottles everywhere and can you believe that the guy who rented it slept on top a huge heap of all this electric equipment up by the ceiling, and they told us he'd once burned his big toe on the light bulb!" Well, you can imagine I spat out my pint and, soon as I could made my excuses, left to check the newspaper. Right enough, behind my back the bastards were advertising my room for rent!'

The Nephew nodded seriously. His heart went out to them, a nutter like this in the house is like a tick with its barbs deep buried in the skin. Nae getting shot of them. 'Mmm.' The Nephew nodded.

216

Just then there was a curious sound outside the window. Female laughter (which is curious sound enough to these two men), but also a low, hollow rumbling on the concrete path paving stones. Along with this, was the magical jingle of bottles, but with a musical lilt. The key in the lock, the 'Hup, two, three' of a male voice.

'It's them,' the radio presenter whispered and pulled a blanket over his head.

Out in the corridor there was a bump and a further jingle of bottles.

'This way, madam,' a low male voice went. A girl's laughter again and then her broad voice. 'Exact change, please,' and another male character laughed and slammed the door heartily.

'His light's on,' a voice sighed mournfully.

'In here, Tracey, in here, please.'

The rumble and magical tinkling swing began once again, followed by a door shutting and silence.

'They've bevvy,' the Nephew announced in awed tones.

'Women too.' The presenter's voice came from under the blanket.

'Let's crash them.'

'You go. I'll stay.'

'I can't go. I don't live here. I need you to introduce me.'

'Tell them you're room service.'

'That's in a hotel you're thinking of, dopey-docus.'

'Oh yes.'

'I've been in a hotel, you know. What was that noise, do you think?'

'I don't know.'

'Wonder who the bint is?'

'I don't know.'

'I'll sally forth,' the Nephew announced and coughed. He

opened the door and stepped out into the corridor that led towards one of the rooms the engineers seemed to have entered.

'Sally who?' he heard the radio presenter mumble, back inside.

The Nephew made his cautious way past several closed rooms until behind one door he heard mumbled words, laughter; he turned and tiptoed back towards the radio presenter's room when suddenly the corridor clipped into perfect darkness, something brushed his cheek, bumped his shirt where the collar hung, damp and open, and suddenly the most searing pain scampered down his chest as if a vicious stinging jellyfish was down there. He leaped. 'In the name of Christ, what now?' as the stinger settled on his stomach, some kind of biting spider, and the Nephew moved arsewards, biffing open the door behind, which suddenly flung out flooding light into the corridor. The Nephew did a little jig, untugged his shirt from his trousers and a hundred-watt bulb fell out and plonked onto the carpet.

From inside the all-lighted-up bedroom, three judgemental faces were stared out at him.

'Jesus. The fucking bulb fell out the light and went down my shirt!' The Nephew looked up in appeal, tears of pain in his eyes, and pointed to the forlorn bulb on the carpet before him. 'That could only ever happen to me.'

The girl, who'd been biting her lip, looked from man to man, then burst out laughing.

'Accident prone, eh?' One of the engineers gave a derisive snort.

'Too right I'm accident prone. Fucking ended up here, didn't I,' the Nephew mumbled.

'Who exactly *are* you?'

'Isn't that him? Oh, that's even more hilarious,' the girl shrieked in laughter.

The Nephew lifted up his shirt and studied the red welts on his belly.

'Nice muscles, lovely.'

'Ah, your housemate there invited me up.' He looked round their faces, stepped in, pushed the door behind him and dropped his voice. 'But he's nuts. Obviously. I tell yous, boys. My heart goes out to you, it really does.'

'You said it, pal, you want to watch that one. Come in, come in shut the door, have a drink!'

'Don't want to rent his room, do you?'

The Nephew took a single step forward and crunched the light bulb.

The girl shrieked more loudly. She was wearing some kind of uniform, tartan waistcoat and matching long skirt, then over by the wall the Nephew saw a drinks trolley, loaded with cans, miniatures, sandwiches, plastic cups, sugar sachets.

'Dinna fret. This is Tracey the Trolley. Get the crack.' The guy pointed at the trolley.

'Quit my job on the railway. Again,' Tracey huffed.

One of the engineers chortled with a beer can near his mouth. 'Walks out on her work for good, takes the train's refreshment trolley with her, craaashing it along the high street. We picked her up giving everything away to drivers on the roundabout!'

'She was doing better business than Beneath the Golden Arches' Drive-Thru!'

'It was raining, and you'd *says* yous had draw. What are you having, burned man?'

'Do you have ice?'

She jauntily up-flipped the lid of a small pot.

'Double gin and tonic then, please.'

'What sandwiches do you have there, love?' the engineers laughed.

'Lemon?'

'Yes, please.'

The two engineers were killing themselves.

'This happened once before, like; had a disagreement about my hours worked, so I walked off the train and out the station, shoving the trolley up the road. It was hysterical. Mr Murchison there, he knows I've a temper, but he's got a soft spot for me at heart, so's he lets me back on. Had to pay back the price of all the stock I gied away. Took me six month out my wages. That first time I took the trolley to someone's party, serving drink on the dance-floor. It was hysterical. That'll be me scunnered for good this time, boys, may as well enjoy ourselves. Near a full trolley, look, nobody's going to buy anything at these prices. There you go, pal,' she tipped out the two miniature gins so her rings and bangles chinkled, and handed the Nephew the plastic tumbler of gin, ice and lemon with the baby can of tonic; she flipped back Bacardi straight out a miniature into her own mouth.

The engineers laughed so much the skin crinkled up on the sides of their teary eyes.

'Where's that draw then, boys?' she smiled.

'You're a discovery, Tracey, a real fucking discovery. Here, here . . . you're nay CID, are you?'

'Hey, don't I know you, you're yon Man Who Walks, are you not? Oh, that's hysterical. I've seen you by the track from the train.'

'Jesus, no!'

'Oh, right enough, you've both eyes.'

The engineers looked at each other and burst out laughing

more, embracing their knees and lifting their boots off the floor. They'd produced the proverbial Rizlas, Golden Virginia tins, and little cellophane-wrapped balls of dope, core fuel of the social machine.

'He's my bloody Uncle, I'm just his Nephew.'

'Oh, righty-o; sorry, darling, sorry.'

'I'm Macushla.'

'What kind of name's that?'

'Thought yous were educated boys. Macushla is the Gaelic, sort of means . . . wee baby, wee darling, eh? The baby of the family, are you the baby of the family, Macushla? Oh. That's hysterical.'

Helplessly the Nephew reddened up with embarrassment. 'That's about it, Trace. Jesus, this is killing me, you don't have germolene or something, do you?'

'Have a blast of draw, pal, kill the pain. Sit yourself down, I'm Jaxter, the monkey here's Liam O'Looney and that's really his name, I'm no joking,' he shouted out a hork of laughter. 'You've got to know Tracey already,' he says, not without a tipple of jealousy.

'Do you want a sanny?'

'No, ta, I'd a big lunch.'

'No? We've ploughman's, spicy chicken, or tuna and cucumber. I wouldn't go for the prawn.'

'Really, no thanks. That guy from the radio, he's completely crazy.'

'They were *telling* me about him, how he's maaaaaad. It's hysterical.'

'He is. Thinks he's presenting radio shows all the time.' The Nephew waited for the Jaxter and Liam to tell the story about the failure of the man's radio station, but they both seriously concentrated on the makings of their draw.

The girl laughed, screwed the top off another miniature. 'Want a cup of tea or coffee? I've a wee boiler in here.'

Nobody replied.

'You haven't seen Uncle? The Man Who Walks. About? Lately?'

'The Man from Uncle,' mumbled the Jaxter, reducing down the lump while holding it in his fingers, but not burning himself in that inexplicable way.

'Who's the Uncle?'

'He's like that one through there. Another, touched by the hand of God and wandering the back roads, the hair out like this, the smile like this, the squint like this, the walk like this.'

'Jesus Christ!'

'Here, the pipe of peace. You must need it.'

Wearily the Nephew did his duty, kneeled piously, head bowed and without speech, took the stem into his mouth, the evil little dropping of whatever balanced on the scalded gauze of the pipe; held the lighter and used what dexterity remained to incinerate the illegal substance, who knows what, that it was illegal was all that may be determined, yet he had to not overly inhale the uncooled smoke. The trolley girl, Tracey, knelt down beside him, her thighs held tight in the long blue sweep of the tartan issue.

'Blow-back, pretty please?'

The Nephew placed his lips upon her turned face, saw freckles on her cheek, brown freckles, like specks of paint, a map of the known universe, but skin beneath, so pale! Lips that felt dreadfully thin, her mouth like a hole of bone after the voluptuousness of Paulette's. And the Buddhist snowboarder's too, if it came to that! Here was another svelte seductress available in her languid hours, when she didn't have her face in

222

a magazine, her arse on the pan and her finger up nothing more adventurous than her minute nostril, thought the Nephew, as he forensically evacuated the smoke from his own lungs through her mouth and down into the inside of her; then he turned away to take a long swally of jumping, clicking, busy gin and tonic.

'Utterly gorg*eous* aftershave, Macushla,' she says as she exhaled and shook her torso so those bangles jingled again.

'So that's what killed the cat.'

'Hear you work on the mobile phone aerials, boys.'

'Aye, cutting the roads up to them and that,' the engineer muttered.

'And look at that, boys, cuff-links! See that, boys? That's a touch of style, that's a wee touch of claaaassss rarely seen in men of these parts these days. And certainly not in my first bloody husband.'

'Where's the second?' asked Liam O'Looney, after a long exhalation of smoke and a final low wheeze. Tracey snapped hungrily through the clouds he exhaled with her teeth.

'Safely tucked up *en casa*. Do you know what *en casa* means . . . Macushla?'

'In the house?'

'Full points, darling. Love you on our team Tuesday night at the pub quiz.'

'Last time I was in the Throbs I won the pub . . .'

'Hoi, back on duty, squire.'

With a mere turn of the head, Macushla took the pipe stem back in his lips, near the thumb of Liam O'Looney.

'We're a confused and brow-beaten people,' announced the Jaxter.

Liam O'Looney turned to him and let his eyes focus on him. 'Why do you say that?'

'Hey! It's not just reserved for the Irish, you shameless

Roman. I was looking there on the handsome, now don't take this wrong, Tracey, the *handsome* thighs, the fine, healthy bearing of the pins of Tracey the Trolley here enclosed as they are in tartan, not the Black Watch tartan, but, and here's my point.'

'Aye, what's your point?'

'Aye.'

It's still the same as the Black Watch, isn't it? It's fake. Here's Tracey, fair Tracey, a fine upstanding example of twenty-first-century Highland womanhood, light of the land, working for the imperial dollar, in uniform? The sleazy tartan to keep the tourists in fantasy land.'

'I like my uniform!' she appealed, looking down at it.

'It's always at the bottom of the pint glasses these conversations . . . no . . . these ruminations appear,' the Nephew said quietly.

'Mr Gin and Tonic's hoisted his colours.'

'Beg your hard-on!' Tracey wiped excitedly at her thighs in the skirt, which, right enough, was beginning to appear more electric blue . . . distinctly inauthentic.

The Nephew chuckled dismissively. 'You're trying to insinuate I'm a North Britisher cause I asked for a gin and tonic from a stolen railway trolley. That smacks of the same puritanical hypocrisy when you hear all these lefties going "Oh, but it's remarkable, so many Scots propped up the empire." Always set ourselves up as angels and fail to maintain. It's another name for Calvinism. Stop this pretence that we're a good people and we'll all get along a lot better.'

'Too right,' Tracey was chewing something. 'Oh boys, no a political discussion. Like Macushla says. Here, I'll take the skirt off. I promise.' Tracey got to her feet, wobbled, the back zip made a little noise like a dying fly and down came the skirt like a tube of cardboard. The Nephew kept looking at the Jaxter who helplessly cast his eyes onto her legs and torso, bound in tights, until she draped the skirt over his head.

Everyone laughed.

'And off comes the waistcoat too since that's so offensive to Willie Wallace here.'

'It *all* offends me, Trace!' O'Looney yelped and fired up another pipeful.

'Had to come off anyways, boys, cause I'm away for a wee piddly tinkle now, so don't be listening. Or thinking about me.'

Up on her tiptoes she walked to the door.

'Don't dilly dally out. There's a weirdo about,' called the Jaxter who found himself neatly, a bit nervously, folding the tartan skirt in his lap.

'A weirdo,' the Nephew whispered.

'Oh, I'll be fine. If I don't come back, Macushla will come and find me, won't you, little darling?'

Macushla looked at her. Her white shirt had fallen down to cover her knickered buttocks. He tried to imagine what endless machinations she would be required to undergo for even the chance of him getting a rise.

She shut the door.

'She's a point. Get some sounds on, Liam. It's like a morgue in here.'

'Jazus. You're well in there, boy.'

'Help yourselves, boys,' the Nephew shrugged.

'Are you crazy, did you not see it, more legs than a bucket full of Colonel Saunders' Chicken. What sounds do you like?'

'Lizzy or Roses or something.'

Womack and Womack went on.

'Ach, gie it up, O'Looney, yous Irish, all like fumbling priests. If you fell into a barrel of women's tits you'd only come out

225

sucking your thumb. Leave her to the Old Piston of the Garrison.'

'Telling you, boys, we'll all get a poke, I mean if we're polite, she's accommodating as fuck and I'm no fussy about dipping my wick in another man's porridge.'

'You can go last then, ya manky Paddy cunt.'

'Here, Macushla, lend us your cuff-links then!' Both the engineers laughed.

'That's the Jaxter ummm,' mumbled Liam.

'What?'

'I don't know. I forgot. This shit's really strong.'

There was a shout from out in the corridor. The Jaxter shot up like a Protestant in the wrong church. 'Fucking Radio Ga Ga's got her!'

There was a curious scampering in the corridor, then the dog with the stripe of paint round its torso pushed its snout into the room and put its muzzle right up to Liam's face who was about to strike a match. Liam screamed and leapt backwards over the sofa, which only excited the dog more as it breenged around, tail slashing at miniatures on the trolley.

Tracey stuck her head in; she'd let her hair down. 'He was scratching to get out the toilet. How'd he get in there?'

'Fucking hell, I'm stoned. I forgot about him. Musta locked him in the toilet by mistake,' the Nephew heard himself mutter, awed.

'He's yours?'

'Your . . . housemate says it was his dog.'

'Don't listen to that crazy. I've never seen it in my life before. He's no fit to look after a dog. Hey, boy. Hiya, boy. Why's it covered in paint?'

Liam O'Looney looked over the back of the sofa. 'It's like that film.'

'What film?'

'Uh, uh,' O'Looney stood, hunched down, turned and said, 'Dog.'

'Eh? What do you mean, uh uh dog? What does that mean, you tattie?'

'You know, Jazus, uh uh dog!' He giggled helplessly.

The Nephew looked from one to the other, he couldn't believe he was like this already.

'Charades. That's what this is. Come on, Mister Pub Quiz Cuff-Links Gin and Tonic. "Uh uh dog". Any . . . suggestions?'

'Uh uh dog. And it's a movie?'

'Yeah.'

'*Lassie.*'

'Nah, nah.'

'*Turner and Hooch.*'

Tracey gingerly re-entered the room. 'Hellooo, doggy doggy doggy, ooooo oi ouch, careful!'

'Peanut butter, Trace!'

'Come on, Trace, charades. Umm, a movie. "Uh uh dog".'

'Three words? Come on, boys, yous are going to bits, give us another blast of yon shit.'

'No, more words.'

'More than three words?'

'Fuck sake, this fucking mutt is going to swipe the dope away, get it out of here.'

'Feed the bastard a bit.'

'Ach, they just conk out and shit themselves. You have to carry them outside.'

'Hi, O'Looney, get over here and put him out in the shed.'

'In the shed?'

'In the "sheh-eh-*duh*".'

'Don't think I can handle it, man.'

'Just take him the fuck out. The door is open, they never lock it in case they have to sleep in it. Away out and put the dog in it.'

'What if it shits everywhere?'

'Good. Just let it go then. I don't give a fuck; get it out of here.'

'Why is there paint on it? Is that paint?'

'Anyone want another drink? Macushla baby, are you okay there, you've gone very quiet.'

'I'll have another can of Tennents . . . '

'Me too.'

'Then we'll get tore in among the miniatures.'

'I'm thinking.'

'*Fluke*.'

'Naaaaaah.' Liam yelled. 'Uh uh, dog,' he motioned, turning round to look at his arse.

'Worms again, Liam?'

'Yes, yes,' he jabbed a finger of success towards the Jaxter but then he slumped into defeat. 'No.'

The Nephew licked his lips and said, 'What do yous make of this film they are doing here then, the *Kidnapped* thing?'

'Oh, we're going to be in that, if there's petrol.'

'The petrol's running out, man.'

'I don't own a car. Come on, let's get more fucked up.' Tracey reached out for the pipe.

'This is the new drug,' the Nephew announced, out loud. 'I had this last night too. And the night before, I think.'

Liam sniggered.

'This is slipped disco, man, this is the brain police.'

'I want to be an extra in that film, and have a musket. The Man Who Walks might be hid in there, in the uniform. Looking like all the others. Looks like something from the eighteenth century. I'll need to go see it. I never go to the cinema.'

'Who's in it?'

'A dog.'

'What? No, in this film they're doing here?'

Oh, Christ knows.'

'I know.'

'Oh, not you.'

'It's this actor but he's mysterious. What's his name?'

'Oh, give us a break, is that his name? Uh uh dog, the rapper?'

'Oh, that's hilarious.'

'What?'

'And what do you mean mysterious?'

'Well, I don't think he has any friends.'

'Oh bollocks.' Jaxter shook his head. 'He hasn't got over the little quails that went down with the Mir space station, the old Lada in orbit, but he's on the hills all day digging up the entire range of species in his JCB. He dug out a rabbit warren one day.'

'That was an accident.'

'So's strictly speaking yous aren't engineers?'

'Fucking right we are, cheeky.'

'Course we are.'

'What do you do yourself then?'

'I toss a few sacks, then hide all day, killing rats in an agric supply warehouse.'

'We rest our case.'

'This actor, I'm telling you, I saw him interviewed once in his Hollywood villa, but it, it was . . . preposterous.'

The Jaxter spluttered, 'It was what?!'

'Preposterous. You could see behind him, there was no

furniture in his fucking house, he was trying to pretend all was well, "I'll make you a coffee, lads, umm, no coffee in this cupboard, where's the kettle?"'

'It doesn't matter, there's a boiler in my trolley.'

'Hush, no, he's telling a story.'

'I thought you'd fallen asleep.'

Her cheek was on the Nephew's thigh.

'Tell you, there was no furniture in his Beverly Hills pad. Sad to think of it. It was being repossessed or something, he has head problems. I felt really sorry for him. He's in it. I have a big heart for him.'

'In what. What is he talking about? Get that dog out.'

'Is he David or Alan?'

'WHO?'

'Tracey, how about getting them out for the boys?'

'All right.'

'See that? Twenty year of women's lib down the drain.'

'Give us more dope, I will.'

'It's a deal. Here then.'

'I'm going out. I'm taking this dog out. Dog. Out!' he pointed.

'How do you think it got paint on it?'

'We had this cat once, with the first husband, but it leaped at the buzzing, got all caught up and wrapped in fly paper and took off out the door. Strangled itself.' She placed an unburned scrap on the pipe and devoured it, leaned over so her ass stuck out next to the Nephew's splayed hand, numb on the dirty carpet, and she put her mouth up on the Jaxter's to do a blow-back into.

Liam watched and mumbled, 'What about the quails on the Mir space station?'

The Jaxter exhaled and murmured, 'Shut him up!'

230

'Right, I'm away out. C'mon, boy, c'mon.'

'Aye, get out.' The Jaxter stretched a leg to flick the door shut, but his leg wouldn't reach and just sort of twitched in space. He was obviously deeply fucked-up too.

'That's hysterical.' Tracey looked at the Nephew.

'If yous are engineers and yous work for the mobile phone company . . . can you get us a free mobile phone? I'll give you a camera for it.'

'We've a fucking box of them there. Some of them don't work. Take a handful. A camera? What lens?'

'Take a photo of me then.'

'He will, when you get them out, instead of bluffing. I think you're all talk, Tracey the Trolley.'

'Right. They're coming out.' She started undoing her shirt buttons.

'Fuck off.'

'Aye, it's next door. Wouldn't mind a deck at those phones.' The Nephew tried to stand.

'Wooah.' Tracey held one of his legs as he tried to stand up.

'Hey, pace yourself, Macushla, still plenty to drink yet, man. Sit yourself down, mate; sit, I'll pass them,' says the Jaxter, but spotting a victim, allowing him to close in on the girl, he began to produce another strong pipeful for the Nephew.

'Hill-walking only good thing about mobiles.'

'How do you mean?'

'Well. Hill-walking. Kills more than any other sport, bullfighting, boxing, horse-jumping, which kills a fair score.'

'Nay loss though, it's all nobbers.'

'Nobbers are okay.'

'Knew it! The gin and tonic speaks.'

'Seen folk up the mountains, two thousand fucking feet, man, in dress shoes, a woman with a handbag on her arm once!'

'So have I; they'll ban boxing but they won't ban hill-walking cause yuppies love it.'

'I've nothing against yuppies. If yuppies means I can get kiwis in my local shop, all the better.'

'I mean, fucking time wasted on it and the money – like the morrow – I'm happy but I'd still ban it.'

'My Uncle survives *everything*. Crosses the mountains in December, fit as a fiddle. Constitution of an ox, nae chance of him dropping dead. Years to go. He'll hop over from Glen Lochy to Loch Lomond right across Ben Lui's flank in an afternoon for ten pints in Arrochar. But he has this thing you won't believe.'

'What, his cock?' she sniggered.

'Nay, when he's pissed or stoned, which he is most of his time, he has this rare balance problem in his inner ear and he can't go up nor down hills, like the slightest incline, not just stairs, the slightest slope. He used to carry a spirit level in his pack, drunk, down on his knee on some backroad taking a sounding! If he tries to go up or down a slope he just falls over. What a laugh. Or it would be if he didn't keep getting up from the falls. He has to make these huge detours, outlandish detours you might call them; miles and miles over the country he roams. When that Uncle of mine is pissed he has to go only in the direction that's flat in front of him, then if he comes to a slope he has to turn back, so when he gets pissed he gets trapped, in one place, for days, and has to sober up a night to escape.'

Tracey and the Jaxter were staring, seemingly enraptured by the description of this ailment, empathising deeply with its obvious disadvantages.

'Poor man.'

'No, not poor. He's rich, cash money stashed everywhere

under fucking rocks, and he's got a big house out Tulloch Ferry
that could have gone to the children, and he's a madman and a
pervert.'

With a heavy voice Tracey asked, 'Ever drunk champagne
out the small of a girl's back?'

'Have you *got* champagne?!' The Nephew looked up.

'No. How about voddy and Irn Bru then? Or a nice wine
punch warmed in the small of my back?'

'A last smoke.'

'Hear, hear, what's-your-name.'

The Jaxter tried to pick up the pipe but dropped it. 'Fuck,'
then leaned forward, stretched his fingers and that green old
pipe was back in the paw.

There was a timid knock on the door.

'Fuck off.'

'Okay. See you the morrow.'

'Oh, it's O'Looney. Come in, you cunt. I thought it was
Radio Ga Ga.'

Liam O'Looney meekly entered the room.

'Where have you been?'

'Was I away long? I've lost all sense.'

'What did?'

'The dog?'

'What dog?'

'Don't worry. I remember what happened.'

'You're just in time.'

'For what?'

'For more.'

'More what?'

'And.'

'Yes?'

'Her . . .'

'But.'

'What?'

'Thought I might go crash for the morrow.'

'Have another *sook*, man, for fuck sake. Tracey's having a blast, aren't you, Trace?'

'Too right. Then . . .' She sat up. 'Then I'm going to kneel and yous are going to mix punch in the small of my back. I've a right little dip there, with golden hairs in it. You start drinking it with a straw, then, eventually, yous just use . . . your mouths.'

The Nephew took first draw, held the smoke down. Tracey moved her face close for a blow-back, but the Nephew held up an admonishing finger, shook his head and turned away to blow out the smoke.

'What a waste.'

The Nephew declared, 'It's not decadence in this land, it's not decadence all around me, that finally wearies me, it's dissolute, not . . . not disillusion. Disso*lution* . . . that's the word. Do you know?' the Nephew went on, 'some soldiers have been unable to identify the, eh, battlefield.' His eye caught something in the corner he'd not spotted before. 'Fuck, it's a drum set!'

'Do you play the drums?' asked Tracey.

The Jaxter nodded, one eye closed, holding his breath to keep smoke down in his lungs.

'Must have a bash at the drums.' The Nephew stood up, took a step forward and crashed down on the drum set with a grand ringing of rivet-bored cymbals and thumps as different parts of the set fell apart and moved in different directions.

'Bingo! Get him off, get him OFF. That's a thousand-pound drum set.'

O'Looney rolled the sprawled Nephew off the drum set and he hit the ground on his back, snoring.

'Get him out of here. Irish, get him out to the "shed".'

'I can't get him out on my own, he weighs a lot.'

Tracey raised a finger. 'Load him on the trolley.'

'Fucking good idea.'

'Get the red wines off though, so's you can make a punch in the small of my back. Poor Macushla though, but I guess yous'll have to do!' She began preparing another pipe.

'Too right, doll. I won't let you down.'

'*Dances with Wolves*!' Liam yelled.

'What?'

'That was the film I was trying to remember.'

'"Uh uh dog" translates as *Dances with Wolves*! Stop smoking this shit, man!'

'You know, uh uh, the dog gets it.'

They stripped the trolley of all alcohol, KitKats, sugar sachets, sandwiches, tonic, lemonade, Coca-Cola, carrot and Madeira cake. Liam and the Jaxter lifted the Nephew onto the top of the refreshments trolley.

'Here, better get his backpack. Check if that camera he was on about is in it.'

'Fuck knows what it's full of.'

'Hang it there and his jacket too, and fling it in the 'shed' with him.'

By holding him in position they wheeled the Nephew out the front door, where the step was small, and round the back under the night where clouds hung low. The rear of Nazareth Heights gave straight onto a land tract and they trundled him a short distance. The trolley made a new, deeper sound and jingled no longer.

The Nephew's head swung far back and he murmured, 'Here. Here would do fine, Paulette.'

'I'll Paulette you!'

The two men reached the 'shed', slid open the door, heaved him up and in. 'Put his jacket on him, it's cold out here.'

Deep in the dark of slumbersome dreams come the same old nightmares; when slipping into the biggest dream of all, consciousness, the Nephew would see the minute little red lights blinking and he was sure he could hear the voices of many, many men in the darknesses surrounding him. Occasionally a wolf presence would come close, lick his face.

There were even the years when The Man Who Walks actually collected the dole, some invalidity benefit, and he was the first in this territory to appeal for a shoe grant – and get one. That was late 70s, maybe even early years of the 80s, before he spun right out of society, burned his treasured wage slips, national insurance number, premium bonds, driving licence and took to scrambling his papier-mâché tunnels in rustling spurts. He kept his passport though, curved into an empty, clean can of North Atlantic pilchards.

As the fortnights came round he'd owe all the winos from the caravan park a good portion of his dole, but he was cunning; when he got the cash The Man Who Walks would always take a taxi thirty miles down the villages, spend a few days drinking his way back home through the hotel bars and lone taverns, sleeping by mountain burns beneath the small railway bridges, in roofless platers' huts or in ballast hoppers shaken by the midnight freight below the mountains. Home, he could be confident there would not be a single penny remaining which they could extort from him.

When his mother's will left him the house and some cash, he knew he had to act quick in reaction to his natural generosity. The Man Who Walks arrived outside the Port railway station in a dazzlingly clean suit and announced to the winos' corner, like Caesar to his people, he was bound for Glasgow, dress circle to see the Moody Blues no less! The

237

winos waved him off with great fanfare (after he shared out a single bottle of cooking brandy). He made a quick exit in a taxi, planning to abandon it at the first station and go forward by train. But chauffeured drinking was to his taste, so drams were taken and generous rounds bought at the Gluepot, the Falls, the old Coaching Inn and the wee brewery the Englishman had at the railway station, as the taxi-driver helped him return to the plastic sheeting he'd rudely tucked into the back seat, but then it was off through the pass to the Turbines and the Tight Line and the hotel opposite, then on to the two stations (Upper and Lower) searching for a train south, and finally the Junction Hotel where the weary taxi-driver, patience exhausted despite the exorbitant fare, cut his losses. Vertical, stiff as a board, his eyes closed, The Man Who Walks got the beer delivery man to wheel him on his crate barrow up the slope and tumble him aboard the train, but it was the northbound, back to the Port! The Man Who Walks was returned outside the station, sharing round a new bottle of brandy with the winos, before the cautious taxi had arrived back! No inheritance money was remaining, his cleaned suit was mud and vomit ennobled.

Once Upon a Time in the West

The Nephew came into woke-ness of the slided shed door and flooded, grey, fish-skin light.

'Whose is the dog? And *who* is that!?'

'Ach, he's okay,' the Jaxter's voice claimed.

The Nephew opened his eyes, squinting. Two astronauts above him. Fair enough.

'Out.'

'The human being, he's just along for the hurl.'

'Get the dog out then.'

More bodies were clambering into the shed. Liam O'Looney's brogue came a-whispering close. 'Macushla my lad, you missed yourself last night.'

The shed began to vibrate heavily. Train coming, refreshments trolley, yacuntya, and the Neph's stomach lurched. The fucking racket. The Nephew sat up, rubbed his eyes.

'Tough night, pal?' a cyclist in his helmet next to him said.

The Nephew belched, just air, managed to nod, felt his stomach move sideways, tried to stand. A cyclist?

Now someone was pushing him back, but the door was just there a step away with fresh air. A mouth was moving in front of him, but no sound. No sound because there was only sound. An incredible almighty fucking racket. The guy must be the radio presenter because he had headphones on and was putting another cyclist's helmet over the Nephew's head.

'You need to stay sat down,' a mysterious voice went in his ear from no identifiable source.

'Need fresh air.'

'Right, just harness him over his backpack.'

The Nephew was harnessed and helped to the shed door. The Black Garrison lay seven or eight hundred feet below him as if he had died and risen again; Neptune's Staircase crawled under his held elbow and a thin coquetry of mist, like the fallen smoke of intense musketry or cannonade, laced the ridges and stitching of the landscape.

'Yacuntsya, I'm in a fucking helicopter!' the Nephew shouted into his headset, leaping backwards to the opposite wall, slow-motioned by the friction-rigged clip harness which made him feel he was being held, invisibly, from behind. He knew fine what was going on! They were taking him, going to throw him down into Loch Ness, its black waters, its steep sides converging like some hideous cleavage till he couldna sink more and was snugged tight, trapped, last bubbles leaving his puffed cheeks!

Static cackle of multiple mirth came back through the headset. The helicopter banked steeply and nosed into the morning, headed north-east over the route of the main road. Down to his left he could see the racks of hand-held radios, their charging lights winking, distant voices would've been coming through them all night.

'Mountain Rescue training, pal,' Jaxter says. 'Come along for the hurl.'

'Like fuck. Get me offof this thing.'

'There's a man here wanting off,' he chuckled. You saw his lips move those words but the sound, reduced down and smaller, came in your ears.

'Teach him not to sleep on RAF property. Go ahead, chuck him down with the rest, onto the roof of Lachy's caravan,' came the posh voice through the helmet earphones. 'Right, fellows, bombs away!'

The helicopter was swinging in an endless pivoty spiral now that made the Nephew grab the superstructure next to him; he stared wildly about. Seven or eight men, all looking like mountain goats: the beards, backpacks, the clipped, red-raw snouts, the layerings of thermal fleeces and climbing boots, bent over the doorway. A winchman sat smiling out in front of him, legs dangling, vapour moved right past the open side door, for fuck sake, and through it came the most intense bright light. They began to throw sealed cans of beer and other debris out. The Nephew gingerly craned up and looked back. They had been worrying a single caravan at the edge of a field. Some cans of beer rested on its mossy roof. A tiny, partially-dressed figure emerged, making violent gestures heavenward. The Nephew found it hard to hold back a sudden whiff of exhilaration, of superiority, over those beneath.

'Where are you wanting down then?'

'We're not taking him back to town. We need to get you on the hills. Cannot decend, there's mist,' the pilot's voice buzzled.

'Spean Bridge football pitch clear up ahead.'

'Winch him down, see if he can score if we bring him in at seventy mile an hour. Ho, ho, ho.'

'Yacuntsya,' the Nephew swallowed. The Mountain Rescue were staring at him, white teeth laughing through their beards.

In the subculture of thumbing it, the best spot for those headed north to or through Inversnecky is well known in this territory: just beyond the Little Chef at Spean Bridge, giving access to two caravan trails: the Laggan route north as it is given in Clough –

> How at the floating-bridge of Laggan, one morning at
>   sunrise,
> Came in default of the ferryman out of her bed a brave lassie;
> And, as Philip and she together were turning the handles,
> Winding the chain by which the boat works over the water,
> Hands intermingled with hands . . .
> They saw lips mingle with lips.

– or the route via the Commando Memorial and to the generous, sheltering, if unpleasant, mega-byres of the Great Glen Cattle Ranch, thus onward by the old railway bed to Fort Augustus and pass Loch Ness on eastern (if one desires a surreptitious entrance into Inversnecky town) or western banks.

The Nephew had no objections as the helicopter descended and bellied to kill speed, towards the football pitch's ill-defined markings in Spean Bridge.

Closer to the helicopter door he could see the wide view the chopper afforded. Why bother saving these daft city cunts offof mountainsides right enough, when they should be scouring the mists for that cunning Uncle of his? And my twenty-seven grand, the Nephew thought.

He leaned down to the winchman and shook his shoulder. The winchman held up a hand, signalling to stay back. The chopper was about ten foot up, the rotor downflow pushing the football pitch flat into a creamy white mass of shivering grass blades.

'He can get a bus back from here, the buses are still running. Don't allow him to take the helmet please,' came in his ears.

The helmet with fitted headphones was being lifted offof him, up past his ears.

He shouted towards the winchman, 'All the territory is looking for this man, my Uncle, this . . . character, this character. Look out for him on the roads, on the lower slopes, walking, skulking like the fucking yeti, a suspicious walker, do you hear me? Look out for a suspicious walker!'

The winchman smiled, shrugged and pointed to the side of his helmet, then jabbed a finger at the earth. The Nephew leaped for the ground and, as he hit it, the downthrust of air fairly whacked him on the shoulders and head. He hunched awkwardly, running away from the rotor's vicinity, turning, giving both hands the traditional thumbs-up to see a variety of non-verbal signs directed back at him: 'great masturbator', from the winchman; 'cocksucker', from O'Looney; traditional Vs from the Jaxter; 'up your arse', from the smiling pilot who was suspended high in the cockpit. The Nephew directed his fingers back in the emblem of a pistol towards the pilot with thumb as the hammer, coming down with slow, but deliberate, finality. The pilot was looking no longer. The engine noise seemed to decrease as the aircraft gained height and peeled suddenly towards the east, its noise faded surprisingly quick.

What an entrance and no a living soul to see it. Typical, yacuntya, the Nephew thought. Suddenly he whacked at his offshore jacket, 'Hoi, my camera, ya bass!' but all he found in the pockets were two mobile phones. He thought these must be top of the range they were so light, but no, they were simply without batteries. He looked towards the helicopter, bright in the sun above the distant mist layers, then his revelation came. He said the words out aloud, in the brightness among yellowed clouds of mist that morning in Spean Bridge as he watched the chopper recede; and the hushed, odd words of revelation were thus: 'Passport curled into an empty, clean can of North Atlantic pilchards.'

And no birds do sing, not even the crows would fly through it, and he'd felt the coldness stepping into it out of the sun. He stood in the eerie quiet and closeness of the mist for some time. It left damp on his face and on the coating of the jacket, but he could see the shimmering sunlight up in the heights of the thickening and thinning vapours above, sense the darkness of the clear blue hope up there, beyond. Not a vehicle had passed in a northerly direction. Only one vehicle had clawed south in a meander downhill, its one headlamp busted out, the other lamp forlorn, seeming uncertain in the mist. Although there was no rain, a torrent was racing down from a deep green pine tree to his left in a constant tattle of droplets.

Northbound vehicular noise approached through the mist, with a headlamp out, yet another! wipers in slow sweep: he canted a thumb. He thought the four-door was slowing in caution and anger at him, hitching in such poor visibility, his back to a slope and wet grass under his feet, but the car reached that slow velocity whereby it just had to be stopping. It stopped almost beside him and the passenger door swung open. But was not this the same car that had just headed south? The very same. Were these travellers lost?

No.

Here was a car sailing the roads well and truly under the sign of Jolly Roger. A driver, two in the rear in the classic formation, the passenger seat horribly bare and all too welcoming. Three men could not have depicted the collective proper noun, Growlers, more perfectly: the old scars from cherished scuffles below the bristles of their shaven heads, like those Aztec highways in Chile, visible from space.

★

The Nephew leaned down and looked in, ran his eyes over the contingent of three. The driver and the other were looking at him, the one in the furthest rear seat was staring straight out the window though only mist moved there, in vapour of such consistency you could see individual motes suspended, moving, as if electrified.

'Oh. Hiya!'

'You'll be a long time waiting for a lift today, boy. Do you not know there's nay petrol left in the country. Come for a drive. Pass your bag there. Pass your bag *there*.'

The Nephew climbed in and the car began again, labouring in first, round the misted corner and then it was into second and third before anyone spoke.

'Some mist, eh? Strange. Eerie even.'

'Birds aren't flying.'

'They do a lovely Olympic Breakfast back in that Little Chef,' the one who'd been looking out the side window spoke.

The Nephew felt his empty stomach pull like fishing gut. He should've had a sanny offof Trace's trolley right enough!

'But their kitchen, their cheffing operation, it's no exactly what you would call flexible. À la carte, you know, an item that is not part of the set menu. I was in catering myself a long time and,' he shifted position on the back seat, 'and the secret of any good kitchen is flexibility.' He coughed.

'I ken who you learned from: Fanny Craddock, eh!'

'The Galloping Gourmet.'

'Excuse my company. Ignore these . . . ignormusses.'

'Ignor*a*muses.'

'I really fancied a syrup piece back there. For ma brekky. Called out this early in the day, eh?' He leaned forward and slapped the driver's shoulder. Then he looked at the Nephew. 'Do you ever fancy a syrupy piece?'

'Once in a blue moon,' the Nephew mumbled.

'Once in a blue moon, eh?'

'Once in a blue moon is what he says, eh?' The one behind him chuckled.

'You're not more partial to a Virol piece?'

'No.'

'No, it says.'

'You listen to the man.'

'No. Emphatic as fuckit!'

'Noh,' he giggled.

'How about syrup of figs, ha ha ha ha ha ha?'

'Oooo, ha ha ha ha ha ha ha ha.'

'You'd be rising up in your seat at the moment, boyo.'

'You'd be shiteing it then, boy.'

'Yeah. Oh, get the man, get him!!!!'

The band Traffic began performing, recorded on their tape cassette stereo fucking system of this car. 'Traffic': was this yet more ironic comment on driving music, *à la* 'harboured by the fisherman', indeed.

The song 'Feelin' Alright' began and the driver magically turned it up by just touching something on the indicators beside the steering wheel. *Another* Dave Mason composition, I do believe. Yacuntya. Is there no end? Another favourite of The Man Who Walks that had infiltrated itself into the very fabric of the family, but had brought little joy in its familiarity.

The men in the car began to sing, the driver first, then the man behind the Nephew, handling a verse each, then together in the chorus. Each sang well, dropping into those plaintive, sad lines. Many hours of leisure, or great car journeyings, must have been dedicated to gaining perfect imitation of Dave Mason's singing. Not without a certain vanity. In the choruses where the men reached a sort of delirious joy they swayed from side to side as the countryside jauntily moved past them.

> You feelin' alright?
> Not feeling too good myself.

The man behind the Nephew clapped, 'Amazing, eh? Amazing that Dave Mason can stand up as a singer next to wee Stevie Winwood.'

'Aye, but it's true, he's good.'

'Hey, hey, now put out your rear fog lights down by your knee there. In clear air they can dazzle a driver behind you. Now you wouldn't want any accidents.'

'No hanky-panky.'

'Anyway. Anyway, call to order and bang to rights I say to her, the waitress, back at the Little Chef, "I would like a syrupy piece, my dear."

'"I'm afraid that's not on the menu," she says.'

'Not on the menu, I say,' repeated the other in the back, behind the Nephew, pulling his hands down over his eyes, and he seemed to rest a moment or even go asleep!

'"Yes, it's not on the menu, you can only order what's on the menu."

'"What's on the menu? Oh, now look, a syrupy piece is a syrupy piece, my dear. I mean, you have sliced bread, haven't you, *haven't* you? There's a representation here in this rather overexposed laminated photograph depicting the colourful glory that is your wonderful Olympic Breakfast in front of me. See. So if you can make your delicious, if rock-hard, fried bread, so well displayed here, you do have sliced white bread of a freshness that doesn't require pure incineration in the disguising mode of toast."'

'A representation, eh? Get the man, huh, huh, huh.' So. Not asleep. At all. In rest mode.

'"Eh," she says "Eh!" and giggles! The education system today.

'"Don't say 'eh' when you work in catering, my dear." I was forced to advise her. "So that much is confirmed and you do have syrup, or at the very least maple syrup, cause here I see pancakes are served à la the United States." Now a real syrup piece cannie consider Yankee maple syrup . . . yeuch, has to be Lyle's syrup every time with the poor dead lion covered in bees, or is it flies, on the tin, the tin with that prise-off lid you had to open with a knife point each time. Remember that sucky feeling, boys, prising the old top off the Lyle's Golden Syrup tin and that dead lion on the tin that so fascinated us all as children, eh? Did it not, gentleman, fascinate us all? All for one and one for all. Out of the strong came forth sweetness.' He dropped his pompous voice and more hushedly says, 'Have they took it off?' His face made polite enquiry round the car. 'Have the World Wildlife Fund or something had the dead lion took off same way the fucking golliwog got took off the jeely jars? Were wee children losing sleep and having nightmares and needing counselling about it?' He turned to the man next to him for some cultural update.

'I won't go down that road.'

'No, don't. You might offend our octoroon guest here. Hoi.'

'Yes?' The Nephew swallowed.

Syrupy Piece was leaning forward, much as the Purple Rinse had, those few days before, though it seemed so very long ago. 'I'll show you my tattoo. Later.' He grinned. 'It has to be said . . .'

'He's going to say it,' went that voice behind the Nephew,

but this time he'd leaned forwards to whisper through the headrest towards the Nephew's ear.

'. . . A syrupy piece, correctly made according to the ancient Scottish recipe, is a thing of beauty. Slices of doughy white bread must be baby soft in their freshness, which means, of course, the butter must be out the old fridge or in off the windowsill long enough so as *never* to blemish that bread in any way. On, that soft but fresh butter smears. Margarine? Margarine! Shoot that man. It has to be butter, then the Lyle's syrup is applied, curled onto the centre of the bread using a teaspoon, letting that little string of syrup coil and accumulate in that wee central, spreading golden heap. Distributed with the knife, repeat with the other slice. Remarkable the way you can study the butter, the knife ridges on it, through the transparent layer of syrup. Placing the slices together. A moment of joy. And if you leave a syrupy piece! Say you've made a big round of them and one has been sitting, the way the edges of the syrup begin to caramelise in the air!'

'Hark at the man!'

'But they still wouldn't give me one, so I had to have an Olympic Breakfast. Bad, niggling start to another day. I must go back and fuck that waitress up the arse and then murder her.'

The men, apart from the Nephew, laughed.

It was so early, still a single star was blinking in disappearance and reappearance as it moved on along the summit of hill ridges at the Nephew's shoulder. To be like the mountains, the Nephew thought. To return the gaze God gave us.

Syrupy Piece, the man in the back right seat, pushed his weight forward to light a joint, inhaled for a while and passed it round.

'No leaving butts in the ashtrays, case we get pulled by the Feds. I'll handle the stash.'

'They wonnie be out the day, look at the roads, no a car on them.'

'Quiet, right enough, just that busted headlight. Is the headlights off?'

'Aye.'

'This is how trouble always starts, some silly wee thing that you get pulled over for.' Syrupy Piece leaned forward again. 'Are you good for the world, Macushla, that's the question you've to learn to ask.'

'More often,' chirped the driver.

'That's right,' he chuckled behind.

'Did you ever watch *Once Upon a Time in the West*, Macushla?'

'Another film buff, the countryside's hoaching with them,' the Nephew groaned.

'Don't be cheeky, laddie. For your own good.'

'*Once Upon a Time in the West*. Spaghetti western, Charles Bronson. Henry Fonda, man.'

'I don't watch movies.'

'He doesn't watch movies.'

'He doesn't watch movies.'

'He doesn't *watch* movies!' The backseat man slapped his own thighs.

'You were always more of a reader, I hear, Macushla, Macushla boy.'

'A reader.'

'Well, listen, *stuff* books, this movie is the works. Henry Fonda says, "You have to learn to live as if you didn't exist." Think about that, Macushla.'

'Think about it,' the Foreman added, looking straight ahead, the speedometer and rev needles in front of him erect, like thistles.

' "Live as if you didn't exist." That means keeping shtoom, Macushla. Whisperin grass you went and told the blabbin trees, man. And the trees weren't meant to know.'

'Anyone seen *I Know Where I'm Going*?' the Nephew asked quietly.

He was ignored for long minutes.

'We know where *you're* going. Fucked if you know,' the Syrupy Piece one whispered.

The Foreman took the joint that was passed forward, and hissed at it, looking straight ahead. Already the Nephew could see the green on the butt.

'Here.'

'No thanks.'

'Take it.'

'No thanks.'

'TAKE IT,' Syrupy Piece screamed from the back, and everyone in the car jumped. 'Breakfast. Even the Foreman takes his toke.'

'That what you call it?' the Nephew says, lifting the joint carefully from the Foreman's fingertips, scrutinising its modesty and sucking its oiliness. He pretended to inhale.

'Inhale for real.'

Verbum sapienti sat est, the Nephew thought.

The Nephew saw an ancient tractor in a field, chalky runs of bird droppings on the fenestrated seat back, where crows and buzzards had used the height to gain vantage point over the field, and hunt.

'Seven Heads. How did the shop get that name?'

'Dunno.'

'Was it not that poet?'

'Oh, here we go; the Professor Macushla'll know.'

'Doesn't watch movies.'

'I believe he was always a reader.'

'I think it was a Gaelic poet, he headed off to Edinburgh or something carrying a barrel of seven severed heads on his back. Remind you of someone we know?' The Nephew shrugged.

Nobody laughed.

'No sign of him then?'

'You tell *us* where your Uncle is, Macushla?'

They've sussed what he's up to, yacuntya; they've realised where The Man Who Walks is heading for; we're driving up there now. They'll catch him there and the money's gone, the Nephew thought.

At Fort Augustus, as he suspected, they hung a right for the eastern banks of Loch Ness, passed the old monastery.

The Nephew really wanted to decipher some more of The Man Who Walks' warblings. He had to admit he was coming to be a little attached to them and he wished badly they existed in some fair copy. Instead he passed the time utilising a game he played in his youth when the caravans moved from site to site. He would locate a small blemish on the side window and he'd pretend this blemish was 'him', running beside the vehicle he travelled in, so when their route presented obstacles on the side of the road, buildings, bridges, gates, bus shelters, he would make the spot on the window which was 'him' fearlessly leap them by ducking his head slightly lower in the seat. He recalled on a long journey in the camper van, he'd once built a small model aeroplane with glue at the table, then succeeded in painting it. He held it out the camper van window to let the wind dry it. When he brought it back in it was completely encrusted with dying greenfly.

'Sit still, for fuck sake, Macushla,' the voice racked from behind.

'Brought our fishing rods,' Syrupy Piece suddenly said. 'Going to stop for a spot poaching on the Awe but nay time, Macushla, nay time. Days trying to track you. According to my wee spies here, didn't the Uncle once use feathers off one your wee birdies for fly-fishing?'

The other two men chuckled.

Syrupy Piece passed forward another lit joint into the Nephew's fingers.

The others laughed on, knowing fine, but the Nephew did not laugh. Huffily the Nephew says, 'Aye. He asks if he could use the feathers for his fly-fishing. I says okay, the tail feathers that have fallen out to the bottom of the cage, but he just took my whole budgie and stuck a hook in it, used her as bait and caught a fucking dogfish too!'

'Your mither told me about then. That was the white bird, aye?' Foreman smiled.

'It used to be white, was stained fucking yellow by the Old Dear's smoking.'

The others all laughed again.

'You're mad about the wee birds, eh, Macushla?'

'They can fly! Whole metabolism is booted up higher than ours. Do you know what kind of strength it would take to fly?'

'St Francis preached to the animals, to the birds, eh, Macushla. Is that not right? Bless the little birdy-wurdies.'

'Right. Birds are important.'

They all laughed.

'Now if you go to Assisi to visit his shrine, they won't allow dogs in. Can you believe that?'

'Book now to avoid disappointment. You should bless them, eh, Macushla. That's your values these days, is it? Bless the birds! You're a principled man then?'

'It's a cruel world.'

'A-fucking-men.'

'Tell them that about when you were little, the chick you got at Kirk Yetholm. That's what started your craze for birds.'

'Aye, tell us that,' went that one behind him and barked a laugh.

'Nothing. Went to visit Queen of the Gypsies in Kirk Yetholm, in her wee house where she sometimes goes, and they were selling chicklets but they'd painted them all different bright colours, so all us kids were screaming for them; none were yellow, they'd painted them bright green, red, blue, all the kids in the camp had one; then, of course, they all suddenly grew into bloody chickens and we wrung their necks and ate them.'

'He's Story for Bedtime, this fellow. Jackanory.'

'I could near weep myself.'

'Bit simple, aren't you, Macushla?'

'And that's The Man Who Walks killed your birds again. You can't be too happy about that.'

'I'm not.'

'What are you going to do about it?'

'Take his other fucking eye out.'

'Radical.'

'Is that right, Macushla? You'll need to find him first.'

'I . . . we'll find him. He's definitely headed for Loch Ness. I had a source in the Garrison there.'

'A source, aye?'

'A fucking source. Listen to it!'

'Sources, is it, boy? Well, you can share with us your wee scheme then?'

'What?'

'Don't come the cunt.'

'What you were on about on the phone yesterday. Your wee nest egg.'

'Ach, that was nothing. I was with this American, I thought he had a valuable book in the car with him. But I was mistaken.'

'He was "mistaken". He doesn't have a scoobie, does he?'

'Macushla, the gob's too big on you. You'll hoik it up like a grogger soon enough, so you may as well spit it out. Where'd you disappear to yesterday afternoon?'

'I was just walking on the hills.'

'Macushla. May I ask you something straight?'

'What?'

'What is this? Don't you believe in the cause any more, son?'

'The cause?'

'The cause. You know the cause better than any man.'

'What cause? There are so many.'

'The cause and the procedure.'

'There. Are. So. Many. They all got mixed up in my head till none meant anything.'

The Foreman passed another joint, coughed quickly and spoke up, 'The legacy of English rule in Scotland is the legacy of poverty. Macushla heard this one day so he goes, "Aye, right enough, the legacy of English rule is poverty." "It's this legacy that has to be fought against," they said. "Aye," said Macushla. So do yous know what Macushla did?'

'What?' asked Syrupy Piece.

'He went out and lobbed a grenade at a tramp.'

The other men all laughed and the car veered a little.

255

'How come yous have petrol?' asked the Nephew in a pleasant tone.

'We've got everything, boy. We've got a big jerry can full of petrol in the boot there, isn't that right, boys?'

'Aye. Ha!'

'Mind McKitterick, the tight-fisted cunt.'

'Associate of ours. Lived on one the islands. He was under a little business pressure about the building of a house. Three mile to his nearest petrol station. He walked it cause his car had been repossessed by us at that time. He was so fucking tight-fisted, when he saw the price of petrol at that station he walked on another five miles to the next petrol station.'

Syrupy Piece says, 'Walked into the forecourt, took the nozzle out the cheapest pump, which was five pence cheaper than five mile back, poured a few litres over his head and set fire to himself before the attendant could get out there.'

'Saft simple cunt.'

'Big jerry can of petrol in the back. Want to see it, Macushla?'

'Nope.' The Nephew thought of his youth again, of them tipping those jerry cans of two-star down into them rat nestings, in the cut rhoddies, those porkers stumbling out, rats flying in arcs, exploding. They flew, but briefly, so briefly.

'Oh, don't worry. We'd put the spliff out. There'd be nay danger of a fire.' They all laughed, except the Nephew.

Before Foyers, the sun was shining and it was a very pleasant day now. On an open stretch of the single track, with a ridge that swept up to the east, they pulled into a passing place and stopped.

'Want to check his bag. Stretch your legs,' Syrupy Piece commanded and he opened his door. The other two got out and seemed to do nothing more sinister than stretch their legs, wander round the bonnet, stick a booted toe out to touch the smashed headlamp.

'You not getting out?' asked the guy who was seated behind him, who he hadn't got a clear dek at yet. The Nephew opened the passenger door, which, after all, hadn't been locked, and stepped into the grassy verge scattered with sheep's purlies. He sized up the cunt who was behind him: legs skinny as fuck, one good crack would take him down and put him to sleep.

The ringleader had the backpack resting on the boot. 'Nasty, very unsocial, Macushla.' He held up the rubber-sheathed knife and lay it gently on the boot on the opposite side of the Nephew. 'Jesus.' Between two fingers he held a pair of the Nephew's boxer shorts. He dropped them on the tarmac. 'More. You must shat yourself a lot, Macushla.' Strangely, this pair he dropped back in the bag, then he tugged out the rustling bin-liner.

'What's this?'

'Typewriter ribbon.'

Syrupy Piece cautiously opened the bin-liner and began to pull at the untranscribed typewriter ribbon, tugging out its amounts higher and higher to his arm's length and letting it clickle down onto the boot and slide to the gravel of the passing place.

'I found it in his house.'

'Whose house?'

'Man Who Walks' house. Who the fuck do yous think? It's . . . writings. Just a load of shit really.'

Syrupy Piece threw the typewriter ribbon to the ground, some of the ribbon got wound on his foot, so he kicked around aggressively to free it. A draft of breeze caught the emptied bin-liner and it made a low float, then began a slow roll forward and over and over down the single track and into the ditch to become a ghost bag. The Nephew watched it, wishing he too could drift away with it. One strip of typewriter ribbon was dragged with the ghost bag, making a tickly noise on the tarmac. Syrupy Piece held up the brightly coloured children's colouring book, sighed. He opened the pages and began to look through it. The guy to the front of the bonnet, smoking beside the Foreman, walked over, looked at the cover of the book.

'What's all this writing in here?'

'A copy of the stuff that's on the typewriter ribbons. Haven't done all those ones you're throwing away yet though.'

The Syrupy Piece and the behind guy stood side by side as the pages of the book were turned.

'It's some crack. Thinks his father was Rudolf Hess at one point, ha!'

Nobody responded. The men looked at one another. 'Who?'

The Foreman passed the latest spliff to the Nephew, so he silently took it and inhaled.

Syrupy Piece folded the colouring book under his arm and lifted the red-checked shirt out of the bag, tossed it into the ditch and lifted the last item out of the bag.

The men looked around at each other and snorted. It was a bottle of Pagan Man aftershave. Syrupy Piece unscrewed the top, sniffed. 'Jeezo. Good taste, Macushla. Always thinking of the ladies.' He put the bottle into his pocket, slid the hunting knife inside his own jacket and spun the backpack into the rear seat. Then he leaned over to get grip and tore the colouring book up its centre. He leaned down again and tried to rip the halves, both his hands forced the rip diagonally, then he hurled the torn book away into the rough moor fringe. Its parts landed quite far apart.

'Check the jacket.'

'Boys, I haven't got the money. Haven't even found the cunt,' he sighed.

The other guy took a step up to him. 'Take it off,' he said.

The Nephew quickly slipped off the jacket and handed it over.

'What's with the cuff-links. Look at the fucking poseur.'

The guy shoved his hands into the pockets, lifting out one, then two mobile phones.

The Nephew turned to the Foreman. 'Presents for you.'

The Foreman looked at the guy. 'Let's see.'

The guy passed the phones over.

'Trash. This fucking lot don't have any decent reception up here, they're only interested in the population centres, where the money is. Like everyone else. Don't you know anything, boy?' But he slid the phones somewhere into his dungarees anyway.

'Nothing else.' The guy folded the jacket and wasn't looking like he'd be giving it back

'Tell you how much I know. He's headed north. Best thing we can do is split up. Yous cover Inversnecky itself. The Railway Club would be the kind of haunt it would head for. One of you could check that out, the other of you scout the town. I'll head for Culloden battlefield. Years ago before he got so bad he was often seen up at the National Trust centre there causing trouble, charging around the battlefield scaring tourists, cause it was him that tells me, if you're running a dog up there, you can only let it take a shite on the English side of the battlefield, not the Scottish.'

The men all laughed at this, so the Nephew smiled and began to feel better about the situation.

'Culloden battlefield, you think you'll find him there, do you?'

'Good chance,' says the Nephew who was working out how he'd shake off these dangerous cunts and cut down to the airport below Culloden. Why ever Prince Charlie's boys fought up on that forsaken moor – like old Prometheus again, splayed out before the gods on his rock, exposed to the merciless heavens, yacuntya, and picked to bits by hoody crows too, like the wounded boys would have been. And if the hoodies don't get you the eagles will, like old Aeschylus on Sicily: an eagle took that tortoise, thought Aeschylus' baldy head was a shiny stone, dropped the tortoise and killed him.

At Inversnecky airport, they might release names of passengers outward bound, and The Man Who Walks is sure to have caused a fuss and to be well remembered, like that time at Abbotsinch airport when they tried to send him to hospital in London and security, alerted by the stench, found all this crushed roadkill in his hand luggage, dead rabbits and crows and a flat hedgehog! Said he didn't trust the food in England!

All the Nephew had to do was get shot of these guys. They'd never suss it, what the sly old bastard was up to. He was getting out for good.

The car moved through Foyers, ignoring Wade's Hut where Johnson and Boswell paused.

'Crowley's house is up here.'

'What?'

'Aleister Crowley's house is up here. In the 60s before it became a private residence The Man Who Walks used to knock around in the ruin with other hippies. Built on the site of what Boswell called the meanest parish kirk he ever saw.'

'Someone turn up the music,' the ringleader groaned.

'Here's a quiet spot for it. On the left there, down on the shore.'

'Aye.'

'This should do it. Put the music off. Listen out for cars.'

The Foreman pulled them into another passing place.

'Boys.'

'Get out.'

The three men got out and, gingerly, the Nephew followed. The Foreman was stood at the front of the car, the two others by the boot. Beside the Nephew was just the banking and birch trees down to the side of Loch Ness.

'Boys, listen.' He turned to the Foreman. 'I know. I could've been working quicker, but I ran into all sort of obstacles: a wasp's nest in a canoe, I was near drowned and that's where I lost the phone, then my legs swole up, a nutter almost killed me in a car crash and I had to horse it out of there before the Feds showed up. I only gave the boy a whack.'

'No out the hospital yet.' The ringleader smiled. 'Not a scratch in a car crash, then you kick seven shades of shite out him! You've a wicked wee touch, lad.'

The others laughed.

'Hijacked by the Mountain Rescue this morn, everywhere I go yous are stuffin spliff in my face. I saw the stuff in the paper.'

'You did?!'

'Yeah, but they can't link that to me.'

'They'll just i.d. you, minute you're back in town, boy.'

'I won't go back. I'm getting restless again, boys. I'll go off for a bit. I'm sorry I couldn't return your money.'

'Macushla. It's no *our* money. Tying up an old couple after you strip them? Not our style. Then you broke Seamus Sheedy's nose. Fucking a hundred yards outside town before you were in fucking trouble. Was there ever anything you could do without ballsing it up? Thankfully, not.'

'It didn't happen like yous think. He tried to get me to suck his fucking cock, man.'

The other three men screamed in laughter.

'Seamus *Sheedy*! He's a shagging machine, man. Women, just *women*, Macushla.'

'Then he's broadening his horizons. Boys, I need you to listen to me.' He turned to the Foreman. 'Did you check his passport? He keeps it in a tin can in that box that he thinks locks. You've got the key though, don't you?'

The Foreman smiled and looked at the others.

'What's his passport to do with it?'

'I think he's walking north. I don't think he's going to bury the money anywhere. I think he'll have it all on him. I believe he's headed for the Inversnecky airport. He makes it there, he can get a flight to anywhere; even if he doesn't have a passport he can get connections at Glasgow. Then you know what that means? Even without a passport he can take they wee Loganairs anywhere, Papa Westray, Islay, Tiree! We'd be searching for him forever and you know he'll squander the lot!'

The men looked at each other. 'So it's not *Culloden*, now it's the *airport*.'

'Telling you, boys, straight for the airport, drive now. We could at least find out where he's gone.'

'We hit a sheep this morn. Come give us a hand.'

The Nephew walked round to the boot as the Foreman stuck in the keys and swung it up. In the space was the flustered, yellow-stained fleece of a dead black-headed sheep, a jerrycan and The Man Who Walks curled in a foetal position, the ragged greatcoat, ankles and wrists tied, a brown slab of parcel tape over his mouth, the Pittsburgh Steelers baseball cap off the head but

clutched, childlike, in his huge hands. The Man Who Walks'
single eye homed in on the Nephew.

'Name of fuck, yous got him! Agh, what a stench!'

'It's no the sheep.'

'We had him in the car, but the smell!'

'And the things it says.'

The Nephew chuckled. 'Well, I'll be fucked. Where'd you
finally catch up with him?'

Syrupy Piece leaned forward and ripped the parcel tape half
off the lips.

'I AM MAXIMILIAN THE THIRD,' that voice yelled. It
blurped to a stop as the guy smoothed his hand back over the fat
lips.

'Got the money?'

'You bet. Nearly twenty-eight.'

'Fuckin beezer!'

'Jeez.' The other men looked at the Nephew and Syrupy
Piece shook his head.

'C'mon, get a hold of this,' the Foreman grunted. The three
men leaned in and got a grip on the sheep as the Nephew stood
back.

'One, two, up. Fuck the weight of it.' They lifted the sheep
out the boot but there was a clatter at their feet. Their three
fishing rods had come out too and fallen to the road.

'Dump it, dump it.' They thumped the sheep down on the
passing place tarmac.

'Ach, it's *fucking* all caught up.' The hooks had got caught in
the wiry sheep wool. Syrupy Piece guy kneeled down, pulled at
the gut leading to the hooks. You saw the tattoo work right up
on the back of his neck.

The Nephew stepped forward and took another look at The
Man Who Walks; source of so much chagrin. His Uncle seemed

asleep again, perfectly resigned to his confinement, but had extended his legs out into the space the dead sheep had occupied. The Nephew turned and looked at the Foreman, looked at the two strangers with him.

The three men each had hold of a rod now, with the gut lines leading to the heap of dead sheep on the ground. Suddenly a car rounded the corner.

'Fuck.'

'Shut the boot, Macushla, shut the boot, for Christ's sake.'

Pleased to have some responsibility entrusted to him, the Nephew put both hands on the boot rim and crashed it shut and The Man Who Walks vanished into a sliding block of shadow.

The Volvo slowed as it approached the three men with the dead sheep on the fishing rods. Its window was winding down.

'Out of petrol, guys?' smiled the English driver. Children's bicycles were attached to the roof-rack.

'No. Fine, thank you,' smiled Syrupy Piece.

'Ah.'

Wife with sunglasses on: now two children in the back seat strained for a view of the men with the sheep on the fishing rods as the Volvo slowly moved in procession past them.

'Bait. For the monster.' Syrupy Piece nodded and smiled towards the loch.

One kid had her nose pressed to the window and started crying. The car moved on, accelerating.

'Christ.' He got the Nephew's knife out and sliced a line.

'Hey, that's a fantastic fly I've got there.'

'You can buy plenty more.' He sliced the other lines. 'Come on, get this *fucking* thing off the road.'

Hunched over, the men hoiked the sheep, then shuffled vergewards. 'Right, on three. One, two and three.' They swung the sheep into the young birch trees, it bent and swished back saplings, hit the ground and rolled over once before stopping.

'Let's go.'

The Foreman opened the boot, a humming sound came out. He threw in the rods violently and slammed the boot closed. They piled back into the car and began motoring onwards.

'Not too fast, don't want to catch them in the Volvo.'

'Bait for the monster.'

'Ha!' barked Syrupy Piece.

'Classic.'

The Nephew's knife came forward, unsheathed, handle first and tap-tapped him on the shoulder. 'You'll be wanting to deal with your Uncle then, Macushla.'

The Nephew turned, looked at his shoulder, where the knife grip lay, as if one of his wee dead budgerigars were perched there.

'We'll need to find some quiet spot. Some lovely wee spot, eh, Macushla?'

'Go this way.'

'Take it then, Macushla.'

Slowly he lifted up his hand and took the unsheathed knife.

They drove. The Nephew wished they could drive on forever, pausing only for refills from the funnel and jerrycan combo, on through Inversnecky and up, over the whale-hump bridges, up true north into the evening lands. He knew what it would be like up there as they ran into the outskirts of a hamlet: the pubescent pink of early sodium lamps and a half moon hung. Luminous dusk humming just behind all the skylines. A trembling rush at the endlessness of possibility which this life presented. Then he felt once more the melancholy; those lonely summers of his youth, no girl by his side, the whole country chorusing with life and nobody to share it all with.

The loss of meditation and hope, which drawing to the end of any journey brings about, took place.

'Here?'

'How about there?'

'Nut, need to get a bit off the road. There, there and over the gate. Quick.'

They creaked the car in along a track between two fields, accelerated down and stopped where the track widened at a gate.

'Ready, Macushla?'

The Syrupy Piece guy opened his door and got out.

The Nephew turned to the Foreman. 'Are you crazy? It was just a turn of phrase. Who is that guy anyway?'

'You done it before.'

'That's just a myth, a fib, I've gone along with it cause it makes me look hard. I never took his eye out. He poked it out on a dead pine tree branch. Jesus, Foreman, he's family. *My* fucking family at least.'

'Family, huh,' the guy who sat behind him was still there.

'Look, it's me that's holding the knife, pal!' The Nephew swivelled and scowled at the guy.

The guy rolled back and raised the sole of his dirty training shoe, which he rammed into the headrest of the passenger seat that violently lurched towards the Nephew's face. The Nephew swung the passenger door open so hard it slammed back and whacked his thigh and then he stood, one foot down in the trackside declivity, but the guy had slid across to the other back door and was out, smiling across the car roof.

'Settle down, girls. Foreman sir, please, get that *thing* out of the boot. I don't want all this blood we're going to see, pishing out all over the car. Is there blood, Macushla? You're the expert. Blood or just kind of goo when you pop an eyeball? I'm genuinely curious.'

The Foreman used the keys to open the boot, leaned in and began undoing The Man Who Walks' feet.

'Don't ungag it, for Christ's sake. I couldn't take that.' The Syrupy Piece guy raised his eyes to heaven, while looking at the Nephew.

'Get up. Get up!' the Foreman shouted, then pulled The Man Who Walks from the boot, his arm linked under his. 'C'mon,' he clattered aside a fishing rod, pulled The Man Who Walks towards the gate.

'Hey, the Macushla. You haven't seen my tattoo yet.'

'Mmm.'

'Wanna see? Boy?'

'Aye, sure.'

Syrupy Piece removed his jacket, tossed it on the car roof, then turned his back. He was wearing some sort of country and western shirt with pointed collars. 'This is from Nudie's, boy.'

'Aye?'

'Been to the States?' He'd turned his back to the Nephew and addressed him over his right shoulder.

'Aye. New York.'

He pulled up his shirt, short fingers digging into the material and his spine arching over as he dragged the shirt up above his shoulders. On his back was a wide tattoo, spread from just above the small of his back, up over the shoulders and further onto parts of his neck: two dogs attacking and turning over a badger, both dogs were pawing at their prey, the dogs' teeth sunk into the curled badger's stomach. 'What do you think? It's no finished. All the blood's getting put in next week!'

'Watch he doesn't stab you in the back,' mumbled the guy who sat behind the Nephew. 'He's got the knife. Or more likely fuck you up the arse.'

The tattoo shook with laughter, 'What do you think, Macushla?'

'Some tattoo. Aye.' Macushla was remembering it was so dark in the woods with Paulette he had no memory of that tattoo at the very bottom of her spine. Was he possibly confusing her with another woman? After all, there were so many. Weren't there?

The man in front of him pulled the shirt fully over his head, tossed it on the ground and turned to Macushla. His face was flushed. 'Ever been badger baiting then, Mr New York?'

'Nut. Heard they bind the badger's claws, otherwise they'd always win,' and he looked over where The Man Who Walks was being led far across the field now. He licked his lips.

'Gives the dogs an edge, I'll admit. But someone always has the edge in life. C'mon, c'*mon*. You want to carry the petrol or will I? JESUS, look at the face on him! Look at the face! Fuck sake, Macushla, we're only joking you.'

The other guy walked towards the gate.

'On you go, Macushla. Fuck sake, man. We're only jesting. We can't leave that thing in the car in case it starts kicking and some Farmer Giles cunt comes along. We're going to find a spot over there, bury the money someplace safe we all know. Except we won't let that crazy fuck see a thing!' He laughed. 'Joke. We won't burn him. You don't have to put his eye out, ya pussy, we'll just not let him see. Let things die down for eight month, a year, come back and dig it up.'

'You're just going to nick it, aye?'

'Oh, come on, man! Saying it didn't cross your mind? All those fat fuckers back home can accumulate twenty-seven smackeroonies for a game of football! Do you really have any sympathy for those lifeless beer swillers who wouldn't give you a lift in the pissing rain, tongues hinging out at young boys half their age running round a field. Those scum can afford it.'

'They haven't gone to the Feds yet?'

'Have they fuck. Those are all in the building and the fishing, black money they never declare, they don't want to be drawing attention to any cash.'

'Where was it all kept in the Mantrap?'

'Need to ask your Uncle that. Get over there.'

The Nephew took the knife and, looking at the man, lay the blade on the roof of the car. 'How did you get in on this, you worked on stuff with the Foreman before?'

'I hear he's enjoying your Old Dear, boy.'

'Aye, what of it?'

'Could be family soon, Macushla. You'd best treat him with respect!' he laughed.

The Nephew turned his back, left the knife behind, clambered the gate and marched across the meadow. There was a fence at the far end, some trees, and the shallow valley climbed out into a steeper slope above. These diddies would need to make sure they didn't bury in a place that was going to be ploughed up. And this flat glen looked liable to flooding too. Fucking stupid place to bury it, the Nephew thought.

Up ahead the guy who sat behind him was gingerly crossing the barbed-wire fence. You could see how scrawny his legs were, yacuntya. Twenty-seven split four ways. Say twice is ten, plus three and a half, split is five, six, nearer seven. Six thousand seven hundred and fifty. This is what you get when all this clan come in. He vaulted the fence in a one-er, hoping the cunt in front would turn back to see. He didn't.

When he caught up, his Uncle was sitting by a thistle clump watching him approach. Foreman was beside him, a slight smile on his face.

It was then the Macushla realised. He said, 'Hi, Uncle. Man Who Walks. You . . . you didn't kill my birds at all, did you? You haven't left town. You've been with these cunts all the time and I've been heading north towards . . . towards nobody. And I'll bet you the Feds are looking for one person in connection with all this. Someone who just walked out of their job the other day. Me.'

The Foreman did a slow hand clap. 'We were hoping the fucking useless Feds would've lifted you by the now.'

Arms spread, the Nephew fell backwards on the tuffety grass, looking up into the sky. All in all, yet another almighty fuck-up. He felt like falling asleep. Heard a pitch, like a scream, rolled his head. The tattooed guy was throwing over the shovels, bound in a canvas sling, and the noise was the squeaking of the wire fence under his weight as he crossed. He lifted the shovels and walked closer. He was wearing the offshore jacket, which he removed and threw down.

'How's about a shot of my jacket. Looks like I'll be needing it on the run?'

The guy walked up and as the Nephew was squinting in the cool, bright light, a large boot kicked him very hard in the mouth. The boot seemed to sink right into his mouth and go still there, and there was sharp, terrible knifing pains on his teeth as something gave.

'It's *my* fucking jacket,' Syrupy Piece, still shirtless with his shaking, angry tattoos, shouted.

The Nephew pushed himself up on his elbows, but now another blow from the right caught behind the ear and there was a low, deep boom in his head as he failed to rise.

The Nephew was aware of a tall figure at his right now, kicking, then another bending, raising the shovel. It was brought down . . . a sledgehammer. The tattooed guy'd aimed for the kneecap but it missed and, instead, the metal head of the hammer came down on the flesh of the Nephew's inner thigh. The muscle broke with a dull, totalising pain, the flesh seemed to compress, completely flat like jelly, and break through the trousers. The Nephew tried a scream but had no breath. Another kick, from the man that was always behind him, made the Nephew flatten out, and another swung hammer broke the edge of the left kneecap and crushed down the side of the knee.

The Nephew held up a hand.

'Fuck you, enough. Haven't started.'

'He doesn't have a scoobie, Colin. He's a denser.'

'Put your foot on his boot there so I can get . . . Foreman, hold him there. Right. Put your foot hard on his boot so I can get on the knee.'

He broke the right kneecap downwards so its bone debris was forced into the joint underneath and the whole joint itself gave way under the perfect hit, rounded joints of bone searing away and a flowering of haemorrhage began where the shin met the knee.

'Don't know what you did to her, cause I can't knock it out of her yet, but I know you were near my wife and girls for days and that's enough for me.'

'He won't get up on that one again, but the other one's no done proper.'

'Watch, Colin. Bleeds too much it can kill them,' the Foreman says a little nervously.

'Get the trousers off him. I can't see where the knees are. They're my fucking trousers too! My aftershave, my girls' colouring book and my fucking WIFE.'

That was the sorest bit, when they pulled the trousers down to his feet and lifted the leg upwards a little. He screamed.

'Good. Hold it still.' He broke the left knee again. Off centre, but it stoved in nicely from the right side, seizing immediate.

The Foreman lit a cigarette. He was kneeling, on one leg as if he was giving attention to a tyre on a car. 'Mentioned a little earner yesterday, Macushla. Share it with us now and he'll stop?'

The Black Book, the Nephew thought, almost comforted at that book resting, hid, in that big house. He could predict the way things were going. Looked like in a few moments he wouldn't be reading any of his beloved books ever again, never mind yon. But that wouldn't stop a blind man in a wheelchair robbing it, yacuntya!

'Going to tell us your earner idea, Macushla?' the Foreman asked.

'Get him over here.' Paulette's husband produced the hunting knife.

'Why'd you go poking near Paulette, laddie?' the Foreman muttered; wearily. 'Colin's a well-known man at home.'

'You're a fool.'

'Aye, you're the fool okay, Macushla. Can't come swanning home after ten year, not knowing the score.'

'Gormless enough to think Man Who Walks could of took the money. Off you went leaving a trail of mess leads right to you and you only.'

'What?'

'Birds.' The Nephew coughed.

'He's still on about his fucking wee parrots. Aye. Colin burned up your wee tweeters. Knew that'd get you going.'

The Nephew spat, breathered, looked up at Colin and says, 'Then I'm glad I pished in your wife's mouth.'

A kick knocked his head sideways.

★

The Nephew squinted. They had a carrier bag there with the money in it. The Foreman was kneeled, transferring the notes in grabfuls of pre-counted wads from the plastic carrier bag and into three backpacks. One was his, yacuntya! The other men stood above watching him, apart from The Man Who Walks who crouched, staring at his Nephew. The Nephew reached out a hand, waved. His Uncle gently lifted a hand, waved back.

When the share-out was done, they let the plastic bag go loose and it filled with air, drifted off gathering speed to become a ghost bag to drift until snagged somewhere.

'Get the other fucking tink over here. Give him the knife. Give it to him!'

Breath hissing through his nose, The Man Who Walks tripped forward and was thrown beside his Nephew.

The Husband whipped the knife butt out over the Nephew towards the Uncle, in offering.

'Ah, hah.' Teasingly the knife was lifted higher as the Nephew tried to grab at it with a trembling hand.

Face of The Man Who Walks! Baseball cap gone. The hair! Leaves and dead crabs in its grey spiked heights. Constant appearance of shock, dirt in the wrinkles, the haunted, prowling expression, already dark skin, weathered by the endlessness of being forced abroad in all weathers into the wider expanses of territory. The eye socket, swollen closed, infected by constantly inserting foreign objects, and crushed peewit's eggs to cool it – like the withered cunt of a dead old whoor, the Nephew thought. The mouth mercifully still taped shut.

'Ah Jesus, ya daftie, poor crazy old harmless . . .' The Nephew coughed and broke a bloody grin at his Uncle. 'These bad bastards have took advantage of you.'

273

'Shut it, gypo.'

The living eye of The Man Who Walks roamed over the face of his younger Nephew, blemished only by the blood on the white teeth. The Man Who Walks brought the point of the knife up and touched the flesh of the younger man's cheek. A hiss of air came out The Man Who Walks' nostril and a long reamer of clear snot followed.

'Go on, Wurzel. Take his *fucking* eye out. Like the Bible says. Take it out, shove it in your own eyehole!'

'Go on, man, don't go in deep or you'll kill him, just poke the point half an inch in, end *his* career poking other men's wives.' The Husband was holding the Nephew's cheeks now, turning his head towards the knife point, his own face up to the Nephew's cheek, and breath flickering, making the eye he wanted to see burst, just blink. The Nephew could feel how the Husband's sweating hands trembled with some unthinkable emotion and he remembered the man would have the burning erection, firmer than any of his life, pushing from his groin and known to all men who torture.

The Nephew closed his eyes, waited for the point to burst through the thin eyelid skin and to see a star he'd never seen before.

Bless the Little Birds

He had crawled all day, fainting only briefly, pulled his own weight on uphill with arms. Slowly progressed through endless dandelions that tickled and mocked his nostrils, made a detour, costly to his strength, round a drystane dyke. Brave towards the endless energy the dull pains in his legs seemed able to muster. What he would've done for a pint! The one The Man Who Walks was doubtless supping at that moment. Deservedly! yacuntya. Deservedly. He'd go on walking more than I ever will.

Another grasp at the clods and he heaved, slid the old corpse forward. 'Michael, row the boat ashore,' as he always had; like the night at Paulette's with the swole feet she had so lovingly anointed. With shit admittedly. Wages of our contentment, severe, man, always severe. 'Got to . . . Accentuate the Positive and . . . Eliminate the negative.'

Ascending the slope up from the river valley had its rewards! As he neared the promising summit, the gradient decreased as the earth gracefully fell back in a lunar curve revealing more and more of the glorious, late-afternoon sky above, and the field flattened off to an awareness of elevation in air all around him, a Lord of our Western Air he felt. It was at this point in his peregrinations that, slowly, very slowly, he spied the strangest thing to his fore, two of his body lengths ahead, which was how things had to be evaluated from now on, where each new pull usually brought so little of interest and cost so much in pain. He lay very still, trying to make out if he was seeing what he was seeing.

He was.

He clawed and hauled closer. Heave-ho. What a country, yacuntya! The gods are sending them to Scotland, but where are they finding them? Up ahead was the moccasin of a man, a man obviously face down, blotto, in the long grass. Fancy meeting you here, yacuntya. Do you have medical experience? A mobile phone that works?

'Hoy, pal, heavy night?' Silence. Another victim of the Argyll mafia? Heave-ho. His face pushed through the verdure, his chest crushed down the dandelions giving clearer vantage. He could near touch the leg of the man. Oh Christ, it was wearing a kilt! Patriotism at a fucking time like this, yacuntya! He reached, took the foot, tugged. The leg came away and sped up to his face. A long plastic leg, its moulded calf reflecting the sun. It was a mannequin in a kilt!

Heave-ho. Pulled himself up to the torso of the dummy, it had a tartan plaid draped over its back, wove from a thin, insubstantial material. Might do the Nephew for the inevitable night under the stars ahead. Hold on a moment. Further, through the grass, the Nephew could see *another* mannequin and, close to him, a sword, a claymore! He heaved forward again and reached out. Wooden sword, just as he thought. He pulled himself up onto the hard mannequin, like the last of some awkward species trying to breed a final generation.

He got some vantage on the fields around him. He managed to push himself up on his arms, like a press-up, and sure enough,

276

the grassland and rougher moor around him was thickly littered with these mannequins in Highland dress, scattered weaponry and even an entire fake horse corpse, its stuffing thrust out of a torn stitching across its belly. Like old Markus the elephant, he thought. And there, sure enough, in the distance, the deep burn of high-fired movie lights, flanked by battalions of reflectors, were blasting down on reality, fighting the natural light with overwhelming, colonising superiority, determined to force a vision on the mundane and curse the consequences.

He was on the battlefield fringes! And now he imagined a spectacular aerial crane shot, lifting above, showing him at the edge of a sea of five thousand corpses which he would need to crawl across, over, between and through the fake blood and mire. He would drag his real blood to reach the cameras and plead. Better than a real sea – the horrifying deep sea – better a sea of fake copses. Wouldn't Bill 'Raincheck' Wright be pleased to see him! Back to the Black Book of Badenoch's home to recuperate! His true level in society. 'Rodger, my friend! I seem to have lost my camera!' Maybe they'd ask the Nephew to take over directing duties for the day, off whatever chump was responsible for this idiocy, the haemorrhaging in the knees making him fevery now. He muttered aloud, 'They could get me upright, like yon Napoleonic French naval captain, both legs torn off by a cannonball, they just propped the poor old bugger up, stuck in a barrel of maize from which he barked orders as he drained away into the bottom, yacuntya!'

The day wouldn't end without him making a grand entrance after all! He'd finally make it into the fucking movie! If he could only get nicely trampled by a little squadron of Cumberland's dragoons, there was the chance of a little insurance fraud too, and if not, surely, he was for once ideally qualified for the perfect job! Squiggle a bottle of tomato ketchup on him: in make-up and ready to please his audience! Yacuntya! Why hadn't he thought of it before? A corpse. Getting paid to be what he already was! Joining those most honest sectors of society who had found vocation in harmony with their characters: judges and whoors!!

He grimaced sideways as the crows wheeled lazily above and came down close to land in their hunched, muscled, forwards glide, reaching claws strained out for the foreign, avaricious earth, seconds before silent touchdown.

'Try and tear my liver out and see what ya get, yacuntya,' the Nephew croaked.

He saw another movie spotlight grow into full fruition, way off to his right across the jumbled crop of corpses, but then, in challenge, the sun was getting low in the sky in another direction, away from medical aid but away from all those lies as well.

Strangely, now in his growing fever, he recalled again that section from the children's colouring book, transcribed from the scrolls of typewriter ribbon:

Movie idea. Bless the Little Birds. Not for Xmas. China, 1959, Chairman Mao Zedong in power. Chinese peasantry ordered into the fields. Enormous flocks of little birds were slowing down the productivity of crops, devouring the wheat and rice. China needed to be more self-sufficient during the Cold War. Mao ordered gangs of peasants, full-time din-makers, into the fields and they began to roam the country, screaming and drumming after the bird flocks, driving them out the fields and into the air so the birds could not rest. So many din-makers one gang would march until they met a gang of din-makers from the next village. West, east, north or south, the birds couldn't settle in any tree or in any field. Soon the entire population of peasantry was abroad, heads turned to the sky, the voice raised, the

278

spoon bashed on the pan until the pans themselves wore out and new ones were brought in by trainload. Bizarre rattles, new fireworks were invented and distributed in the millions. All night, literally for months, from dusk to dawn the peasants, in shifts, stood out in the fields banging their utensils, hour after hour, shouting at the heavens, month after month, until the songs the children had been taught were forgotten for a generation and they never sang again after what followed. The children from that time, even until they were old men, shouted rather than spoke and many became deaf. Lovers lay under trees all night, shouting. A man lived in each tree all along the roadway so no bird could settle there. Houses were built in the trees and children raised there to keep the birds from settling.

And all this time the sky was full of a great, black, single wave of sound, loose with ragged edges, moving as one, thinner towards its rear, shaking that tail to the horizon, until the ground was thick with little birds, who could fly around and around no longer, and rained to the earth, dead with exhaustion. The roofs of the huts, the trees and the fields, the hillsides, the bends in the rivers were darkened with the millions of sparrows that fell. The children with no music kicked the bird corpses aside as they shouted and banged gongs to the school hut, drumming their spoons and spinning their rattles, ready to take over from their brothers and sisters, their mothers and fathers, and plant the crops again.

One spring it really was silent. All the birds of China were dead. All the noise stopped and the world was still. The peasants could return to the crops which grew beautifully, wonderfully abundant. It was going to be the greatest harvest until the locust swarms and other insects arrived, now free of their natural predators: the little birds. The locusts swarms were not driven away by the noise. They were heedless to the terrible choirs as they destroyed the nation's entire crop in a month. Now men fell dead from the trees where they had built their insane houses. More than thirty million people died in that famine. The worst famine in human history.

Och aye, bet ya the good old town looks just the same! the Nephew thought. Oh, to be beside the river once more with those two smiling girls, their hair pinned high revealing pale winter necks, our picnic and river-chilled wine! Singing the songs of redemption and the songs of peace. What ones? Who cares, yacuntya! Tears came into the Macushla's two remaining eyes, beyond mere tears of pain. He clawed himself onwards, through the dummy corpses and towards the ruddy murk of another sunset.

Acknowledgements

Some details of the desert crossings of the Empty Quarter are directly inspired by my notes on Wilfred Thesiger's remarkable book, *Arabian Sands*.

Quotations are from the Everyman editions of Jonathan Swift's *Gulliver's Travels* and Clough's never less than fascinating *The Bothie of Tober-na-Vuolich*, first published in 1848. .
Macushla's Latin quotes can be rendered as, I think:

p. 113: 'The evening is come, rise up young ones' (Catullus)
p. 125: 'Let us see the fields, the happy fields' (Horace, *Epodes*)
p. 251: 'A word is enough for the wise' (proverb)

A portion of this novel first appeared in the *Edinburgh Review*, and another in *The Picador Book of Contemporary Scottish Fiction*.

Also available in Vintage

Alan Warner

THESE DEMENTED LANDS

'Warner's second novel is a classic like his first one...
glorious...powerful'
Independent on Sunday

'Prodigious powers of invention...marvellously dynamic
prose...brilliant visual imagination...A greatly ambitious
novel'
Liam McIlvanny, *Times Literary Supplement*

'A sequel to his acclaimed debut novel, *Morvern Callar*,
These Demented Lands confirms that Alan Warner boasts
an extravagant talent...This novel is set on a Scottish island
that contains a variety of weird landmarks and an hallu-
cinogenic cast of characters – including a DJ who wants to
set up the rave to end all raves, a visitor whose job it is to
assess candidates for sainthood, and the wonderfully
unfazed heroine, Morvern Callar'
Harry Ritchie, *Mail on Sunday*

'Think of the inventiveness of an Iain Banks filtered through
the lurid lens of a David Lynch, with a soundtrack from
Verve and Bob Dylan...*These Demented Lands* is fiction
"on the Outer Rim of *everything*." Rave on, child'
Gavin Wallace, *Scotsman*

VINTAGE

Also available in Vintage

Alan Warner

THE SOPRANOS

'Calculatingly scandalous, wickedly funny'
Independent

'Third and best novel from one of the most exciting young writers in Britain...Hilarious, touching, nasty and beautiful'
Mirror

'*The Sopranos* spans one day in the lives of six schoolgirls from the Port. As part of the choir of their school...they travel by coach to Edinburgh to participate in an inter-school singing competition...Warner provides every nuance of their characters in a sustained tour de force...It is just as though one were eavesdropping...this is the most profound of Warner's books. His sense of place and atmosphere remains extraordinarily intense'
Guardian

'Warner's third novel is as wild as his first...fantastically original...anyone who writes like this earns the right to be read'
Mail on Sunday

'Calculatingly scandalous, wickedly funny, and shot through with a visionary vein...Warner's girls are unforgettable. His song will not go away'
Independent

VINTAGE